THE

THIRD

DAY

Jeff Lovell

TotalRecall Publications, Inc.
1103 Middlecreek
Friendswood, Texas 77546
281-992-3131 281-482-5390 Fax
www.totalrecallpress.com

Copyright © 2016: Jeff Lovell
Edited by: Jacqui Lovell
All rights reserved
ISBN: 978-1-59095-995-4
UPC: 6-43977-69957-2

Library of Congress Control Number: 2016951299

Printed in the United States of America with simultaneous printings in Australia, Canada, and United Kingdom.

FIRST EDITION
1 2 3 4 5 6 7 8 9 10

To Jeff and Louise Johnson, the founder and president of the Israel Today Ministry. His teaching opened my eyes to the relationship of Christianity and Judaism and I owe him more than this dedication can provide.

Shema Yisrael: Adonai elehenu, Adonai Echad.

Award Winning Author

 Jeff Lovell is a native Chicagoan, with 3 degrees from the University of Illinois and an earned doctorate from Vanderbilt University. Jeff taught high school writing and literature for thirty three years and sponsored the school paper, Student Council and several other activities. He ran the drama program at two high schools, teaching and directing and designing sets, lighting and costumes. His specialty in his career focused on Shakespeare. Since he retired from education, Jeff has served as a theatre and film critic for a television station and appears frequently to review theatre and literature.

About The Book

When the heinous pirate Henry Morgan sacked the City of Panama in the seventeenth century, he didn't realize that he was stealing not only a treasure of gold and jewels but also a prayer shawl which had once belonged to Jesus himself. A treasure of gold and jewels was buried with the shawl, which was hidden inside another fabulous treasure. Two young couples accompany a friend who knows where the treasure is hidden, and whose life can possibly be redeemed by the ancient cloak. To complicate the search further, they are pursued by a Cult whose dying leader has a mysterious power to subjugate people and make them his slaves.

PART ONE

The Cymreig

Chapter One

Swim practice—the first one just after Christmas break—had been a monster. Coach Hahn claimed that he'd given the team the extra work in an effort to get the Westwood High School team shaped up for the dual meet season, but everyone knew he thought the team had a chance to place well in the state meet. The squad climbed out of the pool at the shallow end, drank some water and dried off a bit.

Bob Stanton, senior freestyler and team captain, walked to the pool office toweling away the stench of bleach and chlorine. He saw Coach Hahn with his omnipresent cup of coffee unzipping his sweatsuit. Coach set the cup down, hung up his sweat suit and tightened the draw string on his Speedo. Then he took a sip from the cup.

"Yech," remarked Coach. "This damn stuff's bitter." He dumped the cup of coffee down a pool floor drain and rinsed out the cup. "That's strange," he muttered. "I spilled a little more sugar than usual in there. Thought I'd wrecked it."

Bob gave the coach a little snort. "Yeah, Coach," he scoffed. "You drink so much of that stuff I'm surprised your heart doesn't dance a Spanish Flamenco the whole time you're awake."

"Smart kid," muttered the coach, and took an affectionate swipe at his senior freestyler. Bob dodged the slap and ducked out of the office. Coach followed him out and dove into the deep end of the pool.

Bob watched Coach swim a couple of easy warm-up laps as he walked back to the rest of the team. Coach had been a great high school and college swimmer, and his form in the freestyle was still terrific twenty some years later. Coach Hahn lifted weights and stretched with his swimmers and most men his age would have envied his well-toned physique.

Bob, the swim team captain, started the post-workout stretching while the coach swam some laps. Bob looked up as Coach stopped in the middle of the pool. Mr. Hahn drew his knees up and took a breath. Bob heard what sounded like an "Ahhh" and Coach sank beneath the surface.

He didn't come up. *What the. . .*

"Steve!" Bob yelled at the kid nearest the door. "Go get the trainer! Now!" he screamed when the junior freestyler hesitated. Steve Grant ran to the door and out into the pool hallway. "Kenny!" Bob yelled, and pointed to where Coach had gone down. He ran to the edge of the pool.

Kenny Booth turned and looked. His jaw dropped when he saw what Bob was pointing at. "Come on!" he yelled and dove into the pool.

Kenny Booth and Bob hit the water in the same second and sprinted to the far side of the pool. They took surface dives and grabbed Coach, pulling him to the surface.

Bob and Kenny, both experienced life guards, hauled the Coach to the shallow end. Four other guys jumped into the water with them and helped them lift Coach Hahn out. They laid him on a couple of towels and Kenny and Bob started CPR.

Mr. Barsanti, the trainer, ran into the pool area followed by Steve. "Good work, guys," he said. "I called the paramedics, but keep at it until they get here."

Bob and Ken worked hard at the CPR. After a few moments Steve Grant tapped Bob's shoulder. "Bobby. I got it," he said. "Back away."

Bob nodded and slid to the side as Steve and a couple of other guys who had CPR training took over for him and Kenny. He went to stand up, and his legs almost didn't support him. Mr. Barsanti saw him and put an arm around his waist. "Okay, Bobby," he said, his voice quiet but reflecting concern and pride.

"Coach isn't—I mean, it isn't over, is it?" he asked Mr. Barsanti.

Barsanti knew what he meant. "No, we won't give it up," said the trainer. He gripped Bob's shoulder. "Not yet. Not for a while. He couldn't have been under water more than 30 seconds or a minute at the most."

A couple of moments later, Coach coughed and began to breathe on his own. *Thank God,* thought Bob and sighed with profound relief. Coach still looked awful.

The paramedics arrived less than three minutes later although the time seemed an eternity to the team. "Guys," Mr. Barsanti said. "Back up. Give them some room." The paramedics took over.

Bob had been a lifeguard for more than three years, since he was fourteen. Though he'd pulled a lot of people out of the water, he'd never seen one that looked as bad as Coach.

At last the Paramedics wrapped Coach up in blankets. Though he was breathing on his own, he hadn't quite regained consciousness. Bob heard one of them say, "Jeez. The Big One. Look at this guy. Not an ounce of fat."

The Big One? A heart attack? thought Bob, astonished. *Coach*

Hahn? He's in better shape than a lot of the guys on the team.

Bob Stanton started trembling when he stood up from administering CPR to the Coach of the Westwood High School swim team. Then the shakes hit. The experience scared him to the depths of his soul.

Bob walked into his house about a half hour later. His mom came in from the kitchen and greeted her son.

And Bob's composure dissolved. He began to cry, and the sobbing reached down deep into his soul. He hadn't realized how terrified he'd been when the situation unfolded. Choking and crying, he told Mom and Dad what had happened.

A good supper helped Bob feel better and more under control, but still he had to struggle to focus on his Calculus homework. A fine student, Bob had developed the self-discipline to put most personal situations aside in order to complete his assignments. Tonight, though, his mind continued to return again and again to the sight of Coach when they pulled him from the pool. Then the paramedics. The stretcher. The ambulance. The police. The questions.

Bob put his pencil down and stared at the black window of his bedroom. He couldn't see anything outside, but that didn't matter. Something about the situation at the pool kept nagging at him.

In an abrupt moment of insight, he got it. That Maxwell kid. He wasn't there.

Right. Coach had ripped into Maxwell yesterday about loafing through the 200 yard sprints. The junior freestyler had been loafing all week and the younger kids were seeing a terrible example.

Bob called a couple of the guys on the team. They confirmed

his suspicions: yeah, Maxwell had vanished from the pool deck when Coach went down. Once they got Coach out of the pool, the kids all volunteered to do whatever they could. Not Maxwell. Now Bob felt sure Maxwell had been nowhere in sight during the whole thing.

Where the hell could he have gone? And why would he go? Bob couldn't answer any of his own questions.

The school's police counselor and the principal called Bob out of his English Lit class the next morning during first hour. The two men waited in the hall and told Bob to shut the door behind him.

"Bob," said the principal. He gave Bob a firm hand shake and handed Bob a copy of the local paper. He pointed to a story which described the heroic actions of the swim team. Bob gave it a quick scan. "Congratulations and thank you for saving Coach Hahn's life," the principal said.

"Yeah," said Mr. Cooper, the school cop, as he also shook Bob's hand. "You and the other guys did everything right. You and the other guys made us—and by that I mean the whole community— tremendously proud of you."

Bob acknowledged the thanks, but saw that the principal was concerned about something else. He asked the two men if something had happened.

"Yeah," said the school cop."We got the word from the hospital. They think Coach might have been poisoned."

＊ ＊ ＊ ＊ ＊

Two months later

Westwood High School Gymnasium

Marty Hague walked to the gymnasium storage closet,

unlocked it, and put away the scoreboard console. Since this was the last regular game of the basketball season, he felt pretty sure they wouldn't need it again.

Marty, the cross-country and track coach at the high school, ran the scorer's table at the home games. The gym, large and modern, tonight had the stale odor of sweat mingled with disappointment and anger.

So far, the athletic program at Westwood had experienced a tough year. Marty shook his head thinking about how he, as the school's running coach, had to deal with complaining parents all during the cross-country season.

The track season hadn't quite started, but it didn't look like it would be fun either. He'd have to deal with the same kids with the same cruddy attitude, and with them would come same parents who thought their kids were the clone of Jackie Kersey or something. *Yeah*, he thought. *Yeah sure. They're all going to get full ride athletic scholarships to Big Universities, the Big Ten, the SEC, whatever. Right. Kids with their lousy attitudes would be less welcome than a flu epidemic at a Division One University.*

He saw the team's young coach, Lenny Finnegan, talking to reporters at midcourt. He sighed. Lenny, in his first year as head coach, had inherited a lousy team. Jim Bullock, the coach for many years, had retired from coaching at the end of last season. Marty knew why: Jim, near the end of his career, had not wanted to contend with the crummy bunch of athletes that were coming along. To say nothing of their parents.

Like Marty, Lenny had been the victim of unremitting harassment—letters, phone calls, e-mails—from the parents. The most hurtful attack came when the parents of some senior kid bought a bunch of tee shirts which read, "Fire Coach

Finnegan!" The kid and about twenty of his friends had worn them to school. The principal and the school dean made the little jerks turn their shirts inside out and told them that the school would confiscate the shirts if they ever wore them to school again.

Marty shook his head at the irony. The rest of the coaches in the league respected the work Lenny had done. His miserable team won four conference games as well as three or four outside the conference. In terms of size, skills and talent as well as effort, they were far and away the worst team in the conference. As a result, the minimal number of victories amounted to a major accomplishment. Marty had told his wife that Lenny should be the Conference Coach of the Year for winning as many as he did.

Oh well. The playoffs would start next Tuesday. Westwood would get their butts kicked by the number one seed in their bracket. Then the dreadful season would be over at last.

Marty walked back to the Physical Education Department office and chatted with his friends and colleagues. The other coaches drifted out, but Marty decided to shave and grab a shower.

He stood under near scalding water in the coaches' locker room, taking his time to lather up, shampoo, and then shave. As he did, he thought about Saturday, a day off. He sighed with relief: No practice, no having to come back to the school, no big responsibility. He could get up a little later in the morning. He'd take his wife, whom he called Susie Q, into the State Street Diner for some bacon and eggs. Then he could do some chores around the house. Sounded wonderful, he thought.

He turned off the shower and dried off. The gym had been

hot and sweaty. It felt good to rinse off and put on clean socks and underwear and a fresh shirt.

He saw that he was the last guy to leave. Even Gil Westlake, an unmarried guy who seemed to live at the school, had departed. Marty walked out the back door. . .

And froze when he saw the large group of students churning in the parking lot. *Oh, no*, he thought. *Gang fight. This looks bad.*

One boy lay cringing on the asphalt of the parking lot. Some kids were kicking him.

Marty yanked out his cell phone and called 9-1-1. After he reported the big fight, he hung up and bellowed, "Hey, the cops are on the way."

Marty took on his teacher voice as he walked toward the group. He yelled, "I'm a teacher, Mr. Hague. Disperse the group. Beat it. Now."

To his relief, the group dispersed, yelling curses and imprecations. Marty knelt next to the fallen boy. The boy was bleeding around his head and crying. His right arm appeared to be twisted at a funny angle. *Either broken or a severe dislocation,* thought Marty. "Just lay still, Lad," he said. "The cops are on the way. I'll stay right here with. . ."

The first blow struck him behind the right ear. It made a thudding noise and the blow confused Marty. He thought, *what hit me?* The next wallop struck him on the back of the head. He had time to think, "Concussion." His last thought was "Susie?" His wife's face flashed into his mind before consciousness fled. Then he fell forward onto the bleeding boy.

* * * * *

The old, old man walked along a deserted farm road in

Northern Quebec. Summer was still here, but the air had a crisp feeling, like autumn couldn't be too far away. Today was Shabbos, he thought. He hadn't been in a synagogue in a long time, though, and he missed it.

No one would ever guess his real age, but it went back—well, quite a few years, he smiled. Unlike most people, his life hadn't end in a normal time span. He had to wait, the Nazarene had said. He couldn't go to Temple and tell the truth about who he was, why he was still alive, all that he'd seen, and so on.

He shrugged away the feelings of anger and regret and took a deep breath of clean, pure air. He considered Autumn his favorite time of year, beyond all doubt. Up here in Northern Quebec as Fall came on, the air would smell of pines, the maple trees would be a shower of color—bright red, orange, still some green—and he strolled, unhurried, not rushing.

He looked at the sun and realized he had perhaps an hour of daylight left. He turned down a dirt and gravel road, not sure where this one led, but at least the late afternoon sun felt warm on his face.

Though he was older than anyone on the planet, no one would know it by looking at him. He stood a bit more than five and a half feet tall, but people saw him as lithe, well-muscled, with almost no body fat. He appeared to be the picture of health.

His mind continued to be as sharp as a Surelock Vermin Trap, also. He had memorized the Jewish canon, the Tanach, many years before. As he walked day by day, he would recite the scripture. Today, for example, he'd been working through the book of Leviticus.

He spent his days feeling chilled, almost freezing cold,

though. He should have been dead long ago, and his body knew it, but he couldn't let go of life. Unlike every other mortal on the planet, he couldn't surrender to death, to lie down and cast himself into the abyss. At least, not until a day that had been promised.

A tear formed in his eye, and then rolled down his cheek. He tried again—as he did several times a day—to apologize, to say that he knew that he had done wrong, bitter and nasty, but like his body, his soul seemed frozen. Though almost amazing in his articulation, there were so many words in Torah.

Once, years before, he'd thought about going to live in the Caribbean, say, St. Vincent's, maybe Barbadoes. Before he could gain control of the thought, his mind turned to the closing years of the seventeenth century, Morgan, the ship known as *Satisfaction*.

But the cold didn't ease in the beautiful islands of Hawaii, of the Caribbean, of Greece and the Mediterranean, among the lovely people, the bright sun, the delicious food. Indeed, he felt much worse. The voice came in his depression and sent him on missions to help other people. He tried, but as it had been for centuries, he couldn't resist.

The old man shook his head and once more found himself walking along the road in Northern Quebec. A car pulled alongside and a farmer leaned out and addressed him in French. The walking man knew French, of course, but the Quebecois accent had always been difficult for him.

"Do you want a ride, Neighbor?" asked the farmer.

"No, thank you," said the man. "I don't mind walking."

"It is starting to get on toward dark," said the Farmer.

"Yes," said the man.

"Do you have a place to stay?"

He thanked the farmer for his concern but, no, he admitted, he had no place to stay. He slept outside almost every night.

The farmer shifted his car's transmission into 'park' and climbed out. He put out his hand. "Call me Beaujourn," he said.

"Cepha," said the man, and shook the farmer's gnarled hand. This kindness happened with some frequency. No one ever saw Cepha as a threat.

Cepha accepted a ride and slept under an old blanket in the farmer's barn that night. In return he helped with milking, mucked out stalls for the stock, and slept in the loft in the barn that night. He smiled, thinking about his father, who had also been a farmer. Cepha had grown up doing farm work. It suited him well.

Jews should always be farmers, he reflected. It really seems to be part of our makeup. He smiled, thinking of other times when he'd helped out at farms in other countries, in other centuries, using other tools.

Again the next day he helped with chores, ate three fine meals, and slept again in the barn—

But when morning came, he knew he had to leave. The Voice came, and he had no choice but to obey. He got up before dawn and scrawled a good bye and thank you note. He had walked several miles before the sun came up.

As usual, however, The Voice spoke: *Geneva, Illinois, U. S. A. Find Clint. Find Nicole.* The voice went silent again and, as usual, it gave him no choice whatsoever.

He turned south. He found a major highway and a car stopped—as one always did—and the driver offered him a ride down to Montreal. Cepha accepted with gratitude.

The Voice didn't speak again. Cepha would know, somehow, when he'd found Nicole, and he'd know when he found Clint. Something on this order had happened many times; too many to count, in the long years since It had happened.

Cepha never ate much, but today he felt hungry. He climbed out of the car when it reached Montreal, thanked the driver and walked until he found a grocery store. He went around back to the store's dumpster and found an apple and a loaf of day old rye bread. He began walking again and ate as he walked.

The impromptu lunch satisfied his hunger and he began the long walk toward London, Ontario. From there he'd cross to Detroit and begin walking southwest to Geneva, IL.

Nicole and Clint, he said to himself, fixing them in his memory. Those were the names. He had to find the people who went with them.

Chapter Two

McClelland "Mickey" Logan sat on the couch in his family room chatting with his close friend Rusty Ivers, a lieutenant in the Illinois State Police. Rusty, out of uniform today, seemed a bit distracted as they conversed about baseball, the weather and their families.

Rusty asked him, "McKenna still lives here, right?"

"Yeah," said Mickey, smiling as he always did when he thought about his niece. "She loves teaching at Westwood. She's doing well, from all we can tell."

Rusty smiled, but lapsed into a distracted silence. After a few moments, Mickey grinned at his friend. "Okay, Rusty," he said. "What's up?"

Rusty looked up. "What do you mean?"

"Something's on your mind, I can tell," grinned Logan. "You only act like this when you have something at the station preoccupying you. So, Lieutenant, what gives?"

"Uh-huh," said Rusty. He tapped the edge of his cup. "Now understand, the main reason I came to see you is because I wanted to visit with you and Rand."

"I hear a 'but' coming," smiled Logan.

"Okay, right," said Rusty. "Here it comes. I'd like you to give me some background on a case we just picked up."

"Me?" Logan drew back, surprised. "You need my help on a case?"

"Yeah," said Rusty. "You worked at Westwood High School

for what, eight, nine years?"

"Westwood?" Logan blinked. "Yeah, I did. I taught English and drama, and directed the plays. Why do you want information about Westwood?"

Rusty rubbed the tip of his nose, thoughtful. "One of your former colleagues had an accident last week," he said. "A wheel came off the passenger side of the front end and he lost control. His car ran off the road and hit an old oak tree. He totaled the car, but he was damned lucky he didn't get killed, Mickey. The doctors tell us he'll be okay."

"Who is it?"

"He's named Mel Robbins," returned Rusty. "He's one of the football coaches. I think he also taught physical education."

Logan stared at him for a moment in disbelief. "Mel?" he asked. "He's the *head* football coach and a terrific guy."

"Yeah. The school plans to appoint an interim head coach today. Mel won't be coaching for a long time, if at all."

Logan shook his head in disbelief. "Yeah, I know him well," he told Rusty. "He's a good friend. He's close to retirement— well, maybe two, three years. He's an excellent coach, too."

Rusty raised his eyebrows in surprise. "You think he's excellent?" he asked. Mickey nodded. "He doesn't have a super record, just a little better than a .500 winning percentage. That's not all that sensational."

Logan shook his head. "Yeah, but it's better than it looks," he said. "Westwood plays in one of the toughest conferences in the state. They compete against schools with much bigger enrollment. Also, the community has a miserable park district, so they don't have any programs for kids like we do here. Most of the freshman boys come in without having played any organized football."

"Do you know a guy named Gil Westlake?" asked Rusty.

"Yeah, I do," nodded Mickey. "That's the guy I told you about, the one McKenna's dating. She seems pretty serious about him, from what I can tell. Why do you ask?"

"The people at Westwood think the principal will appoint him as head football coach today or tomorrow," said Rusty.

"No kidding? Well, good for him."

Paula Ivers came out to the family room with a carafe of coffee. She poured some for her husband and Logan. Logan watched her with a smile, startled as always by how beautiful she was. Paula and Mickey had never dated but they'd been close friends in high school. Her marriage to an abusive clod named Frankie Capriatti ended when he was murdered in an insurance plot. Paula had met and married Rusty, the cop who had investigated the murder of her first husband. Frankie, not only an abuser, had also denied her children. Her bubbling excitement about her pregnancy with Rusty charmed Logan and his wife Rand.

"Jeez, Rusty," said Logan. "I thought your wife was good-looking when we were kids in high school. She was dazzling when you got married. But she's even more gorgeous now that she's pregnant."

Paula blushed and the two men chuckled at her. She smiled and said, "Irish blarney, Logan. Nothing but flattery."

"On the contrary," said Mickey. "A well-deserved tribute." Paula leaned over and gave him a little hug, then kissed his cheek.

"Thank you, you old goat," she said, giggling.

"Why, you—" Logan growled as he took a playful swing at

her posterior, which she dodged. She stuck her tongue out at him and went back into the kitchen, laughing.

"Anyhow," said Rusty, "the parents in the community have been all over Mel Robbins for the last few years. He was 2-9 two years ago and only won three games last year," said Rusty.

"I know about the team," Logan said. "I still check the scores in the papers. But, Rusty, he won the conference four years out of eleven before those last two years. He got enough wins in two other years to get to the state playoffs. That's a hell of an accomplishment. Don't let anyone kid you. Mel knows football and he knows how to coach. The kids love him and respect him."

"Love and respect," Rusty jeered. "Good luck telling that to the parents of the kids he has now. They've had letter writing campaigns, petitions, and everything: calling the principal, the district superintendent, and the school board. They've sent him anonymous letters, made crank calls to his wife and kids..."

"Doesn't surprise me," said Logan. "The community is a strange one. The housing ranges from crummy trailer parks to five hundred thousand dollar homes. A lot of schools have a texture, a consistent sociology, but not Westwood. Don't get me wrong, I enjoyed most of my experience there. I taught a lot of terrific kids, but we had psychopathic jerks as well. Parental support ranges from enthusiastic to indifferent."

Something clicked in Logan's mind. "What got you involved with this?" he asked. "You don't take charge of routine auto accidents, do you?"

"That's just it," said his friend. "We don't think the accident can be called routine. I'm pretty well convinced it's a homicide attempt."

Logan leaned back in his chair, trying to absorb this information. "My God, Rusty, you think somebody tried to kill Mel Robbins?" he managed.

"I'm afraid so, Mick," said Rusty. "We looked hard at the car. Like I said, a wheel came off the front. We're pretty sure someone loosened the lug nuts so that the wheel would fall off."

"Couldn't that happen anyhow?"

"Mel took the car to Ira's station for an oil change three or four days before the accident. Ira rotated the tires. I talked to Ira and he was just dumbfounded. I have no doubt he tightened the tire down, Mick. He has a routine that he follows when he rotates. He starts at the Driver side front tire and works his way around. All the other lug nuts are tight. He's too good a mechanic."

"I used to trade with Ira all the time when I worked up at Westwood," said Mickey. "Yeah. You're right."

"Mel has a fine driving record, too," said Rusty.

"Yeah," said Mickey. "I bet he hasn't gotten three tickets in his life."

Rusty smiled. "Not even two. His wife told me he got a speeding ticket in a speed trap in some two-bit jerkwater town in Mississippi when he was twenty-two years old. The speed limit went from 55 to 30 in the space of one hundred yards. He was slowing when he got picked up. Cost him like $50. He wrote a letter to the governor of the state, he was so mad."

Logan nodded.

"He was driving a classic Dodge Challenger he bought in 1971," Rusty said, and Logan smiled. He remembered the car well. "Took care of it as if it was one of his kids. The thing is a wreck after the accident. Totaled for sure."

"What a shame. I remember how much he loved that thing."

"Well, for sure he could have been killed in this accident," said Rusty. "He's the father of three great kids and now he's a grandfather. Losing him would devastate his family."

Rusty and Logan talked for a while, Logan trying to give him a handle on the school where Mel worked.

Chapter Three

Nicole Sadler had to admit that her brother Mickey Logan had been right. Her senior by some fifteen years, he had begged her not to marry the miserable lout named Brad, who'd turned out to be a boorish drunken oaf.

She winced as she thought about the last conversation she'd had with Mickey two long years ago. "Pumpkin, I know you're in love," he said. "It's hard to get past that and look at reality. But let me urge you. Please try to see this through my eyes."

"What do you know?" she said. "How can you know what Brad's like inside? He needs me. He needs someone to believe in him, to support him and give him a reason to live."

"You aren't a missionary, Pumpkin," he said. "Please, let's consider the facts. You graduated from college and high school with high honors. You've got a dynamite job. He just managed to finish high school and works at the Quik-Lube for minimum wage. You get tipsy on half a glass of wine. He drinks beer by the six-pack and he's been arrested twice for drunk driving. You're a committed Christian and he thinks that's stupid."

"What do you know about marriage?" She lashed out. "Look at you—never married? No relationships? Who are you to advise me?"

She couldn't stand the next part of the memory. Her brother hung his head for a moment and when he looked up, she saw that his eyes had filled with tears. "You're right, Pumpkin."

"You see?" she sneered.

"I'm nothing but a brother," he nodded. "Nothing but a man who has loved you since our parents died when you were ten years old. I'm the guy who raised and cared for you since then. I'm the guy who paid for your education, who paid for proms, who never missed one of your softball games. See, I think all that ought to count for something, don't you?"

Now the tears started down his cheek. Nicole felt her stomach fall. She considered taking it all back, apologizing, hugging her brother—

No. She wanted to marry Brad. She turned her back and walked out the door.

Her brother and sisters didn't come to the wedding. She didn't invite them. Brad's parents invited a ton of people, but made no offer to help with the expense. She had to take out a loan to pay for the wedding. When she thought about how Mickey would have paid for it without hesitation, she winced, but again hardened herself.

Brad got so drunk at the reception he had to be helped to the car. Well, *dragged* would have been the better word, she winced. He spent the night sick and vomiting at the two-bit hotel where they spent their one night honeymoon. The alcohol poisoning made him so sick that they couldn't consummate the marriage until two nights later at their apartment, a dreary two-bedroom hovel that made the hotel look luxurious.

Well, at least they consummated it that night, she thought. She'd moved to another bed in another room after a couple of nights and intimacy had ceased for the most part.

They'd gotten a fair bit of money as wedding gifts, but it had vanished, or to be more exact, he wasted it. Night after night he came home with expensive liquor, narcotics and pornography.

When the money ran out, he stole money from her purse. So she put him on an allowance. Then he got fired from the Quik-Lube job. Then he got fired from another job pumping gas. Then he decided not to look for another job.

She tried reasoning. Rational arguments. Then begging and pleading. Finally she resorted to threats with which she had no intention of following through. She came to realize that he liked being off work, lying around eating chips, watching TV, saying to hell with shaving and grooming, taking money out of her purse and going out to watch TV games at sports bars with his vulgar drunken friends.

This morning, she dragged herself out of the bed and went out to the living room. The television was still on and she found Brad passed out, sprawled snoring on the couch. She turned the TV off and began picking up the detritus from his six pack and chips and Slim-Jims.

She came out of the shower and began to dress for work. She went to her closet and took out a slacks outfit, but after a moment's consideration, put it back. Tonight she'd go to the last meeting of her Organizational Theory class, the second to last course she needed to take to earn her Masters of Business Administration degree. That meant three hours with Professor Frey, who was tall, handsome, a gifted lecturer, funny and personable. She couldn't wait. He seemed to like her, to her delight, and she'd worked especially hard in this class so that he'd be pleased with her.

She took out her best outfit. Short and black and sophisticated, every time she wore it she received several compliments. Professor Frey might like it. Besides, her ego could use a little boost.

She went to pick up her purse and briefcase and found that her husband had gone into the kitchen. She went in to say goodbye and he snarled profanity at her.

"What's that for?" she asked. Not that he treated her with any sort of courtesy at any time.

"I'm taking off," he said.

"You're what?" she managed after a few stunned seconds.

"You heard me," he sneered. "I've had enough of you and your smart mouth, your straight A's, your snotty attitude."

Again she stared in stunned amazement for a few moments. "What on earth are you talking about?" she said, fighting hot tears of hurt that rose to her eyes. "I've done everything I can to support you and encourage you."

He snorted with contempt. "Like hell," he said. "You've done nothing but hold me back."

"Don't go," she said. "Things are about to get better, you'll see. I'll be finished with the MBA in a couple of months. Then we can get you going on finishing your degree. I'll support you in it."

He snorted in contempt, told her to go to Hell and took a sip of coffee. Nicole began to cry. She walked out of the kitchen, picked up her keys and briefcase and left.

She took the elevator down to the first floor of the apartment building, though as a rule she walked down the steps. She looked at her lovely SUV in the lot across from her and toyed with taking it so Dale wouldn't. Then she decided to take her car. *He's threatened before,* she thought. *He's just hung over and not thinking.* She looked down. Yes, she had the keys to the Explorer. She'd taken the two sets when he'd begun driving drunk again and let him have the car mostly when she could be sure he wouldn't drive drunk.

Maybe that's what he's talking about. Okay, maybe it was a little unkind, but she doled the keys when she could be sure he wouldn't wreck the car. Thank God he hadn't been arrested for DUI since they'd been married, but she knew that was only because he'd been lucky.

We have to get his life going, she thought. And again she heard her brother Mickey's voice in her mind: *You aren't a missionary, Pumpkin.*

She walked out into a blast of cold, wet air. It would be autumn soon, but winter in the Chicago area seemed perpetual. The joke was that Chicago had two seasons: Winter, then July and August. She smiled a little. People also said the two seasons were winter and road construction.

The miserable rust bucket she drove started up, rather to her surprise. And relief. It got terrific gas mileage, and she drove it to save some money. She loved the Explorer, but it was nowhere as cost-efficient as this dreadful thing. She pulled down the shift lever and the transmission clunked into reverse. Now she turned to look for traffic in the parking lot—

And screamed when she saw three old women standing right behind the car.

Nicole jammed on the brakes, threw the car into park and jumped out. "Oh my god," she cried. "I'm so sorry. I didn't..." her voice trailed off.

No one was there.

Nicole Sadler felt a shiver run through her whole body. "Where did they go?" she said out loud.

A neighbor walking his dog looked up from 30 or 35 feet away. "What?"

"Those old women," Nicole said. "They were standing behind my car." He gave her a look that implied that a full psychiatric evaluation would not come amiss.

Nicole stood in the parking lot for a few more moments, looking around in bewilderment. She reviewed the situation several times. Had she dreamed the women?

No. It was too windy and cold outside and she was too upset. For sure she hadn't fallen asleep in the icy parking lot.

At last she rallied. She took a deep breath and got back into the wretched car.

Nicole pulled into the parking lot at work and hurried in to her work station. She was most concerned to take care of her bank accounts. She went on line and transferred all her money from the checking account she shared with Dale into a secret account she'd maintained for several months. In moments her savings and the checking account were safe, hidden where Dale couldn't find them. A few more key strokes cancelled the Visa and MasterCard and a few other credit cards.

Only then did she relax and clarify her thoughts. "What am I worried about?" she said aloud. "He couldn't use the Internet on the best day he ever had."

Unnoticed, her boss came to stand in the corridor behind her office station. "What did you say, Nicole?" asked Mr. Chandler.

"Oh!" she said, startled. He smiled and offered to apologize, but she waved the apology aside. "Just a little jumpy, I guess," she said.

"You look very professional today," he said, still grinning. She knew he didn't mean any disrespect and that the compliment was genuine. Mr. Chandler always treated her with the regard of a perfect gentleman. She contrived a smile and made some excuse about concentrating on something. He laughed and they chatted for a moment or two. When he went back to his office she navigated to the firm's website and got going on her work for the day.

Then she remembered the three old women she'd seen standing behind her car and shivered. "What happened this morning?" she said out loud. But the vision wouldn't lend itself to any explanation.

It *had* happened. She *had* seen the women. She could identify their clothing, the color of their hair, the sneering laughs…

Then she thought about Dale. She hesitated a moment, then picked up the phone, telling herself that the right thing to do was call and apologize for the nastiness that morning. . .

Then she remembered him telling her to go to hell. *No*, she said to herself and replaced the phone. *No. I didn't provoke that hideous rudeness. He's the one who needs to apologize.*

At lunch, though, her salad tasted like notebook paper. She struggled all day to focus on a couple of contracts she needed to get done. At last 5:00 P. M. came and she packed up her desk for the evening. A couple of people dropped by her desk on the way home and expressed concern for her and she realized that her attempts to appear normal had been unsuccessful. The whole office thought that her marriage had hit the rocks. They were wrong. It was on the boulders, down the ravine, over the cliff, and she knew it.

Nicole headed down to her little car, a nine year old martyr to rust and corrosion. She had to use her considerable automotive skills to tune it up and keep it running. She even kept tools and jumper cables in the trunk in case of an emergency.

Her brother Mickey had taught her how to work on cars, use power tools and lots of other mechanical things. She liked working with her hands, but not on this thing. Every time she tried to start it, she lived in fear that she'd be stranded in the middle of nowhere and need to do some sort of mechanical intervention in the freezing rain or snow.

But tonight, for some reason, it started right away. She drove out of the company's parking lot and headed to the Community College where the MBA extension class was held. She pulled into a Mickey D's and bought a burger and chocolate shake. She ate at a table in the restaurant while taking a look at the newspaper which she had brought to work with her. She didn't enjoy the fast food dinner which lay in her stomach like a construction block.

When she arrived at the college, she parked and hurried to the door in a blast of wind that slashed the parking lot. She saw three women walking a few steps to the left as she ran and hurried by them, running tip-toe in her high heels.

"Excuse me," she said as she hurried by. They didn't say anything. She opened the door and started in, but realized that she couldn't let the door slam in the face of the women, who were right behind her.

She turned and smiled at them—

They weren't there. No one was there. She stood all alone in the door way. The sidewalk lay empty.

Nicole's hand flew to her mouth as she just managed to stifle a scream. She turned and ran into the building.

Nicole found a washroom and went into a stall. She knelt in front of a bowl and vomited. When the spasm passed, she rose and walked to a mirror, just managing to stifle a grin. Her hair looked like a rat's nest, her makeup was smeared and she felt wretched.

She worked for a few moments to repair the ravages of the nausea and the terror. She decided at last the effort held little chance of success, and made her way to the door and went out into the hallway—

And ran right into Professor Frey.

"Oh!" she said, staggering on her high heels a little. Frey reacted like lightning and caught her arm to keep her from falling.

"Nice to see you too," he grinned.

Nicole made a lame attempt to apologize and he laughed. "Cut it out," he said. "I'm okay. But if you have a lawyer's card, just in case I decide to sue..." Nicole hurried to open her purse but he laughed and assured her he was kidding. "Come on," he said. "Let me walk you to class." He took her arm in a gentle grip at the elbow.

Oh God and I look like the last few hours of a misspent life, she said to herself. Before she went into the exam, she stopped at a drinking fountain and drank enough water to keep her stomach from growling during the exam.

She knew she was rattled and not at her best. She had to get herself going. Nicole thought about her brother and the lessons he'd given her in acting. She cleared her mind and focused her thoughts.

At the end of the exam, Nicole brought the test to the desk. "Can you stay for just a few moments after class?" Professor Frey whispered. She nodded and excused herself to the washroom. Using her brain, thinking of something else, and focusing on doing well had calmed her down. Now, she fixed her hair and makeup before returning to the classroom.

When the test period ended, Professor Frey thanked the class for a good effort and said good bye. He received a nice round of applause and as the class left, several people shook his hand and thanked him for a great class. *Well, it was*, she thought. *The best one in the program.*

Then she found herself alone in the classroom with the Professor, who held up a finger to say, "Just a moment." Frey grinned at her and packed up his briefcase. He opened the door for her and said, "Let me walk you to your car."

Oh yuck, she thought. *He'll see that miserable wreck I drive.*

"How'd you do on the exam?" he asked.

She shrugged. "I guess okay," she said. "I studied hard for it."

"That doesn't surprise me," he said with a smile. They arrived at the car. She felt lucky that he didn't comment on the heap of corrosion. Then she realized: a true gentleman stood with her. He wouldn't do or say anything to hurt or embarrass her.

"Nicole," he said. "I wanted to say this to you in private. I was afraid that I'd sound too much like you are the teacher's pet."

She gave a wan smile.

"Congratulations on a very fine effort in the class," he said. "You made me proud of you with the leadership you displayed, your introspection and the pleasure you seemed to take in the class. I asked to speak to you so that I could encourage you to go on with your education. I really think that you ought to pursue a doctorate, and I'd be very happy to help..."

He broke off when Nicole began to cry. The whole day

rushed in on her and the sweet compliment as well as the affection he'd shown her undid her. She held her briefcase in front of her and sobbed, blind with embarrassment at crying in front of the man she respected so much.

"What's wrong?" he asked, and she heard the concern in his voice. "Did I insult you?"

"No," she managed. "No. I'm glad you spoke to me. I had a terrible day."

"Huh," he said, handing her a handkerchief. "Problems at work?"

She shook her head. "No," she sobbed. "My husband told me he planned to leave me today. I'm..." she couldn't go on. He put a gentle arm around her shoulder and she leaned against him and let him hug her as she wept.

"I'm so sorry," he said. His voice, quiet and kind, made her feel better.

"Thank you," she returned, wishing she could stay leaning against him for the next several hours or so.

"Any children?" he asked in that low, gentle voice.

"No," she said. "Thank heaven."

A moment later she rallied. "I have to go," she said, though she didn't know why. She didn't want to go home.

"Could I drive you?" he offered.

She shook her head. He opened the door and helped her in.

"Look, you be careful," he said. "You're pretty upset. Do you have far to go tonight?"

"No," she said. "No, and I'll be okay, I promise."

He closed the door and waited while she started the car. She waved her thanks and he waved to say good night. Then he tapped on the window with his keys. She rolled down the window. "Do you have a card?" he asked. "I'll e-mail your grade in the class."

She nodded and pulled a business card out of her wallet. She pulled out a ball-point pen and jotted her home address and e-mail address on the back. He handed her his card in return. She drove off and looked in the rear view mirror.

"Now I'll never see him again," she said, and again tears formed in her eyes. Then she turned the corner and the school faded. So did Professor Frey.

Nicole pulled up in front of her apartment building, her stomach churning. She didn't see the Explorer in the lot. *So, he managed to get a key*, she muttered to herself. Then she realized. Of course, she thought: He'd taken her keys to the Explorer and had duplicate keys made.

Nicole walked into the lobby and used her key to go through the security door. She crossed the lobby to the elevator and pushed the button—

The doors crashed open almost at once, startling her. She took a step to walk inside, but stopped when she saw three old women blocking her entrance.

Now she felt fear.

"Excuse me," she murmured, trying not to show her fear. The three old women backed to the other side of the elevator. Nicole walked in and pushed the button for the third floor. "Can I push your number?" She asked the old women, trying to be pleasant and not show her terror.

"No," said one of them.

Silence. The doors slid shut and the elevator started up.

"Do you live in the building?" she asked.

"Oh yes," said another.

"We're always here," said the third. They laughed. She'd been expecting a witch's cackle from them, and the laugh indeed sounded like a revolting giggle.

Nicole turned back to watch the numbers above the door. The damn elevator always crawled up the shaft, but she felt like she was riding on a giant snail now.

At last the doors opened for her floor. She stepped out, glad to be away from the women, and then remembered her manners. She turned to say "Good night" —

For the third time that day, she gave a little scream. The women weren't there. No one stood in the elevator behind her.

A deep chill of terror struck her, leaving her numb for a few moments.

Nicole turned and ran toward her apartment, terrified. Her emotions were now at the point where she didn't think she could take much more.

She pulled out her key and pushed it into the lock. As she pushed, though, the door fell open in front of her.

The door had been left open. What on earth…

Nicole's fear didn't ease as she walked in. She flipped on the hall light switch, but nothing happened. Her eyes adjusted, and in the dim light from the hallway, she could see that the apartment was empty.

Brad hadn't just left. He had taken everything. The couch. The lamps. The 55 inch Samsung LCD-HD Television that had cost her almost $2000. The end tables. The stereo and its cabinet were gone.

Into the bedroom. He'd taken the dresser and dumped her clothes on the floor. He stole the bed, too, and the rest of the furniture.

None of it was worth much, but it had been hers. She'd paid for it, not him. How could he—

Then she remembered. *Oh no!* She plowed through the clothes and found her jewelry box. It was empty. He'd taken everything out of it.

She fell to her knees, trying not to wail with the pain. He'd taken her necklace, the special gift from her Grandma and Grampa. Every year, on her birthday, for Christmas or other special days, they'd bought her a tiny pearl. The pearl had been something special for her, something they did just for Nicole. Her brother and her sisters got other gifts, but the little necklace had been special just for her.

She ran sobbing into the bathroom and vomited again. Nothing but yellowish, disgusting bile now.

Nicole went into the living room and wandered around in a daze. She couldn't think of what to do.

"What are you doing here, Miss?" said a male voice from the hallway.

Nicole turned and saw two large men standing there. She backed up against the wall, too terrified to say anything.

The men came in and stood in front of her. "Miss?" one of them said.

Now Nicole spotted the truth. They were policemen. "I'm sorry," she managed. "You startled me. I live here."

The policemen exchanged glances. "You live in this apartment?" the older of the two men said, sounding suspicious.

Nicole looked around and spotted her purse where she'd dropped it next to the door. She reached in and pulled out her wallet, then extracted her drivers' license. She handed it to one of the men. He looked at it and nodded.

"Nicole?" said a voice from the door. The group turned and saw an older woman standing there, looking bewildered. "What are you doing here?"

Nicole stammered for a second, but managed to ask, "Why shouldn't I be here, Mrs. Wessex?"

Now Mr. Wessex spoke up. "Why, we saw your husband moving things out. He said you were moving away."

The policeman asked, "What's going on here, please?"

Nicole swallowed. "I live here with my husband," she managed. "But I don't know where he went."

"He left you, it appears," grunted the other policeman, "And decided to take everything."

Nicole looked at him, and nodded. Then, for the first time in her life, she fainted.

Nicole came to as an ammonia smell assaulted her nostrils. She found herself lying on the floor and the two policemen knelt beside her. One of them held a small capsule he'd broken under her nose. One of them, she noticed, had pulled her skirt down for modesty.

"He left me," she said. They nodded.

"Miss, I'd like to take you to the hospital," said the younger of the two cops. The two policemen took her arms and helped her up. She tried her legs out and found she could stand without problem.

"No thank you," she said. "I'm okay. I'm just so stunned."

"I think you ought to be checked out," he said. "You just fainted, and–"

"I can take it from here, Officers," said a different voice.

The group turned. "Professor Frey," whispered Nicole.

"Who are you, Sir?" asked a policeman.

"I'm her professor and her friend," said Professor Frey.

The policemen looked at one another, then Nicole. "You know this man, Miss?"

"Yes, thank you," she said. "I'll be all right. Thank you so much for your kindness, officers."

It took a few more moments, but at last the policemen agreed. "Let me just make sure I understand," said the younger cop. "Your husband left you and took everything."

"Right," said Nicole.

"Do you want to report it stolen?" asked the other

"I hadn't thought about it," she said. She looked at Frey. He nodded. "I think so," she said.

The younger cop nodded. "Okay," he said. "Why don't you come in to the station tomorrow and make a report? You know, when your thinking clears up?"

Nicole nodded. In a few moments, the two policemen left. Mr. and Mrs. Wessex offered to help in any way they could and then also said goodnight.

When they left, Nicole turned to Professor Frey. She hesitated for just a few seconds, but then ran to him. She came into his strong embrace and relished it for a few wonderful moments. "What are you doing here?" she asked.

"I take it you're not glad to see me, then?" he smiled.

"No, no, I didn't mean that," she said. "I just…"

"I started for home," said Frey. "But then I thought that, well, you're still my student, so I have a bit of responsibility for you, so maybe I should follow you home. You were pretty distraught, so I took your business card, plugged your address into my GPS, and it led me here."

"Thank you," said Nicole. "I'm so grateful to you."

"Can you pack up some things?" he asked.

"What do you mean?"

"I think I ought to take you some place where you can relax a bit more," he smiled. "Sleeping on the carpet could be a little uncomfortable."

"Where could we go?" As she said it, she realized that wherever he took her, it would be okay, as long as he came with her.

"My mom lives pretty close, like a half hour away," he said. "She's used to me coming and going at strange hours. Let's go there."

Nicole nodded. Professor Frey found a suitcase in the bedroom and Nicole picked out some clothes from the pile on the floor. She packed a few toiletries as well as her hairbrush and toothbrush, then went into the washroom and changed into some jeans and a sweater.

Frey took her keys and locked up the apartment, then led her to the elevator.

"What's wrong?" he asked. "Oh my Gosh, you're as white as the polar ice cap."

Nicole looked into the elevator. No one was in there. "I'm sorry," she said. "It's just that I haven't had anything to eat. I guess I'm a little hungry."

Frey nodded. "I think I can fix that," he smiled.

They went into the parking lot and he took her arm to lead her toward a car. Nicole stared.

"Now what?" he grinned.

"I love your car," she said. "I've never seen such a nice '81 TransAm."

He laughed out loud. "That's great," he laughed. "It's my pride and joy. It's got a 4.9 liter turbocharged engine. Four speed stick shift."

"Do you like to work on cars?"

"Oh yes. I've restored several cars. I'd have to call this one my favorite, though."

"I can see why," she said.

"Can I assume that you are something of a gearhead as well?" he asked, with a huge smile.

"Yes," she said. "I used to help my brother work on his car and I tune our cars, change the oil, things like that. I loved it. . ." Then she thought of how much she missed her brother Mickey, who had taught her. She choked back a little sob.

"That's neat," he said. "Cars have always fascinated me too."

"Can I drive this one some time?" she asked.

"I'd be delighted," he said. "But not tonight. You relax and let me drive."

She nodded and lowered herself into the car, relishing the warm leather upholstery. He adjusted her seat to let her recline. He put her bag in the back seat and pulled out a blanket. He tucked it around her.

He started the car and the heater began to pump out warmth. She glanced to the right and saw her own car...

The three old women stood there, sneering at her and waving. Nicole gave an involuntary little scream. Frey turned at once. "What is it?" he asked.

"The people," she gasped. "The ones standing by my car." She turned away and looked at him.

He looked past her. "No one's there, Nicole."

She whirled back around and stared. He was right. The old women were gone.

She couldn't speak. *Who are they*? She asked herself. *What do they want*?

Frey put a hand on her shoulder. "Are you okay?" he asked.

She managed a nod. He started the car and she heard the powerful engine throb into life. He put the car in reverse and backed out. Nicole looked again at her wretched car. The women were gone.

He spoke to her, being gentle and soothing until the terror subsided. His voice and presence made her feel much better, but these continued visions of three—witches?—bewildered and frightened her.

Frey took her to a small neighborhood restaurant and ordered her a nice dinner. She sipped at a glass of wine while he drank a Beefeater Martini with a couple of bleu cheese olives. At last he said, "Are you okay?"

She nodded. "I'm fine," she said. "I've had a few scary moments all day, I guess."

"Yeah, when the person you love betrays you, the pain goes deep, that's for sure," he agreed.

"I never loved him," she whispered, and realized it was true.

"I know it's not my business," Frey said. "But why did you marry him, then?"

"Let me answer that another time," she said, and the tears welled in her eyes.

About midnight they pulled up in front of a large house. Frey got out first, pulled her bag out of the backseat, then came around and opened the door for her. He took her into the house and led her upstairs.

"I'm putting you in my old bedroom," he smiled. "I'll get you some towels and stuff."

Nicole nodded, opened her suitcase and took out some pajamas. Frey came back. "You'll find the washroom right across the hall," he said. She nodded and went to the washroom to change into her pajamas and brush her teeth. He smiled and told her goodnight. He turned to leave, but she caught his arm.

"Thank you, Professor Frey," she whispered. "I don't know what I would have done without you." She reached her arms around his neck and hugged him. The hug went on longer than she had intended and turned into something tender. She had a hard time letting go.

"Good night, Nicole," he said. "And don't worry. You're absolutely safe here. The old women can't bother you here."

Frey shut the door as he left and Nicole slid down into the bed, relaxing a little. The hug had been wonderful. She had a brief thought about inviting him into the bed with her but rejected the thought.

"No," she whispered to herself. "He'd think I wanted to make love, and I don't think I could do that. Not tonight, anyhow."

Just before she fell asleep she jerked her eyes open. "How did he know about the old women?" she said aloud. "He didn't see them."

She forced herself to relax and drift off, though. Frey was right. She felt safe.

Chapter Four

The car's glass pack muffler screamed in the street outside the window and jerked Clint Byrne awake. *Cripes*, he thought. *Like I don't have a hard enough time sleeping without some kid drag racing at 1:00 in the morning.*

Clint sighed and got out of bed. He drew a bottle of water out of the little fridge in his kitchen and went back into the bedroom.

He'd been under attack again. The nightmares had been violent tonight and he didn't relish going back to sleep. He sat in a chair by the window and listened to some of the sounds of the night, breathing in some of the fresh air.

Clint Byrne had been making a success of his life by almost all measures. An outstanding high school and college athlete. A Phi Beta Kappa student at his college. A good job now. Savings account, good investments.

So why am I so lonely? He wondered.

He looked out into the street with a little trepidation. Sometimes, when loneliness almost overwhelmed him, he'd hear the mocking laugh of the three old women and they'd terrify him. He saw them in dreams when he was little, then through his teenage years. When his college threw him out after his freshman year of college, they began to come to stand just outside of the range of his sight.

He'd hear the echoes of mocking, nasty laughter and turn quickly, but they'd be gone. Yet there was always a hole—like a shimmer in the air, as if smoke had risen into the atmosphere.

They knew just how to attack him: right through the biggest screw-up of his life. They'd fire away, accusing him, belittling him, ridiculing at him. It was worst in his recurrent dream.

In the dream, he once again became a freshman in college. Clint had received a great deal of financial aid because of his football ability and an exceptional grade point average in high school.

Even though the family would by no means be considered poor—on the contrary—his father begrudged him every quarter that his financial aid and his part-time jobs couldn't cover. Not that the parsimoniousness came as a surprise. His parents had never seemed to like him, even when he was little. They'd made it clear that they were delighted that he was leaving home.

Nonetheless, his first semester had been a rousing success in every way. He made good grades. He'd taken over as varsity quarterback in the third game. With his leadership, the team won most of their games that season. Clint became the toast of the campus. His parents never made it to a game.

He'd been invited to parties and fraternity rush programs. At the beginning of the second semester, he pledged the fraternity to which most of the athletes belonged. Not only had he suffered through the downright cruel pledging procedure, but his grades began to plummet. He didn't pay a lot of attention in class or do much classwork.

For the first time in his life, he felt accepted and important. At college, things were better than they'd been at home or at his high school. People seemed to like him.

He'd gotten involved in the party life at the school, drinking, going to campus parties, raising hell five or six nights a week.

Then, it was final exam time. He realized that he didn't know anything in two of the classes. He worked out an elaborate plan to cheat his way through those two exams. It worked to perfection. He'd passed everything.

Except someone in both classes had turned him in. The cheating was exposed when the professors re-examined the test papers.

He found himself in the dean's office. "The school," the dean told him, "can't tolerate cheating."

"No, of course not," he said.

"We are suspending you from the university for one semester."

"I understand."

"Your grades in the two classes will be recorded as F's," said the dean. "You are also suspended for the next semester, that is, the fall semester."

"Yes, sir," Clint mumbled. He didn't know what to say. He'd never before failed any course in grade school or high school. Indeed most of his grades had been A's, with a smattering of B's. He'd always been a fine student.

"You may return for the second semester next winter. Goodbye." The dean stood, and Clint left.

* * * * *

Clint stood up and stretched. His lonely apartment contained a bed, a closet, a stove and tiny refrigerator, a bathroom with a washbasin that doubled as his kitchen sink, and a tiny shower.

His mind roamed back to the aftermath of the suspension.

* * * * *

His parents, who really didn't want him at home anyhow,

were ready to kick him into the street. Clint's father didn't show any sympathy. "Swell. You can get to work. Or join the army."

"But, Dad!"

"What do you mean, 'but'? There's no 'but'. No discussion."

"Look, I'll get a job. Meantime, I'll go to the community college and take some classes. Then I can go back to the university in January. I'll cut back on the classes. I'll work."

"You betcher butt you will. I'm not paying a damn thing for your college anymore." Dad looked gleeful. Clint got it, now. His father had been looking for an excuse to stop supporting his son's education. His chance had come.

"Can I stay in my room?" he asked.

"'Fraid not," said his father. "Better get an apartment, a room."

"But I don't have any money," he said. "Not even a job."

"You said you were going to work," his father pointed out.

"We decided to make your old room a guest bedroom," said his mother. "You could set something up in the basement, though."

"What!" said his father, giving his wife a look of disapproval for this suggestion.

"You've got your pillows and sheets from college," his mother continued. "You might as well get some use from them."

"You pay room and board, though," asserted his father. Clint agreed.

Clint found an army cot in the attic. He scrounged a bedside table on garbage pickup day. Then he rewired an old lamp.

He set up a room in his parents' unfinished basement. He hung a few sheets to afford him a little privacy, but he didn't need to bother. Most of his family didn't come down there if he was there anyhow.

A neighbor who'd always liked Clint gave him an old car that the owner wasn't using. Clint spent some time tuning the engine and doing basic repairs, agreeing to pay the owner what he could when he got a job. His parents made him park the car in the alley behind the house.

He enrolled for the summer term at the community college. He took the two classes he'd flunked at the university and worked his brains out on them. To his surprise, he aced them both.

The college employed him as a custodian, sweeping floors at night. He also ran the lunch counter in the student union from 11:00 to 2:00 every day. When it wasn't busy, he studied. The school paid him minimum wage, but they waived tuition for him.

Rejected by his family, Clint withdrew from life. He didn't date, didn't try to make friends, or go to dances or movies. He worked out at the gym and lifted weights and ran three to five miles a day. When he wasn't working or at class, he stayed in his room or studied at the library. His family didn't care. Only Joyce, his twelve-year-old sister, in the beginning stages of rebellion against her family, came to visit and talk with him on occasion.

Clint, with little distraction, developed first-rate study habits. He became a superlative student. He received outstanding grades in all his classes at the community college, despite his work hours.

Now, however, the *other* dream started to come every night. The dream of the dean's office continued, but his lifetime recurrent dream of a huge snake—mud colored, red-eyed, tongue flicking out at him—became a nightly visitor.

His most vivid childhood memory involved a huge snake visiting his bedroom. This dream had come first when he was two and a half years old. His parents had told him it was ridiculous. In the dream the snake would rear by the side of the bed, hissing, red eyed, talking to him, threatening to kill him. He would struggle to wake up, and he'd find himself drenched with sweat. He'd have to change t-shirts and battle to fall back asleep.

His family, not understanding, ridiculed him at times like this. His mother and stepbrother told him that he should learn to live with the nightmares.

As a child, these dreams terrified him. He was afraid to go to sleep.

* * * * *

Clint sipped at the bottle of water. He remembered the bitter rejection that had come at the end of the semester.

Clint's academic efforts earned him Trustee Honors, which were granted to students with straight A's. His parents didn't care. They asked when he was leaving.

He went to the basement, where he worked to pack to return to the university.

"If I killed myself, would anyone care?" he asked his reflection in the mirror he'd set up above the laundry tub.

"Probably not," said the reflection and nodded at him.

A girl he'd dreamed about for years came to the dreams that night. She hugged him. "No," she said. "You can't kill yourself. Not a chance."

"Why?" he asked her.

"Because I love you," his best friend told him. "And we'll meet some day."

"But my parents hate me. They wish I was dead."

"It's your eyes," she said. "They're just afraid of what you can do with them."

* * * * *

Clint sat at his kitchen table. *My best friend*, he thought, taking a swig at the bottle of water: *a fantasy girl who comes to me when things get scary or when I'm at my worst.* But after that lovely, vivid dream he didn't think about suicide again.

* * * * *

In January, a few days before he was supposed to return back to the university, the phone rang. He'd gone to his room to finish packing. His mother called him to the phone, telling him, as usual, not to linger. The room and board money he paid didn't include the privilege of using the phone.

"Hey, Clint, Jim Borton here," said the president of Clint's fraternity. "I'm going to be in your area today."

"Great," said Clint. "Can you come over?"

"Yes, I'd like to see you. Let's meet somewhere for a cup of coffee."

"Sure," said Clint. He gave Borton directions to the coffee shop called The Brass Ring and arranged to meet him at two o'clock.

Clint found himself feeling more than a little mystified. Clint lived a significant distance from the University and Borton, he remembered, lived somewhere on the east coast. He couldn't figure out why Borton would have come all the way to his hometown. *Oh, well, guess I'll find out.*

He entered the coffee shop a little after two and saw Borton at the back of the restaurant, with a half empty cup of coffee in front of him. He walked back to the table. "Clint," Borton said, motioning him to a chair. He didn't shake hands. Clint dropped his outstretched hand, puzzled. He saw that Borton didn't return his smile.

"Yeah, hi, Jim," he said. "Good to see you."

"Thanks."

A silence descended for a moment. Now, Clint began to feel uneasy. "Everybody okay?" he asked.

"Yeah," grunted Borton.

After another silence, Clint tried to make some conversation. It failed. "Is there some problem?" he asked.

Borton seemed to make up his mind. "Yeah, there is," Borton nodded. "Where are you planning to live when you come back next week?"

The question took Clint aback. "Well, at the fraternity house, I guess," he stammered, trying to figure this out. "I don't have any other plans, didn't even think—"

"Then, yes, you've got a problem," said Borton.

"What does that mean?"

"We took a vote last week. You're out of the fraternity. You'll need to make other arrangements for where you'll stay."

"What. . ."

"We did it for your own good," Jim said. "We figured you wouldn't want to live with a bunch of guys who don't want you around, right?"

Clint sat staring, too stunned to speak. At last he managed, "You don't want me around?"

Jim stood, and again didn't shake hands. As he turned to leave, he said, "See you."

Clint recovered. "Just a minute, Jim," he said, his voice hard.

"What?" said Borton, turning back. Clint extended his hand. Borton hesitated, then took the hand. He looked into Clint's eyes—

* * * * *

In the next instant, Jim Borton found himself standing on the dusty main street of a frontier town, hands bound behind him.

"You no-good polecat," snarled the man who stood in front of him. "We oughta string you up right here."

"Naw," yelled someone else, standing on Borton's left side. This man launched a vicious kick with a pointed boot to Borton's backside that sent him sprawling face first into the dust. The crowd standing around broke into loud, raucous laughter. "Hanging's too good for the sumbitch."

"Where am I?" said Borton, so confused that he couldn't think. Rough hands yanked him to his feet.

"You know damn well where you are. You hornswoggled that poor man. We don't take to that around these parts," yelled another voice.

Someone came forward with a knife. He slashed a few times, and some men tore the clothes from Borton's back. In moments he stood naked on the street while the lynch mob jeered and hooted. Small boys ran forward and lashed his back and naked buttocks with hickory switches.

"Is it ready?" bawled the leader of the group, who, Borton now noticed, wore a six pointed star on his chest.

"Yup. Grab the brushes, men," someone yelled.

Rough hands dragged Borton down the street as the crowd kicked and pummeled him. He saw a fire with a black cauldron perched on top of it. Now he smelled the boiling tar.

Borton's stomach fell with fear and his bladder let go, to the hilarity of the crowd lining the street. He'd heard the expression "tar and feather" but hadn't realized what it meant until this moment.

He began to beg and plead. The people ignored him.

His pleas turned to shrieks for mercy. "Like the mercy yuh showed that young man?" mocked the sheriff. "He made a mistake and you took ever'thang he had." The crowd mocked Borton's pleas.

Now two men grabbed his shoulders. Two more grabbed his ankles. They lifted him and dumped him onto the ground, knocking the wind out of him. The same four men held him down, kneeling on his arms and legs.

Now the tar. Borton, no wind in his lungs, couldn't manage to scream as the mob brushed the first wave of hot tar onto his naked skin. More. Still more.

He heard the screams of delight from the crowd as his flesh seared. The smell of burning skin invaded his nostrils, nauseating him. This tar would leave brutal scars for the rest of his life. One of the men who held him down cut open two pillows. They shook the feathers onto his scalded skin.

Now they turned him over. "To hell with the brushes," said a voice. "Just pour it."

The men turned him over. He managed to scream until his voice grew hoarse with shrieking, as the scorching tar hit his skin. Laughter drowned out his screams in a moment, however, when the sheriff poured boiling tar onto his groin.

"He ain't gonna be using that little thang much more!" yelled a man, and the laughter redoubled.

He wished he could pass out, but the men shook two more

pillows full of feathers onto his tar covered body.

Now the crowd lashed him to a railroad tie, his skin burned with boiling tar and covered with feathers. Three men lifted the railroad tie to their shoulders, and he saw they were heading for the river. When they arrived the men threw the rail into the river. They turned him upright and secured his rail to a few more timbers.

"Well, good luck, Borton, yuh no-good-sumbitch," said the sheriff's voice. "'Speck yuh'll be in Cairo by morning. If the raft don't turn over and drown yuh." The crowd laughed. The sheriff gave the logs a shove with the heel of his boot. The makeshift raft floated out into the Mississippi River, and the jeers of the crowd continued. . .

* * * * *

Then Jim Borton found himself standing in a coffee shop. He wasn't floating on a crude raft in the Mississippi River nor had he been tarred and feathered.

"Good God," he managed. "What happened?"

"What do you mean, what happened?" bellowed Clint. "You just threw me out of the fraternity. You humiliated me. You left me without any options about where to live. Feel good now?"

"What the hell. . ." stammered Jim, still dazed by the horrific vision.

"No. Not what the hell," said Clint Byrne. "You go to hell. Tell the rest of those disgusting bastards to go to hell with you." Clint stood but Jim didn't move. Clint put his hand against Jim's chest and shoved him aside. Jim crashed into a chair and fell to one knee. Clint didn't look back as he left the restaurant.

Clint had to smile a little as he walked out of the restaurant. He had left the link open so that Borton would remember the terrifying vision.

Borton would have that nightmare for weeks. *Only a little vindictive*, he thought.

Clint drove home. He told his parents what had happened and asked permission to stay for another few months.

They weren't pleased. They also weren't sympathetic to learn that he'd been tossed out of the fraternity. His father chortled with sarcasm. "Doesn't surprise me. Who'd want a cheater living with them?" Clint began to cry, now. His parents left the room.

Clint retreated to his basement bedroom. He didn't come upstairs to get his dinner. He sat on his bed. Then, he turned to his suitcase and boxes. He started to unpack.

Late that night, as he tried to fall asleep, the episode with Borton kept flashing into his mind. *Why did I do that to Jim? Not that he didn't deserve it. But I was just mean. Nasty.* The tears of rejection, anger, and despair overwhelmed him.

In a dream that night, the Snake and the witches tormented him without mercy. They again suggested that he kill himself. They even presented him with several options. He could hang himself in the basement. Slash his wrists. Take an overdose of something. No one would find him for days.

The girl, the one he met only in his dreams, came to him. They faced down the Snake and the Three Witches, as usual. Then she held him and comforted him. "You can't give in, Gareth," she said. "You've got to move on."

"But so many people. . ."

"Not me. We're going to meet some day, too, I promise."

"Who are you?" he asked, holding her close in the vivid dream.

She hesitated, thinking. Then she seemed to remember. "Viviane," she said.

Clint decided not to go back to the University that semester. He re-enrolled in the community college, rather to the delight of the faculty at the school, many of whom made a point of welcoming him. He kept his jobs and again did well. He received straight A's again.

But he kept conversation at a minimum and didn't make many friends. He went to school and the library, to work, and to the basement in his parents' home. His parents and his siblings made it clear that they were still ashamed of him.

He came to the painful conclusion that football was over for him for life. Tears rose as he thought of how much the sport had meant to him over the years.

The weeks plodded on and became months, the unhappy time dragging out like a rusty knife in his soul. Rejected by his family, not pursuing any new friends, Clint's spirit continued to shrivel within him. The Snake visited his dreams every night, accusing him, assuring him that no one would ever love him or care for him. He tried hard to tell himself that it was a delusion, only a horrible dream. His only friend, the girl with the red hair and sapphire eyes, came to comfort him many nights in his dreams.

Clint burrowed into his studies. People noticed that he had become one of the best students at the college.

When May arrived, he dreamed one night of Viviane. They sat together at a picnic table in a park overlooking the ocean. A lighthouse stood nearby, and they threw bread crumbs to sea gulls. "You know you have to make a decision about school for this fall," she said. A huge wave crashed, and he said he knew.

"You have to apply, find housing and try for financial aid."

He agreed, but he said, "I don't know where to begin. I can't bring myself to consider going back to the school with the fraternity that threw me out."

Viviane took his arm and leaned her head on his shoulder. "Why don't you go to see Mickey?" she asked.

He hadn't thought of it, and somehow he felt comfortable that she knew about Dr. Logan, a faculty member at his old high school. "Look, Gareth," she said, "You've got to get going on this. Come on. You don't have to be afraid."

The dream ended, much to his regret. He found himself alone in the cold, dismal basement of his parents' home. He didn't sit next to someone who loved him. He lived in the house that had been a spiritual Newgate for him most of his life.

The next afternoon he rallied and went to see his high school mentor, Mickey Logan, as school ended for the day.

"Hi, Dr. Logan. Am I coming at a bad time?"

Logan looked up. His face broke into a wide grin as he realized who his visitor was. "Clint! Good to see you," he beamed. "Well, yeah, I'm running late—-"

"Oh. Sorry. I just thought—"

"What's wrong?" Logan peered at his face.

"No, I can't take up your time. You're busy—"

"Let me make a call. Sit here. I'll be right back—" Then Logan left the room, his voice trailing down the school hallway.

When Logan came back, Clint fumbled through the story of his suspension from the university. He told Logan about his screw-up with cheating. No, he was guilty, deserved to be punished. Then he told Logan about how the fraternity tossed him out.

"Why, the crummy jerks," said Logan. "They didn't think the University punished you enough? They had to humiliate you?"

"I guess so," Clint said.

"And *I* guess we're lucky they didn't tar and feather you," grunted Logan. "You're better off without those bums." Clint considered this for a second. Then, he had to agree.

Clint went on, smiling a little as he told Logan about the community college. Yeah, very good grades, he did fine in his classes. Parents wouldn't help, no. He considered himself lucky they hadn't thrown him out of the house. They still might.

Thinking of his parents and family did him in. To his humiliation, Clint began to cry in front of his friend and mentor.

Logan didn't say anything for a few moments. Then he came over to sit next to the young man and put an arm around his shoulder. The gentle hug, given with unfamiliar affection and comfort, made him cry more.

"I'm sorry, Dr. Logan," he managed at last. "I don't know what to do. I know I let you down."

"Let me down? Don't be silly. You just screwed up, made a big mistake. You paid for that mistake. You aren't going to do that again, are you?"

"No, I couldn't. I wouldn't let myself."

Logan smiled at him. "So you learned a lesson, huh?"

"That's for sure," Clint agreed.

"Stay here," said Logan, pulling out his billfold. He removed a business card. "Let me make a call." Logan left the room and returned in ten minutes.

"Okay," he said. "I just called my buddy Terry Deal at Weller College. We went to grad school together."

"I've heard it's a good school," said Clint. "Small place, right?"

"About 1200 students," agreed Logan. "Division 3 NCAA. It'd be a bit different from what you were used to at the university."

Clint nodded but he didn't understand why Logan would call someone at Weller College.

"Terry's the college provost," said Logan. "Go and see him tomorrow. He's expecting you. I'm pretty sure, based on what you told me about your academics, that he'll take you, get you set up with admissions and financial aid. He's a good guy. You'll like him."

Clint sat dumbfounded, searching for the right thing to say. "Th-thank you," he managed.

"Forget it. You need someone to look out for you a little. You deserve it, too. Have you got a car?" Logan asked.

"Yeah, it isn't much to look at but—"

"Will it make it to Weller?"

"Sure," said Clint. "But I'll get there if I have to walk."

"It's about 200 miles. You'd have to walk a long way," Logan joked. Clint still didn't know what to say. He stammered out another thanks. Logan grinned.

The next day, Clint found the registrar's office at the community college. They xeroxed him a copy of his transcript. He drove to Weller College and met Professor Deal.

Deal sat him down and chatted with Clint about his friend Mickey Logan. Then he asked for Clint's grades. His unofficial transcript of the past year impressed Deal.

"Let me ask you something," said Deal. "Are you going to take an Associate of Arts degree? Looks like if you'd take a couple of courses this summer you'd qualify for an A. A. after the summer semester."

"A what?" asked Clint.

"An associate of Arts degree," said Deal. "No, it's not the same as a bachelor's, but it'll help with transfer of grades and courses."

"I hadn't thought about it," said Clint.

"If you can swing it, I'd recommend it," nodded Deal. "That way everything will transfer here, grades and all."

Clint thanked Deal for the advice. The Provost waved his hand and said, "You're welcome."

Then, he leaned back and put his fingertips together. He looked Clint in the eye. "What happened when you were a freshman at the university?"

Clint looked down at the floor. He told himself, *I can't lie. I'm past that in my life, no matter what the consequences. If they don't take me here, at least I didn't lie.* He drew himself up straight, looked back into Deal's eyes, and took a deep breath.

He didn't hold back. He related the whole incident.

His heart fell when Deal didn't respond at first. Deal toyed with a pencil and made a note or two on a legal pad before him. At last, though, Deal nodded. "You going to do that again?" His voice was soft, but clear.

"No," Clint assured him. "Nothing could tempt me back into living like that, or cheating to get ahead."

Deal put him at ease with a nod and a small smile. "Okay," he said.

Deal showed him around the small campus and then took him to lunch at the Student Union. After they finished, Deal took him to the admissions office and got Clint going with the necessary applications and paperwork. After Clint filled out an application, Deal walked with him to the housing and financial aid offices. It took a few more weeks, but Clint got accepted, received some financial aid, and set up housing. At the end of the summer, he moved to the Weller Campus.

He realized that he had left home for good. He saw no way he could go back. As soon as he absorbed that fact of his life, he felt better. He wouldn't return home for vacations and holidays, not even summers. Nor did his family ask him to.

* * * * *

Clint gave up, realizing he wasn't going to fall asleep again soon. He rolled out of bed and walked across his little room. He pulled a chair over to the window and sat down, looking out at the night, listening to the sounds of the night. He heard a car go by and glanced at the street. *Another kid's car*, he thought, seeing exotic paint and big tires. He heard the car's glass-pack muffler throbbing loud in the stillness.

He looked at his watch and saw that it was 2:00 A. M.

He picked up the half empty bottle of water, thought about Weller, and smiled. A good memory. He needed to be cheered up.

* * * * *

Clint arrived at the Weller College campus a few days before the start of classes for the fall semester. He'd gone to summer school and finished the year at the community college with straight A's. As Professor Deal suggested, he took an Associate of Arts degree at the community college. He'd completed most of his general education requirements and was ready to spend the next two years focused on his major, which he figured would be history. He'd begun to think maybe he'd like to be a teacher and football coach when he graduated.

Clint unloaded his car. It took just a few trips, since he didn't have much to carry. He began to unpack and settle into a little bedroom with a small refrigerator. A knock at the door startled him. He opened the door and found a man, about 5' 8", smiling and pleasant, standing in the hallway.

"Yes?" said Clint, thinking, *Oh brother. This has to be a salesman.*

"Clint?" the man asked.

"Uh, huh," he said, a bit guarded.

"I'm Steve Miller," said the man, extending his hand. "I'm the football coach here at Weller. I'm glad I caught you here. Can I come in and visit with you for a minute or two?"

Clint relaxed a little, shook Miller's hand, and invited the man in. "I apologize for the mess, Coach," he said. "I'm not really a complete slob, I promise. I just arrived in town."

Miller waved his hand, chuckling, and sat on a worn-out couch while Clint pulled over a cheap kitchen chair. "Nothing fancy, huh?" he said.

Clint liked the man at once, and said, "I couldn't afford the Ritz. I'm paying for college on my own."

"I know," said Miller. "Terry has told me about you."

"Dr. Deal?" said Clint, somewhat surprised. "He remembers me?" Miller nodded.

After a few moments of chit chat, the coach came to the point. "Look, Clint, would you consider playing football again?"

Clint had been figuring that he'd reached the end of his football career. The question jolted him. "I haven't even thought about it," he shrugged. "It didn't occur to me."

"That's why I'm here," said Coach Miller. "Our regular quarterback came up lame yesterday. I'm pretty sure he tore an Achilles tendon."

"Ouch," said Clint. He knew that the quarterback had to be in terrible pain.

Miller nodded. "We had another quarterback, a senior, but he's ineligible this semester. Academic problems. We have a guy who played some in high school who's filling in, but he's a natural cornerback on defense. We need someone who can play pretty quick.

"I called Terry Deal in admissions today to see if he could find someone for us. Well, things are different here in Division 3 College football. He told me we had a new kid on campus who'd played a little quarterback." He smiled and winked at Clint. "I checked, and you're okay for transfer eligibility. What do you think?"

The question surprised Clint and he didn't know what to say. The idea of playing football again thrilled him to his socks. "Jeez," managed Clint. "I've been running and lifting, but I'm not in football shape. I'd need a few weeks to get ready."

"Sure," Miller said. "How about starting today? We practice at two-thirty."

Clint agreed to come to that afternoon's practice. Miller drove him to the field house and led him to the football locker room where an equipment man outfitted him. They even had a pair of cleats for him.

Then he walked into the training room, where an octogenarian who introduced himself as the team physician, Doc Harrington, gave him a physical complete with rubber gloves, lubricants and stethoscopes.

"He's fine," said Doc to Miller. "Get his butt out of here. The ball game is on." He turned the training room radio up.

"White Sox?" said Clint. Harrington's face lit up.

"You a White Sox fan?" he asked. Clint nodded, and explained that he'd followed the White Sox since he had been in third grade.

"I knew I liked this kid," he told Miller, who grinned.

Clint knew it would be tough. Indeed, the workout, the first of its kind he'd participated in since he'd left the university, came close to killing him. The temperature on the field exceeded 90 degrees and the humidity brought on perspiration as soon as he put on the helmet. He didn't do any blocking or tackling, but ran and exercised with the rest of the team.

Still, it felt good. Football had been a refuge for him beginning when he was in sixth grade. The pain of his parents' obvious contempt for him eased when he put on the pads.

Miller came over to him after calisthenics. "Want to do some throwing?"

Clint, breathing hard, wheezed agreement.

"Baldessero," Miller yelled at a freshman. "Play some catch." He flipped a football to Clint.

Clint spread his fingers over the football's laces, relishing the feel of the leather. He threw some light passes to Baldessero. His arm limbered.

As he threw the football, he discovered that more than just his arm loosened up. Clint felt a familiar joy and warmth spreading through his system. After about twenty throws, he reached back and zipped the ball to the freshman.

"Ow," said Baldessero, laughing as he caught one perfect spiral, the best pass Clint had thrown.

Miller wandered over. "Well?" he asked Baldessero.

"He can throw, that's for sure," said Baldessero, flexing his fingers.

"Want to take some snaps?" Miller asked Clint.

"Sure," said Clint.

For the next hour, Clint took snaps from the reserve center and threw passes to the wide receivers and running backs who weren't on the practice field.

After the workout Clint showered and walked home. He fell asleep that evening right after dinner. But he set his alarm clock and made the early morning practice.

His throwing arm ached with a dull pain at first, but as he warmed up, the twinge subsided. He knew that he had to stretch the muscles out for a few days.

Several of the other players came over and introduced themselves. Their welcome made Clint feel at home. Still he decided to keep to himself for the most part.

He watched practice for quite a while, evaluating the group to himself. To his mild surprise, the team had the potential to be pretty good. They hustled, hit hard, ran sprints with enthusiasm and seemed happy. The players weren't as big as they were at the university, but made up for it with speed and energy.

Cliff Lever, the sophomore who was filling in at quarterback, came over and shook hands. "Get in shape in a hurry," said Cliff. "I'm not a quarterback. I do defense."

"You look pretty good to me," said Clint.

"Okay, consider this a threat," teased Cliff. "Get your butt in shape, now."

Classes started a few days later. He found the courses stimulating, even exciting. The professors were personable but challenging.

Within a week of workouts, Clint found himself rounding into condition. At practice, when he wasn't on the field, he studied the team's playbook. It was a straightforward offensive system, similar to the one he'd played at the university, and he picked it up without difficulty.

The team dropped its first game. The offense struggled to score a touchdown and kick one field goal.

"Clint," Miller shouted over the noise of the Weller crowd, a few minutes into the second quarter of the second game. Weller was down by a touchdown to a conference rival, Gresham College. Clint hadn't played yet, still learning the system.

"Coach," yelled Clint, yanking his helmet on and running over to Miller.

"Get in there at quarterback for a series," said the coach. "You're ready. Get us back into the game." He gave Clint a few simple plays to run.

"Yes sir," mumbled Clint. His stomach felt empty and he feared he might throw up with nervous fear. *You can do this*, he argued to himself. *You're ready, Coach said.*

His first play in two years was a disaster. Clint fumbled the snap from center but managed to fall on the ball for a five yard loss. *Damn it*, he thought as he got up. *Get your head in the football game, Idiot!* But the sick feeling in his stomach wouldn't go away.

In the huddle, he heard one of the guys mutter, "What, we giving this game away?" Another started to answer.

The nasty crack jolted Clint into football mode. The fear transformed into competitive passion. The buck fever dropped away like a filthy garment. He felt cool and clean. Some months later, he came to understand that his entire life changed in the next ten minutes of that football game. Doing what he loved to do, sweating hard, and taking charge made him feel confident and poised. He took charge of the game.

"Shut up in the huddle," he snapped. "I'm the only one who talks." The players' heads jerked up at him in surprise. But they shut up, too. They knew he was right. The quarterback was the only one who spoke unless spoken to in the huddle.

He called a pass play. Before he gave the snap count, he said, "I want those yards back. Get your heads up and do your jobs. On three. Ready?"

"Go!" The team responded, and clapped their hands together, but not with the enthusiasm Clint hoped they'd feel. *I need to do something to gain their confidence,* he decided.

The team sauntered up to the line of scrimmage as the defense moved to their positions. Clint, standing tall, saw the Weller left cornerback wince as he turned to face the center of the field and put some pressure on his left foot. *A bum ankle,* he thought. *Heh, heh, heh.*

Clint turned to his right and looked hard at the wide receiver who was lining up opposite the cornerback. Then, he gave the verbal signal for the wide receiver to go deep.

The wide receiver just stared at him for a moment, his surprise obvious. Then he wiped his left hand on his thigh pads, the signal that he understood.

Clint ducked under the center. He growled the snap count. The center smacked the ball into his hand. He began to back pedal as the offensive line grunted and shoved.

The wide receiver, the fastest guy on the team, shot down the right sideline. He gained two steps on the lame cornerback within a few strides. Clint set his feet and drilled the ball to him on a straight line. In the next second, a Gresham lineman hit him in the back and slammed him hard to the ground.

Clint, buried under 280 pounds of defensive lineman, didn't see the wide receiver make the catch in full stride and gain twenty-three yards before the free safety tackled him. He heard the Weller crowd yelling with approval and knew the play had succeeded. In fact, it was Weller's best offensive play so far that season.

The defensive lineman rolled off. Clint turned his head and started to say "Good lick," as players did when the other team hit hard and clean.

Before he could speak, the defensive lineman jammed a knee hard into Clint's back, driving his breath away. He slapped the back of Clint's helmet and shoved Clint's facemask into the turf as he rose to his feet. "Get used to it, Pretty Boy," he leered. "I'm going to be all over your candy ass today." The Weller crowd yelled disapproval at the tackle.

"Watch your mouth, number 68," bellowed an official. Number 68, whose jersey bore the name of Mullin, sneered at the official, then Clint, and turned away.

Clint, angry and dazed, managed to rise to one knee, gasping for breath. He felt as if his head was packed with cotton. He looked at the sideline, where Miller stood talking into his headphones. The coach gave him a grin. Clint thought about coming out for a play to catch his breath and started to signal the coach.

Then Clint saw them. The three old women. Right behind Miller.

He knew why they were there. They wanted to see him scared, humiliated.

He put his hand down. He decided to face his fear. Now, that moment.

I'm not going to be scared, He said in an undertone, looking right at the old women. *Not a chance,* he thought. *Not going to happen. Not today. Not ever. No one's going to bully me again. Never again.*

He breathed deep twice, his lungs aching, as the offensive guard, whose name was Burgess, came over red-faced. Burgess had let Mullin through the line. He helped Clint to his feet and cleared dirt from Clint's facemask.

"Sorry," said the guard. "I didn't. . ."

Clint shook his head to clear his mind and finished wiping the mud off his facemask. His breath came back. "You didn't block that fat jerk," sneered Clint. "He told me he's going to be on me all day."

The guard's face turned brick red. "Look, I said I'm . . ." he began.

"I'm okay," said Clint. He saw the guard relax. He let his voice become gentler. "Forget sorry. Get your mind in the game. We go from here."

"Okay," said the guard. "Bring it to me. He ain't going to touch you again today, I tell you that."

"That's more like it," Clint told him and clipped the guard on his shoulder pads.

Clint jogged toward the huddle. The wide receiver came over to him. "Good call," he said. "I'm open all day on that guy."

Clint nodded. In high school, he'd gotten in the habit of walking away from the huddle for a few seconds to give himself a chance to think about what play he wanted to use. He walked away from the huddle a couple of steps and grinned to himself.

He knew what he wanted to do.

He almost felt sorry for the fat defensive lineman.

But not quite.

He looked back at Coach Miller for a second, met his eye and grinned. Coach nodded as if he knew what Clint was thinking. *I don't have to accept bullies*, Clint resolved again. *I'm not going to.*

He ducked into the huddle and knelt to call the play. The ten other players gazed at him. He was on trial for this team. He wasn't scared.

"That fat guy, number 68, hit me in the head and shoved my face into the mud," he said to them, and gave them a broad smirk. "He told me he's going to be on me all day. We're going to bring him a little heat." The team murmured agreement.

Clint called a quarterback draw play, with a full trap on the defensive tackle. The players grinned.

Clint took the snap, dropped back seven steps, and ran straight at Mullin. He saw the tackle leer, ready to smack Clint as hard as he could. Mullin didn't see Ross, the guard who'd missed on the previous play, who lunged hard and blocked the tackle with a vicious jolt to the midsection. The center slammed into Mullin's left side in the same moment. The tackle sprawled hard to the ground with the two players on top of him. Ross drove his left shoulder pad into Mullin's midriff. Mullin's "Oof" could be heard all over the field and made the Gresham fans murmur with sympathy. In the split second after Mullin hit the ground, Clint ran through the opening. The Gresham strong safety tackled him after an eight yard gain.

The tackle didn't hurt. Clint's head now felt clear and sharp. He felt the competitive juices flowing.

On the other hand, three guys had to help Mullin to his feet.

He stood up, shaky, wheezing and gasping for breath.

Clint moved fast. He called a dive play through the lineman's position. Again two blockers smashed Mullin hard to the ground and the running back gained five yards for another first down. Again Mullin had to be helped to his feet. The fury on Mullin's face made Clint grin to himself.

Now the Weller team began to smack each other on the shoulder pads and helmets. *Attitude is getting better*, Clint thought with satisfaction.

Clint ducked into the huddle. "Okay, good job. Ross. Can we get that fat guy out of here?"

Ross smirked. "Yeah, he's steaming mad, cussing and yelling. Bring it on."

Clint nodded. "Okay, listen," he said. Clint called the play. But before they broke the huddle, he told them what he was going to do. The linemen were surprised at first, but then grinned.

The center snapped the ball to Clint, who dropped back seven long paces. He stood. Ross, the offensive guard, released his block, and Mullin charged hard through the line, intent on Clint. He came on, arms upraised, snarling, and looked right into Clint's eyes.

In the next instant, Mullin saw a roaring tiger where Weller's quarterback had stood. The huge cat reared up and emitted a deafening roar. Mullin lost his stride for just a second, but it was enough.

Clint slid his back foot to make it look like he slipped while trying to set his throwing stance. Using every ounce of arm strength he possessed, Clint gunned the football right into the tackle's facemask.

The face mask bent with the impact, but prevented Mullin from having the projectile smash his nose. Stunned, Mullin staggered, then fell backwards to the ground as the whistle blew to end the play.

"You did that on purpose!" yelled one of the other defensive linemen.

"Sorry," said Clint, stepping over the moaning defensive tackle, making it look like he was concerned. He leaned over and spoke into Mullin's dazed face. "Foot slipped. That happens with us pretty boys. At least, pretty boys who don't like loud mouthed bullies."

The defensive tackle struggled to his feet. He drew back his fist and swung a haymaker at Clint, who leaned back and avoided the punch without trouble. Mullin, still somewhat shaken by the vision and being hit in the face with a football, staggered off balance. The Gresham players grabbed him and held him back while Clint turned with exaggerated nonchalance and walked away. Whistles blew and penalty flags soared around the fat tackle. The referee threw the tackle out of the game. He assessed a fifteen yard penalty to Gresham for unsportsmanlike conduct.

Mullin didn't go quietly. The Weller team heard him yelling vulgarities and imprecations about how he would exact vengeance. Now the coach ran over, and began pushing Mullin off the field. Mullin yelled something about a tiger. The Weller team laughed, perhaps too hard, but like everyone else had no idea what Mullin meant.

Clint looked at the sideline to Miller. The coach gave him a knowing grin and nodded to him as he talked into the headphone.

Clint looked around and grinned to himself also. The three witches had vanished.

The tackle hobbled off the field, supported by the trainer and another player. A cascade of boos from the Weller fans accompanied Mullin's exit. "How'd you dream that up?" asked the running back, smirking.

"Not me," said Clint. "Sammy Baugh, a Hall-of-Fame quarterback for the Washington Redskins did it in 1948, I think, in the days before facemasks. I can't take credit, I'm afraid." The team, dead quiet now, huddled and turned to their new quarterback. To his gratification, Clint saw that the players had joined hands in the huddle. He knelt to call the play and felt the players on either side of him put their hands on his shoulder pads.

Three plays later, Clint took the ball himself over the goal line on a quarterback sneak. The Gresham defense didn't even touch him. The Weller players slapped his shoulder pads and helmet in celebration. The Weller crowd cheered, energized by the well-executed drive.

When Clint came off the field, Coach Miller met him. "How do you feel?"

"Great," said Clint, unable to contain a huge grin. He spoke the truth. He felt better than he had in eighteen months.

"Want to come out?" said the coach, amused.

"Hell no, I don't want to come out." Miller laughed and talked with him about what they wanted to do when Weller got the ball back. When they did, Clint went in and directed the offense to another touchdown. Clint played quarterback until only a few minutes were left in the game, when Baldassero came in for him to mop up. Weller won, 42-16.

After the game, the Weller players lined up to shake hands with the other team. Mullin, who'd sulked on the sidelines, didn't come out to shake hands. Clint led the team through the line. Then, accompanied by Ross and a couple of other linemen, he walked over to the Gresham sidelines to seek Mullin out. The tackle walked away, refusing to shake hands. Clint shook his head and his teammates laughed at the snub.

After the handshake ritual, Coach Miller called the team together for a meeting in the end zone. He called Clint up to the front. He awarded him the game ball. The Weller players applauded.

Clint thanked the coach, and then called to Ross Burgess, the offensive guard, who came forward. "Here," Clint said, holding out the ball.

Ross stared at the ball. "Whattaya doing?" he asked, bewildered.

"I know why we won this game," said Clint. "It's easy to look good at quarterback when you've got linemen in front of you."

Ross, red with embarrassment, took the ball and shook Clint's hand. Again the team clapped and whistled. When the meeting broke up, Ross hauled Clint over to meet his parents and his girlfriend, who were standing just behind the team meeting. "Mom, Dad, Janet," he said. "I want you to meet our new quarterback, Clint."

Mr. and Mrs. Burgess shook hands with Clint. "Did your parents come to the game, Clint?" asked Mr. Burgess.

"Yes," said Mrs. Burgess. "Please introduce us."

Clint shook his head. "I'm sorry," he said. "They don't come to my games. Never have."

Ross's parents looked surprised for a moment. Then Mr. Burgess glanced at his wife. She knew what he meant and nodded. She said, "Clint, we're taking Ross and Janet out for supper at a restaurant. Would you like to come with us?"

Clint felt tears just behind his eyes. "Thanks, that's terrific of you," he choked. "I wish I could. But I work on Saturday night."

After visiting for a few moments, Clint excused himself. A couple of reporters asked to talk to Weller's new quarterback. He sent them to talk to Ross and the receivers and running back. He trudged alone to the locker room and showered. He went to work two hours later, and waited tables until one o'clock in the morning.

That night, he dreamed of Viviane and told her about the game in his dream. She hugged him, thrilled at how well he'd done.

For the rest of the season, the Weller football team lost two more games, but won six others behind Clint. The local press made quite a fuss over the new quarterback, who continued to give credit to his teammates. The reporters described him as shy and withdrawn.

His teammates became protective of him. "Clint's just quiet, real intent," Ross Burgess told one of the reporters. "He focuses on his grades and doing his job at quarterback."

That didn't bother Clint. Over the next several weeks, his teammates offered many times to include him in activities, but he kept himself intent on his academics, unable to forget what had happened at the University.

His parents and his siblings never came to a game. They didn't know, or care, that Clint was named to the All-Conference team. Coach Miller tried to contact them to let them know that Clint would be honored at the end of season banquet. His teammates elected him the Weller Rookie of the Year. The parents didn't respond to Miller's invitation. When Miller telephoned, they told him they would be busy.

After the football season, he fell into a work and training and study routine that kept him busy. He excelled at Weller that year, despite working at a grocery during the week and waiting tables on the weekend, struggling to find time to run, to lift weights and stay in condition.

The dream of the cheating episode never faded. The snake dream continued. Both would haunt him for the next several years.

However, in time he began to make friends. He and Ross ate dinner together several nights a week, and his other teammates joined them more and more. He even began to go out on dates. Nothing serious, he told himself. Somehow though he knew he wasn't going to love anyone until he met the real Viviane.

One of Clint's history professors, Dr. Clifford, became his academic advisor. He pulled Clint aside after class one day.

"Clint," said Dr. Clifford. "You've got a remarkable aptitude for history. You ought to be thinking about graduate school, a master's degree at least, a doctorate if possible."

Clint promised to think it over. But he couldn't imagine how he'd ever be able to afford graduate school. College drained almost all of his resources.

Still, he did love the study of world history. In particular, he focused on seventeenth century England, which led him to an interest in the age of piracy and the spice wars.

One day, he ran across the name Henry Morgan, a vicious pirate. To his amazement, he learned that Morgan had been knighted and made Governor of Jamaica. Clint wrote several research papers about some famous pirates, especially Morgan.

Morgan, he learned, had become the terror of the Spanish Main, bloodthirsty, vicious and merciless. Still, he had a fine reputation as a seaman, and ended his life as the governor of the British Protectorate of Jamaica.

His most famous exploit, Clint learned, involved The Sack of Panama, in which he destroyed Panama City, raped it clear of gold and silver and murdered without mercy. In particular, he robbed a cathedral of its gold and silver. His greatest treasure came when he stole a life sized statue of the Virgin Mary, cast from solid gold.

The statue, Clint learned, had never been recovered. No one knew what had happened to it.

Clint discovered, as the school year rolled on, that he had a surprising gift of language. He studied French, and even took courses in Latin, then Spanish. He became proficient in all the languages, fluent in Spanish.

In early May, Coach Miller and his wife Ruth surprised him with a visit at his apartment. "Did you sign a lease for this year on this place?" asked Miller.

"No, not yet. I imagine I will," said Clint.

"How about moving in with us?" asked Ruth.

Clint couldn't have been more surprised. Gratified and touched to his soul, he mounted a feeble protest at first. "I couldn't put you out like that. You—"

Miller interrupted. "Cut it out. We've got a spare bedroom, since our daughter married in January. You wouldn't be in the way whatsoever. What do you say?"

Mrs. Miller, a twinkle in her eye, said, "Of course, you'll pay room and board, you understand."

"You bet you will," nodded her husband, cackling and rubbing his hands together. Clint knew that Coach loved making the offer and then teasing him, and he appreciated the kindness and consideration. All three laughed.

Clint, thrilled, agreed at once and shook hands with the couple. Within a couple of days, he'd moved his belongings to the Millers' home. He paid them nominal room and board. The Millers treated him like a son, including him in family events and in celebrations. They surrounded him with the feeling of being part of a family.

Clint went to summer school at Weller and took two classes. He worked for a construction company owned by a Weller alumnus to earn money.

Professor Deal called him in July and asked him to come to the office the next morning. Clint went in to see Deal, nervous. "Clint," said Deal, shaking hands, "relax. I've got good news."

"Thanks," said Clint, a little ashamed. Deal introduced him to Stan Bricher, the head of the financial aid office, who also shook Clint's hand. The two men made a little chitchat about the football team.

After several minutes, Clint couldn't take it anymore. "What's up, then?" he asked. "You didn't call me in to talk football, did you?"

"No," said Deal, and the two professors chuckled. "We're just teasing you. Here's what's up. Weller just awarded you a full academic scholarship. We'll cover tuition, fees, and a little for books and supplies."

Clint couldn't get the words out for a few moments. "For real?" he said.

"Oh, yes," said Dr. Bricher. "You've become one of our top students. Congratulations. Keep up the good work. In class, not just on the football field."

At last, Clint could cut back on his work hours.

During his senior year, Clint directed the football team to a 9-1 season and the conference championship. The highlight victory, the team asserted to him, was the last game in which Weller eked out a difficult and close win over their arch-rivals from Gresham. They learned that Mullin, Clint's nemesis from the previous season, had not returned to the school that year. The game, although tough and hardnosed, proceeded with fairness and good competitiveness.

The conference coaches named him as quarterback on the all-conference team and his teammates honored him again. They voted him the Most Valuable Player award. His parents again didn't respond to the invitation to the season ending banquet.

"Congratulations, Clint," said Coach Miller, when he called Clint forward at the end of season banquet. Clint's teammates and their parents were standing and applauding.

"Coach," said Clint, struggling to maintain his composure, accepting the award as his teammates and their parents continued to clap and whistle. "I can't begin to thank you enough for seeking me out last year."

"There's something else," said Coach. He turned and quieted the audience. "Don't sit down just yet," he said. "Now, Clint doesn't know what I'm about to say. One of the highest honors the NCAA gives to a student-athlete is All-American. To superb students, they also award Academic All-American honors. This award comes with a full scholarship to graduate school."

The audience murmured. Miller beamed and said, "I imagine you've guessed it. We're proud to announce that Clint has been chosen as a first team Academic All-American."

The banquet audience applauded and cheered. Coach Miller handed Clint a certificate and again shook his hand. Then, he signaled for quiet. "That certificate is going to look pretty good on Clint's wall. But I have another surprise for Clint also. He's been selected to be the quarterback on the second team National Division III All-American squad."

Then, he hugged the young man, who now couldn't hold the tears back. The audience cheered louder.

Coach Miller asked Clint to say a few words. He wiped his eyes and managed to say a thank you to the team. Then he gathered courage.

"Many of you know, I imagine, that my family has pretty well tossed me out. They never came to my games, and they made it clear that they had no interest in this team. That hurt more than I can say. But in the last two years the people in this room, and in the college, have helped me overcome that hurt. The Weller community has been more than kind to me, more than I can repay. Thank you for letting me experience what a family, and a community feels like." The audience applauded.

"These All-American awards will be prized possessions, of course, but not because they honor me. Rather, I'll use them to remember this wonderful experience at Weller. I'll honor them because of my teammates, the coaches, and the Weller community. I'll never forget you."

Clint returned to his chair, the cheers and applause of the banquet audience still ringing in his ears.

After the banquet, Clint's teammates invited him to come

out with them for drinks and more celebrating. He declined at first, but then, when Ross and a few others pressed him, he gave in. He limited himself to drinking cola, but joined in the celebration.

As the year progressed, Clint started attending a church in town with Coach Miller and his wife. He volunteered to work at a homeless shelter in town.

Clint's appalling shell of loneliness vanished as the year progressed.

He was inducted to Phi Beta Kappa, graduated *summa cum laude* and Coach Miller and his wife had a celebration picnic for him. Many of his teammates and several faculty members came and congratulated him.

His parents didn't come to the party or send a gift or even write him a note to acknowledge his success.

They continued to exile him as they had all his life, since he'd been a little child. The cheating episode had sharpened their dislike. They couldn't seem to bring themselves to forgive him. His brothers and sister weren't interested in him.

He discovered, to his surprise, that he didn't care.

* * * * *

Clint, in his little room, found that the memory had relaxed him. Now, he felt ready to sleep again. He went back to bed. He hoped he'd see the red-haired girl in his dreams.

Chapter Five

Nicole heard a mild tap on her door. She looked at the clock on the bedside table. 8:00. She'd slept well, she realized.

"Come in," she said.

The door opened and a woman entered carrying a large terry-cloth robe. "Hi," she said. "Luke was right." Who? Then Nicole got it. Professor Frey had to have a first name. She tried it a little.

"Right about what?" she smiled back.

"He told me you were lovely," said the woman.

Nicole blushed at the compliment. "Thank you," she said. "I'm sure I'm not especially lovely at this moment, of course." The woman smiled.

"Why don't you put on this bathrobe," said the woman. "Come on down and have some coffee."

Nicole shrugged. "I think I just want to go back to sleep—"

"No," said the woman. "No, you mustn't do that."

"I beg—" Nicole began.

"Did you sleep last night?" asked the woman.

"Well, yes, very well," nodded Nicole.

"My dear girl," said the woman. "I know your heart is broken. But you mustn't sleep more than you need."

"What do you mean?"

"I'm a social worker," said the woman. "Depressed people tend to sleep far more than they need. They get into a rut, and it's very hard to get out of that habit."

"I see," murmured Nicole.

"So put on this robe and come down stairs."

Nicole complied and found Luke sitting at the kitchen table, a stack of final exams in front of him.

"Luke, on your feet," said the woman. "Where are your manners, for heaven's sake?"

Luke grinned and pulled a chair out for Nicole at the table. "My mother remains incapable of surrendering her maternal contempt for my adult manners. I apologize for being lost in my work."

The woman snorted. "Nicole, let me introduce my mother, Ruth," said Luke. Nicole saw that they had a friendly teasing relationship and smiled at them.

"Please," said Nicole, "what should I call you?"

"My patients call me Dr. Frey," said the woman. "But I'd be pleased if you call me Ruth."

Nicole smiled and shook the woman's hand. She sat and accepted a cup of coffee from Luke.

"If you two will excuse me, I have a busy day," said Ruth and left the kitchen.

Nicole looked at Luke and gave a wan smile. "Can I call you Luke?" she asked.

"I'd be honored," he said.

She sat in silence for a few moments, and felt the tears welling as the events of the last 24 hours surged in on her. "Oh Luke, what do I do?"

"Well, I think you ought to start with putting a new lock on your apartment door," he shrugged. She agreed. "Then you should get some legal protection."

"I don't have a clue where to begin there," she said.

Luke pulled out his billfold. "I can recommend an attorney," he said, extracting a business card and tossing it to her.

"Cinnamon Fixx," she read. Luke nodded.

"Yeah, she's as sharp as a scalpel," Luke said. "She took care of my divorce."

"You're divorced?"

"For a couple of years," he said.

"I'm sorry," she said.

"Look, why don't you call Cinnamon now?" he smiled.

"Well…" she hedged.

Luke took out his cell phone and dialed the number on the card. He chatted for a few moments, and then handed the phone to Nicole.

"Hello?" mumbled Nicole.

"Hi, Nicole," said a dark, smoky voice. "I'm Cinnamon. Luke tells me you could use a little help."

"Yes," said Nicole. "I guess I could."

"Okay," said Cinnamon. "I can make some time this morning. Can you get down here in an hour or so?"

Nicole conferred with Luke, who nodded and said he'd drive her.

Luke took back the phone, chatted for a few moments and said goodbye. He turned to Nicole. "How about some breakfast?"

Luke and Nicole pulled into the parking lot at the large office building a few minutes before the appointment. Luke led her to the office.

"I'll wait out in the lobby," he said.

"No," said Nicole. "Would you please come with me?"

"Are you sure?" said Luke. "This interview could get pretty

personal." She nodded and held his hand as they walked into the office.

"Nicole Sadler to see Cinnamon Fixx," he told the receptionist.

She grinned at him, punched a couple of numbers on the phone, waited a second and spoke into it. "You can go right in," said the receptionist. "I'll show you."

Nicole had been expecting perhaps a middle-aged matron, with silvery hair and two dozen or more extra pounds. The woman who met them was about Luke's age, tall with an excellent figure, stylish blond hair and a flattering gray business suit. "Hi," she said with a radiant smile. "I'm Cinnamon."

Nicole shook her hand, trying hard not to look astonished at the unexpected beauty of the young lawyer.

"Luke, it's good to see you," Cinnamon said. "How's Ruth?"

"She's fine, Cin," said Luke, grinning at his friend Cinnamon. "She asked me to say hi to you."

The two friends chatted as Cinnamon brought them back into her office and seated them on a leather sofa. She sat on a wing chair opposite them, opened a legal pad and said, "Tell me."

Nicole began to tell the story of her failed marriage, trying to be as objective as possible. Cinnamon interrupted from time to time with questions and comments.

"He told you to go to hell?" she asked, shaking her head.

Nicole nodded and continued.

"So you were supporting him, in essence?" Cinnamon asked. Nicole assented.

Cinnamon didn't react to anything Nicole said, but made notes on the legal pad. From time to time, however, Luke shook his head in disgust. When Nicole reached the part where she came home and found the Explorer missing, something clicked. She began to cry, and Luke put an arm around her shoulders for comfort. He gave her a handkerchief and embraced her a bit tighter, but still made no comment.

After fifteen minutes or so, Cinnamon excused herself and picked up a phone. She tapped a button, listened for a second and said, "Linda, see if you can find Jack, will you please?" She thanked Linda and hung up.

"Your investigator?" said Luke.

Cinnamon nodded. "I'd like to have him try to locate your furniture and the Explorer if he can," she said to Nicole.

"Except for the Explorer, none of it was worth too much," said Nicole. "The only other thing I really care about is the little pearl necklace."

"Who owns the Explorer?" Cinnamon asked.

"I put the title in my name," said Nicole, but then understood the import of the question. "O my gosh, I'm still on the hook for the payments, aren't I?"

Cinnamon shrugged and suggested that they report it stolen. She called her paralegal and told her to contact the police and the insurance company.

The conversation resumed for several minutes before the phone next to Cinnamon rang.

"Yes, Linda," said Cinnamon, and listened for a minute. "Fine, send him in."

The door opened and a middle aged man, balding with a paunch, came in. He wore a wrinkled suit that seemed to double as his pajamas, an out of date tie, and he looked like he needed a shave. "Nicole, Say hi to my investigator, Jack Earle," grinned Cinnamon. "Jack, we're representing Nicole in a divorce suit."

Jack shook hands, greeted Luke and took a chair while Cinnamon brought him up to date on the case. He made notes, asked an occasional question, and shook his head in disgust. He departed, promising to do his best.

Linda brought in some coffee, while Cinnamon and Luke chatted about old times for a few moments. Cinnamon asked, "Nicole, may I know your maiden name?"

The question took Nicole by surprise, but she said, "Logan."

Cinnamon nodded. "I thought so."

"Why?"

"You have a brother named Mickey, am I right?"

"Well, yes," said Nicole. "I gather you know him."

"Yes, I do," grinned Cinnamon. "I thought I saw a family resemblance."

"I suppose that's true," said Nicole. "I haven't seen him in a couple of years, though. How do you know him?"

"He's married to my sister," said Cinnamon, and Nicole's jaw dropped. "I see them or talk to them a couple of times a week."

"Oh!" exclaimed Nicole.

"Didn't you know he's married?" asked Cinnamon.

"No," said Nicole. "We haven't stayed in touch for a couple of years."

"Would you like to talk to him?" asked Luke.

"I don't think he'd even speak to me," said Nicole, and tears welled in her eyes.

"I know him pretty well," said Cinnamon. "I think he'd be glad to speak to you."

A half hour later, Mickey Logan, his wife Miranda and their son walked into Cinnamon's office. Mickey hugged his sister for some time as she told him what happened. Nicole kept waiting for her brother to say, "I told you so," but he never did.

Chapter Six

Clint woke up late, the phone shrieking in his ear. He mumbled something into the receiver that might have sounded like "hello", but he was too sluggish to care. He'd had a bad night of dreams. "That you, Byrne?" said a voice he hadn't heard in a long time—since he was a senior in high school, as far as he could remember.

"Moran? Is that you?" he said. Paul Moran, a football friend, was one of the guys he'd hung around with in high school.

"Yeah, you old …" said Paul.

Clint interrupted before the obligatory profanity could complete his friend's greeting. "Good to hear from you, too, Paul."

The old friends spent a few moments swapping insults and greetings. "How'd you find me?" asked Clint. He climbed out of bed and put on some water to boil.

"Saw your picture in the paper," said his friend. "Big spread about you winning some sort of sales award. So I checked on line and found your phone number."

"Oh, right," said Clint. "You want to have dinner or something?" He pulled down a jar of instant coffee, then put a spoonful of coffee into his favorite mug.

"Well, I thought maybe you'd want to come to Westwood's game tonight."

"I haven't been to one since I was a senior, what, eight years ago?"

"I know, but it's the first home game of the season," said his friend. "They've played two away games. There's a big dance afterward, I guess."

"You aren't asking me to go to the dance with you, are you?"

His friend laughed. "No, but a whole bunch of guys meet there every year for this game. You know most of them, I imagine." The water began to boil, and Clint poured some into his coffee cup.

Clint smiled to think of his success in high school football: all conference, all area, special mention all-state quarterback. He'd gotten good grades, been pretty well liked.

"I suppose it'd be good to see all those guys again," he said. "Yeah sure, what time?"

Clint got held up by a business deal and arrived a little late. He pulled into the parking lot at Westwood High School at almost eight o'clock, as the game was about to go into the second quarter. He walked to the field and paid the nominal entrance fee, noting that no one recognized him from several years ago.

He made his way to the bleachers and the group greeted him with considerable warmth. He told stories about college, football, his career and heard other news. He stole a glance at the field when he could, but the game wasn't going well. Westwood was down by two touchdowns as the first half entered its waning moments.

The conversation among his friends settled into familiar patterns, things they'd been discussing since they were freshmen at the school. Clint lost interest in a few moments and tried to watch the game.

To his surprise, he didn't see the man who had been his coach on the sidelines. Puzzled, he nudged Paul Moran. "Did something happen to Coach Robbins?"

"You didn't hear?" said his friend. "Geez, all the papers ran the story. He had a real bad car accident. He wound up in the hospital. Lucky to be alive."

Clint stared in surprise. "That bad, huh?"

"I think the right front wheel on his car came off," said Paul.

"That Challenger of his?" asked Clint, his mouth open. Paul nodded. "You've got to be kidding! He took care of that thing like it was one of his kids."

"I know," his friend said. "The cops have been investigating, but nothing yet." He went back into a conversation with Alan Vickers, seated on the other side from Clint.

Clint shook his head and looked at the field, where the gun sounded and the teams left the field. Everyone in the bleachers stood and applauded as the marching band took the field and began a superb program. Clint had to smile, realizing that it was the first time he'd seen the Westwood band perform since he'd been a sophomore at the high school...

Then he saw Mickey Logan, his mentor and friend. He hadn't seen him in years. He stood next to a tall woman, chatting back and forth with her. He looked to his right and saw that no one would miss him.

He stood and walked down a couple of stairs. "Dr. Logan?" he said, shy, afraid that the man wouldn't recognize him.

The man turned and smiled. The smile turned into an ear to ear grin as Logan recognized him. "My God. Clint Byrne," he said, extending his hand. "How are you, Clint?"

Clint, flattered that the man remembered him, shook hands

and told him he was fine. Logan turned to the woman next to him and said, "Rand. I want you to meet one of my distinguished former students." Rand Logan shook Clint's hand, pulled him in between them and grinned at him.

They visited for a few moments. Rand took Clint's arm and pointed out a ten-year-old boy standing on the sidelines and holding a football. "My son Joey," she smiled. "Coach asked him to be the ball boy for the team this year. We haven't missed a moment of the first two games." Logan and Rand laughed.

Rand turned to someone next to her and asked her to move over. "Sit with us, Clint," she said, in a smoky voice. "McKenna, say hi to Clint," she said to the girl who sat next to her.

The girl reached over and took Clint's hand. She looked into his eyes and gave him a big smile.

Logan was saying something, but Clint didn't hear it. He had a hard time breathing. The young woman stunned him. She wore a red and white shorts outfit that revealed a beautiful figure and long athletic legs.

He heard a voice saying, "Clint." He realized that Logan was speaking to him.

"Oh," he said. "Sorry, Dr. Logan."

"Clint, would I be correct in assuming that you'd like to sit with us?" said Logan. Clint managed to nod. He and McKenna moved to sit on the bleachers in front of Logan and his wife. He couldn't see the amused smiles that his mentor exchanged with his wife.

Clint managed to get himself under control and started a conversation with McKenna. She smiled at him as he looked for topics that wouldn't bore her.

"Clint, what's your last name?" she asked him.

"Byrne," he said.

"Right, I thought so," she said.

"Huh?"

"Yeah, Mickey talks about you often," she said. "He's very proud of you."

"Really?"

"Yeah," she said. "I've been living with them the last couple of years."

"Sounds good."

"Yeah," she said. "I teach English here at Westwood, and my mom and dad live some distance from here, so it's just easier to live with Mickey and Karen since they're only ten minutes away. I pay them room and board, of course, but I don't think they really care if I do."

Clint couldn't stop thinking that he'd met this young woman before, but he dismissed the idea.

The band left the field after a terrific half time show. Clint told McKenna how impressed he was. "I haven't seen many marching band shows," he said.

"Westwood's band wins prizes all the time," she noted. "They're terrific."

As they chatted, it began to dawn on Clint that the football game they were watching had become competitive. The Westwood team rallied and scored three touchdowns in the third quarter. The game transformed from a rout into a duel. McKenna, Rand and Mickey joined him in cheering, yelling themselves hoarse.

In the closing moments, Westwood scored a touchdown to take a two point lead. On their subsequent possession, the other team scored a long touchdown on a surprise play that caught the Westwood defense flat-footed. Now Westwood was down by three. One minute to go.

Westwood took the kickoff and brought it out to the thirty-yard line. Two plays gained little. Then Westwood's quarterback dumped a short pass off to the right side receiver, a kid named Tim Wellborn. The other team's safety hit him hard but didn't wrap his arms around him to complete the tackle.

Tim staggered for a few steps but shook off the tackle and kept his feet. Then he got his balance. He took off, hitting full stride in a couple of steps. The Westwood fans leapt to their feet as he streaked down the sideline. He had two men to beat. He cut toward the middle of the field and they lost their angle on him. *A terrific move by a high school kid,* thought Clint.

Tim accelerated to the goal line. A cornerback from the other team hit him in desperation at the five-yard line.

Again Tim staggered and took three more steps. He fell over the goal line for the touchdown. It had been a gutty, tough and determined play by the young man. Clint made a note on his Blackberry to call Coach Miller at Weller College and tell him about the quarterback and the wide receiver, as well as a couple of the defensive players. They weren't big, but they impressed Clint with their hustle and aggressiveness.

The game ended as time ran out on a desperate drive by the other team. The Westwood stands cheered in delight. McKenna hugged Clint as they jumped up and down in excitement.

When things calmed down, Logan put his hand on Clint's shoulder. "Clint," Logan said, "We haven't had dinner yet. Have you eaten?"

In the excitement of the game, he hadn't thought about hunger, but now he realized that he'd become ravenous. He said, "No, I haven't. I'm starving."

"Then why don't you come with us?" said Logan. "We're going to Gino's for pizza as soon as our son finishes up here. Shouldn't be too long."

Clint glanced at McKenna. She smiled to encourage him. "Please come, Clint. I'd enjoy your company."

"Are you sure I wouldn't be in the way?"

At that moment Joey, Logan's 10-year-old son came over. Soaked with sweat and delirious with happiness, Clint grinned at how Westwood's last minute win thrilled the boy.

Mickey introduced Clint to him. He told Joey how Clint had been the quarterback on the Westwood team some years ago. Joey's delight flattered Clint, who grinned and accepted Logan's invitation to go out for a bite with his family.

"Great. We've got that settled," said McKenna. "Let me tell Gil we're going ahead and we'll meet him there." She jogged away.

Clint turned to Logan. "Who's Gil?" he asked.

"Gil Westlake, her sort of boyfriend. He's one of the assistant coaches."

"Oh, shoot, Dr. Logan, I can't come then. I'd be a third wheel. I'd feel awkward."

"Don't be silly. You're coming with me, to catch up. Also: Clint, you're 25 years old. You can call me Mickey."

Clint hesitated. "But. . ."

Then Pete Morley, the head coach, came over and Mickey and he exchanged greetings. "Pete," said Mickey. "Do you remember this guy?"

Pete turned to Clint and peered at him. His face lit up with delight. "Clint Byrne! For gosh sakes, how are you doing?"

Clint shook hands, and then filled Pete in on things about his job and so forth. "How do you know Mickey?"

"He and I were good friends when he taught here," said Pete. "We've stayed friends since he left."

Clint nodded. "Mr. Morley," he began, but Pete cut him off.

"Clint, you're old enough to call me Pete," he laughed.

Clint chuckled also and told Pete that he wanted to let Weller's head coach know about the players he'd observed.

"Yeah," said Pete. "Those guys ought to play college ball, for sure, like Division III. Here's a couple more possibilities." And he mentioned a few other players whom he thought would do well in a small college program and whose grades would allow them to be admitted to the school.

"Where's McKenna?" asked Pete.

"You know her?" asked Clint.

"She student taught here in the English department, and now she's on the faculty. She's a great young woman," said Pete.

"Yeah," said Mickey. "She's been dating Gil Westlake."

"Oh," said Pete, his smile fading.

"What's up?" asked Mickey.

"Gil's not in a great mood. He didn't get the head coaching job here, you remember—"

"Right," said Mickey.

"—And tonight I moved him to coach the sophomore team. I brought Bill Wyatt over to the varsity."

"That sounds like a good deal for Gil, doesn't it?" said Mickey.

"Yeah, it'll give him some head coaching experience. I thought he'd be pleased. But he didn't take it well." After another moment or two Pete excused himself and shook hands with Clint and Mickey as he departed.

Clint turned to see McKenna on the other side of the field talking to one of the young coaches who sulked and frowned. *Frowning at McKenna?* thought Clint in amazement. The coach had the look of a wounded martyr on his face, eyes cast skyward like the medieval portrait of St. Sebastian about to receive the seventeenth arrow.

McKenna's smile faded and then she looked damned mad. She put her hands on her hips and let Gil have it.

Clint couldn't hear her words, but he didn't need to. *Ouch,* he thought, and winced for Gil. Whatever Gil had said to her had plunged him into deep, blistering hot water with her. Clint found himself feeling glad she wasn't angry at him.

In another moment, McKenna waved her hands back and forth in front of her, like a referee calling for a timeout. Then she threw up her hands and walked away, leaving Gil standing there, stunned into silence.

She stormed back to Mickey and Clint. "Okay," McKenna said. "Let's go."

"What about—" began Mickey.

"I told him you were coming, Clint. He got mad. He's being an ass."

"Oh," said Mickey.

"I told him to give serious consideration to going to hell." She turned and walked away.

Logan caught Clint's eye and grinned. "Rand and I didn't think Gil was the guy for her anyhow," he said in a confidential whisper.

"Oh," said Clint.

They followed her to Mickey's car. "McKenna, would you like to ride with me?" asked Clint. "I mean, Joey's a nice kid, but sitting in the same car with him. . ." he grinned at the sweaty nine-year-old and pinched his nose. The kid laughed and took a swipe at him.

"Sure, I'd love to," said McKenna, recovering her good mood. He led her to his car. While he drove, he had to struggle not to stare at her splendid legs in the shorts outfit.

"You saw the fight I had," she said.

"Well, I didn't mean to," he said. "I'm afraid I couldn't help but notice, though."

"I'm still mad," she said.

"Not at me, I hope," Clint smiled.

"No, no, of course not," she said. "Okay, I'll tell you."

"It's none of my business—" he began, but she interrupted.

"He told me that he'd made reservations for him and me at the Sybaris," she said. "I told him I didn't want to go."

"What's the Sybaris?" he asked, puzzled.

"Oh," she shrugged, "it's a sex motel. Round beds, silk sheets, movies, hot tubs, a couple of the suites have pools—like that."

"You mean, kind of sleazy?"

"Oh no," she said. "Not at all. It's very lovely. But it's for married people."

"Uh, huh," he said. He noticed that he felt intense jealousy. What on earth? He thought. "I haven't been dating him very long," she said. "A couple of months, maybe. I like him—or at least I did—but I told him I wasn't ready to make the commitment that comes with making love," she said. "He began behaving like an idiot. I let him have it."

"I did see that part," he smiled.

"I'm sorry," she said. "I shouldn't have made a scene."

"I don't blame him," said Clint. "As for wanting to take you to the Sybaris, I'm sure most of the men at the game felt the way he did."

She looked at him, saw the corners of his mouth twitching, and gave him a little whack on the arm. "Thank you," she said. "I think."

"It's a compliment, McKenna," he chuckled. He began to make conversation, and managed to seem somewhat coherent. He told her about his job, his MBA, his apartment. When they arrived at the restaurant, they located Fixx and his family without difficulty.

At 11:00, Fixx and his wife made excuses, took their son, and rose to leave. Clint insisted on grabbing the check. Then, "McKenna, would you like to stay? Maybe we could go out for a little while?"

McKenna hesitated for perhaps a third of a second before she agreed and said good night to her aunt and uncle. Joey, perhaps a quarter inch from falling asleep, murmured something that might have been goodnight as they left.

Clint took McKenna to a dance club and they danced until almost three o'clock, when McKenna told him that she had to get a few hours of sleep. He drove her home, following the directions that she gave him at the restaurant. She fell asleep within moments of him backing the car out of the lot.

To his delight, McKenna leaned against his shoulder for the drive home. Her head bumped against his shoulder. He considered it a life highlight.

At Fixx's house, he woke her with a gentle shake and

enjoyed watching her stretch to wake up. He took her to the door, opened it and turned to say "Good night."

Except that she came to his arms, put her arms around him and they began to kiss as if that was the next item on the evening's agenda.

Chapter Seven

Cepha thanked the truck driver and stepped down from the passenger side of a Peterbilt semi whose driver was making a delivery at the loading dock of a Home Depot in Batavia, Illinois. The truck had just left Randall Road, a major north-south link in the western suburbs of Chicago. Cepha thought he might walk into Geneva, find a restaurant, and see if he could scrounge some food in exchange for some work, maybe.

How strange, he thought, not by any means for the first time. When he had a job that benefitted others, that served other people, The Voice allowed him to rest for a time. He had been able to go to a few universities, from which he graduated, then to some medical schools, from which he'd also graduated, done an internship and then a residency, and then achieved doctoral degrees in history and psychology and biology. He sometimes would just begin to feel that his wandering was over.

Then, The Voice would come.

He'd been on all the continents, in the major cities, sailed the oceans, but never could he stop for good. He had to keep wandering, walking, surviving and waiting. He didn't like to think about some of the hideous disasters he'd witnessed. He knew that some authors had linked him to the calamities, as if they were his fault, saying that when he showed up, unpleasant things would happen.

Cepha walked around to the front of the store and entered

through the contractor entrance. He found a coffee pot and drew a cup of dark, scalding coffee. He wore jeans, heavy boots and a brown coat, and he took off some lined work gloves and stuffed them into his pocket. The woman behind the counter greeted him and he chatted with her for a few moments before setting off to walk through the store. She'd mistaken him for a contractor, he knew, but that was okay. He had a variety of identities.

As he went, he looked at employee name tags but saw no one named Clint and no one named Nicole. That didn't surprise or bother him. They'd show up. He'd learned patience over the years.

He found himself in the tool department and wandered down the aisle, looking at the power tools, the measuring devices, screwdrivers, wrenches. He paused in front of a display of hammers and saw a large mallet made of hard rubber. Tears came to his eyes as he relived the day when he saw the Roman centurion kneel on the arm of the young Jew and drive the huge spike through the Jew's wrist into crossbeam of the wooden cross—

Cepha shook his head to clear the pain of the vision, one which had haunted him almost every day. He couldn't face it now any better than he could then.

Cepha finished his coffee and walked out of the huge store. He saw a sign which said "Help Wanted"—

Hmm. He'd worked as a clerk on occasion. Maybe...

No, The Feeling came. *Keep moving. Don't stop here.*

Cepha walked down to the east-west road on the south side of the huge store. He saw that it was called Fabyan Parkway and tried to remember if he'd walked it before. He found a brown bag which contained the remains of someone's lunch: half of a roast beef sandwich with some yellow cheese, half an apple and an unwanted candy bar. It made a sparse breakfast as he walked along the road toward the rising sun.

He came to a bridge. It hadn't been here the last time he'd come to this area, and it stood a long way above the river.

Cepha walked to the center of the span and looked over into the Fox River. The water, a swift flow of cold water from the north, rushed down toward the Illinois River, and then would go on to the Mississippi.

He stood and considered. He hadn't tried this for some time.

He climbed to the top of the guard rail and jumped into the surging Fox River.

Chapter Eight

Ruth Frey drove to a homeless shelter in Palatine, Illinois, not too far from her home, where she visited and worked with some of the desperate, defeated people who had nowhere else to go. It always made her sad, but in a couple of cases today, she saw that perhaps a few might have the potential to get back on their feet and do something to get their lives moving again.

She had just climbed back into her little car and started down Route 53, intending to head into Hanover Park and to visit another shelter there when her cell phone rang. She assumed that it would be her son, but to her surprise the caller was a longtime friend who headed up another homeless shelter in the town of Aurora, just south of Batavia.

"Ruth, it's good to hear your voice," said Joan Little, the administrator, and the two friends made a little small talk, catching up on family and personal matters. At last, Joan asked Ruth, "Did you plan to come here today?"

"I hadn't planned on it, but I could if you need me to," said Ruth into her Bluetooth earpiece.

"I wish you would," Joan said. "I have someone here that I really think you ought to see."

"Why, what's up?" said Ruth, puzzled at this suggestion. Joan had never made such a request of her.

"We have a man who tried to commit suicide in Batavia," Joan went on. "He jumped off the Fabyan Road Bridge over the

Fox River in Batavia."

Ruth got a picture in her mind. "And he survived that?" she said.

"Not only survived," said Joan. "He's fine. No broken bones, no sprained ankles, no hypothermia."

"Hypothermia?" asked Ruth.

"Yes," said Joan. "The Fox is as cold as melted snow at this time of year. Not only that, it's only four or five feet deep where he went in, and the bottom is flat rock. He *should* be pretty beaten up, but he's fine. Not even a sniffle. No bruises. He stayed in the water for quite a while until the police got a diver to haul him out."

Ruth stared at the road for a few moments, speechless. Suicides were not unknown to this area, but to survive intact—

"Okay," she said. "I'll be there in a half hour."

"I called David Hanes, too," said Joan. "I told him about this man and he became pretty mysterious. He said he'd come as soon as he could. I think he's on his way now."

"It'll be good to see him," said Ruth. They hung up and Ruth puzzled about the conversation. How could someone survive such a fall unharmed?

She had to smile as she thought about David Hanes. Now the pastor of a large church in North Aurora, David had a remarkable story. Addicted to drugs, homeless, uneducated, the police had found him in a San Francisco public toilet, passed out under the urinals, incoherent and babbling. The police had taken him to a hospital, and then to a detox unit at another hospital.

As he recovered, a man—David never knew his name—came into his room and began to talk to him about getting his life going. The man gave him a Bible, prayed with him, and David's whole life changed.

The last time he saw the man, David asked for his name. "I go by many names," the man had said.

The enigmatic answer challenged David too much to respond in anything like a rational way. He managed to nod, and he tried to focus on the man sitting across from him.

He had a moment of looking into the man's eyes and saw depth, age, sadness. David asked, "How did you know about me?"

"I can't explain, David," said the man. "No, I would like to, but I can't."

"Will I ever see you again?" asked David.

The man hesitated. "I think so," he said. "Go on with your life. Get it going." Then he left the room and David never saw him again.

David, released from custody, the hospital, and the drug habit, went back to college. He finished his bachelor's degree, then went on to seminary and became ordained. Over the next several years, he had become the senior pastor of a successful church and he enjoyed a fine reputation. His key interest in his ministry involved helping homeless people to resurrect their lives as he had.

Well, if anyone can counsel this man at the shelter, it would be David, beyond doubt, Ruth thought.

As she drove she picked up her cell phone and speed dialed her son.

"Professor Frey," he said.

"It's your mother," she said into her Bluetooth earpiece. "Is everything okay?"

"Yeah," he said. "Nicole took the rest of the week off, and she's staying with her brother and sister-in-law for a few days. I'm going over there about four o'clock."

"I'm down in Aurora," said Ruth. "I have to see a person on a very strange assignment. Would you like to have dinner?"

"I take it you wouldn't mind if I brought Nicole," he said.

"Of course not," she sniffed. "I'd be angry if you didn't."

Luke laughed and agreed to meet her at a restaurant about 6 o'clock.

When she hung up, Ruth smiled to herself. She had enjoyed meeting the young woman named Nicole and hoped her son wouldn't blow it with her. His divorce had damaged him, for sure. But she saw the way he smiled when he looked at Nicole, the soft glow in his eyes, and the gentle way he talked to her. She knew him well enough to know that he'd developed strong feelings for her.

In love already? She wondered. Well, it wasn't impossible, she shrugged.

Ruth pulled into the parking lot at the Homeless Shelter and made her way to the office of her friend Joan.

She and her friend chatted about some people whom Ruth had been assisting for the last few weeks. Then David came in, smiling, but she could see a little apprehension in his face.

"What's wrong?" she had to ask at last.

"I have a hunch about who this person could be," David said. "I'm a little nervous."

"Well, let's go, then," said Joan, and led them back into the shelter.

A man lay on a bed, staring at the ceiling, his eyes unfocused, as if his mind wasn't really engaged. Ruth wasn't surprised to see the expression. So many people that she dealt with had nothing to live for, nothing to engage their interest whatever. Some were so crazy that she didn't know why they weren't locked up.

"Cepha," said Joan. He turned and fixed each of them in turn with a disinterested stare. However, he paused as his eyes met those of Ruth. She gave him a smile, but then he looked away.

"What is it?" he said.

"Some of my friends want to meet you," Joan said.

Cepha swung his legs onto the floor and stood. He had good manners, thought Ruth. At least he didn't tell us to go to hell.

Joan introduced David first. Her pastor friend stood staring at Cepha, almost as if he recognized him. Cepha stared back and broke into a smile. "You've become a clergyman, have you not?" Cepha asked.

"Yes," said David. "But I'm not wearing clericals. How would you know that?"

Cepha shrugged and shook David's hand. "I know you, David," he said. "I know you. I'm very glad to see you." David let his eyes drop to the ground. He nodded.

"I believe that, yes, Cepha," said David. "Yes, you're right."

Cepha smiled. "San Francisco, was it not?" he asked. David nodded again.

Then Cepha turned to Ruth, who stood by watching this encounter, puzzled. She realized that the two men had a relationship that somehow transcended anything she understood. "May I know your name?" Cepha asked her. His manners were impeccable. Though he spoke excellent English, Ruth heard the merest hint of an accent. She guessed that he might not be American born.

"I'm Dr. Ruth Frey," she said, and took his hand.

"Another doctor?" he said. "I thought they all agreed I was fine."

"My doctorate is in sociology," she said. "I work as a social worker."

"Sociology," he mused. "That's a degree I don't have."

"Do you have a Ph. D.?" she asked.

"Yes, a few of them," he smiled. "And a couple of doctor of medicine degrees, as well."

Ruth drew back in some surprise. He didn't look old enough to have that much education.

"Tell me something," said Cepha. "Am I not correct in saying you know a young woman named Nicole?"

Ruth's mouth dropped open for a moment. Then she nodded. "Yes, I do," she said. "My son is seeing a young woman named Nicole."

"Yes," said Cepha. "I thought so. Anyhow, what did you want to know?" He wasn't discourteous with the question. Ruth couldn't take offense.

"I want to know who you are," said Ruth.

He shrugged with a little grin. "You do not believe that I am named Cepha?"

"I did some research this time, Cepha," David said. "Some people name you Cartiphilus the gate keeper. Another name is Ahaseurus. I recall that some name you Malchus, as well."

Cepha, looking surprised, gave David a broad smile. "Pastor, you have indeed become a scholar," he said. "I am very proud. My real name is indeed Malchus, though I haven't used that name for some time."

"Can we speak in private?" asked Ruth.

"Yes, of course," said Cepha. "I have nothing to hide. But I'm afraid I'll have to leave soon."

"Why?" asked Ruth.

"I have an assignment," said Cepha.

Ruth stared for a moment. "What do you mean?"

Cepha lifted his shoulders. "Sometimes—a few times a year—The Voice speaks to me. Then I have to go where it tells me." He gave David a look, and David nodded back, as if in understanding.

Ruth puzzled over this as Joan showed them to a conference room. Cepha and David chatted until David said, "Can we help you?"

"No one has ever been able to do so," said Cepha. "I fear that The Curse will persist for some time."

"Have you tried saying you're sorry?" said David.

Cepha looked at him. "I'd like to, Pastor. I'd like to confess that I turned my back on the one who healed my ear, who kept me from being killed. But—" he paused. "Have you read *Macbeth*?"

"Yes," said Ruth and David nodded.

"Do you remember how Macbeth heard Duncan's prayer, yet because he intended to murder the King, he could not pronounce 'Amen'?"

"Yes," said Ruth. "I do remember the scene."

"Shakespeare could have taken that line from my life. Like Macbeth, I can't pronounce the words I want to. I want to say I am sorry. I want to apologize. Yet I cannot. My heart remains frozen in the place when I pronounced my curse on the Nazarene."

"Can anything help you?" asked Ruth.

"Are you saying you believe me?" said Cepha, with a wry smile.

"Should I not?" she asked.

"Why should you?" he countered.

"You are my patient," said Ruth, covering his hand with hers and giving it a gentle squeeze. "If you lie to me, I cannot help you."

He smiled. "Do you not think me mad?"

"No," she said. "I have no evidence to contradict your story. Yet I learned that you were standing in the Fox River for over an hour. You should have been killed or hurt by that fall."

"I hadn't tried that in some time," he said.

"You try killing yourself often?" said David.

"Less so now than the first several centuries."

Ruth thought. "Why do you have to leave here?"

"I never stay anywhere more than a few hours. I wear out my welcome."

"Can you tell us what happened?" asked David.

"What happened?" asked Cepha. "What do you mean?"

"The night before the crucifixion," said David.

Cepha shrugged. "I came to the garden," he said. "I followed the soldiers there. When we arrived, we found the Nazarene standing in the moonlight."

"You saw the betrayal, then," said Ruth.

"I'm sure you mean Iscariot," said Cepha, and now Ruth saw a tear roll down his cheek. "My betrayal. . ." Then he didn't go on.

"Peter drew his sword, didn't he," said David, his voice gentle. "And struck."

Cepha nodded.

"He cut off your ear," said David. Cepha nodded.

"And the Nazarene healed you, didn't he," David asked in low voice.

Cepha didn't move. "Can you tell us what happened the next day?" asked Ruth.

"I saw him coming, staggering under the weight of the cross," said Cepha, his voice so low they had to struggle to hear. "I stood by the side of the road, jeering with everyone else. He missed a step and fell. The cross fell against my leg and barked my shin. I. . ."

"Cepha?" said Ruth, when he didn't go on.

He shook his head, unable to continue.

"Shall I finish the story?" said David. Cepha nodded. "You lost your temper and hit the Nazarene with a backhand. You accompanied the blow with a bitter curse. He said—"

"'I am going, and you shall stay until I return,'" mumbled Cepha.

The room fell silent for a few moments. "Could you not repent? Say you are sorry?" asked Ruth.

"Yes," said David. "Why not?"

Cepha looked up at them. "When I struck him, something happened," he said. "My heart and my body and my soul were frozen in that moment. I don't experience physical aging. I don't have the ability to say I'm sorry."

A silence of several moments ensued. "Could you stay here for a while?" asked Ruth.

"Why?"

"So I can figure out how to help you," she said.

"You cannot," said Cepha. "Why would you, at that?"

"I consider you my patient," she said. "I help my patients when I can."

He smiled, but it was not a smile of condescension or indulgence. Rather, Ruth's words appeared to touch him in a unique way. "Thank you, Dr. Frey," he said. "Your kindness does you much credit."

"Could you find a way to stay?"

He shrugged. "Once in a while, I am allowed to rest for some time, yes."

Joan spoke up. "You said you trained as a medical doctor." He agreed. "What if you stay to help here at the Center with medical care?"

Cepha thought. "Yes, that might be okay." He thought a bit more, and then shrugged, "I could try."

Fifteen minutes later, Ruth turned again onto Randall Road and headed north toward the restaurant where she would meet her son and Nicole. "What on earth?" she said aloud, as she stopped at a traffic light. A horn blipped behind her and she lifted a hand in apology. She had to struggle to focus on driving.

She arrived at the restaurant and walked into the bar area, where she ordered a martini. She sipped it and thought about the man at the shelter.

Cepha. David knew him. Cepha had done something for David.

What had he done?

Cepha, until an hour or so ago, had been a legend for Ruth. A myth. Condemned to walk the earth without a home, unable to stay in one place more than a few hours, sleeping and eating as he could, without family, without hope—

She sipped the martini, lost in thought. "How can I help

you," she asked. "How can I melt a heart that has been frozen for centuries?"

Or was it? He'd been kind to David at some time in the past. David didn't want to talk about it. Probably, Ruth thought, the situation transcended a ready explanation.

She didn't see her son approach her, nor hear his greeting. He had to give her arm a gentle prod. "Mom!" he said. "Wake up!"

"Oh!" said Ruth. "Oh, I'm sorry, Dear," she said. She turned and hugged her son and the lovely young woman named Nicole.

"How are you, Dear?" Ruth asked.

Nicole smiled and they chatted until Luke got a little impatient. "Let's get a table, shall we?"

Once they were seated, they ordered cocktails and started to unwind together. Ruth spoke up. "Any luck with finding your belongings, Nicole?" asked Ruth.

She shrugged in answer. "Maybe. Jack found some of the stuff in a Salvation Army store, and he thinks he has a line on tracking down the Explorer…"

Salvation Army. A homeless shelter. A man on a cot, a blank stare on his face, lost in some world—

"Mom."

What has he seen? Where has he roamed? People almost always associate his name and legend with major disasters—

"Mom!" yelled Luke.

"Oh!" yipped Ruth.

"Mom," Luke said. "We've been talking to you. Are you aware of what we've been saying?"

"I'm sorry, Dears," Ruth apologized, and they smiled at her.

"Mom, this isn't like you," said Luke. "What's happened?"

Ruth thought for a second. "Let me tell you a story…"

* * * * *

The three rascals walked out of town and met the old man on the bridge. They insulted him and reviled him as a filthy Jew.

The man stood listening, calm, oblivious and didn't rise to their taunts. At last, they told him that they were on a mission to kill Death, the enemy of all men.

He didn't think it strange, from what they could tell. "Go over the bridge," he said. "I left Death by that huge oak you see yonder."

Without thanking him, they ran to the huge oak. Beneath it, they found a chest full of gold. They lost all thought of the search for Death.

One went into town, where he bought a dram of poison and bread and wine. He spiked the wine with the poison. When he arrived back at the oak, the other two killed him with knives. Then, they drank the poisoned wine.

* * * * *

"*The Pardoner's Tale*," said Nicole. "By Geoffrey Chaucer."

"Quite right," nodded Ruth.

"Mom, I've known you all my life," said Luke. "Therefore, I know that you have a point in telling us this story somewhere in there."

She nodded. "Yes. The old man they met at the bridge. . ."

"Many people think Chaucer re-told the legend of the Wandering Jew," said Nicole. She smiled at Luke. "English minor," she explained. "Many people consider *The Pardoner's Tale* one of the greatest short stories of all time."

"Quite right," nodded Ruth again.

"Mom, I know you think in abstracts sometimes," said Luke. "Therefore I'm hoping that you'll give us some hint of why we should give thought to a 600 year old story, a myth."

"Well, that's just it," Ruth said. "It isn't a myth."

Silence descended on the table. At that moment the waitress showed up with an appetizer, artichoke hearts in a cream sauce on toast points. The group ate for a few seconds. "Yummy," said Nicole.

"Umm," said Ruth.

Nicole took a sip of water and said, "What do you mean when you say it isn't a myth?"

Luke spoke up. "I think Mom means that people consider the story a parable about Israel, wandering friendless in the world, condemned to wander until…"

"It isn't a parable either," said Ruth.

Now Luke turned to her. "Okay," he said. "Then explain."

"The old man at the bridge," said Ruth. "The Wandering Jew. He's real."

Again Luke and Nicole stared at her. "Real?" said Nicole.

"Mom?" said Luke.

"The Wandering Jew. He's not a myth. He's not a parable. He's a real person. I've met him."

Ruth told her son and Nicole about Cepha, the man at the shelter who was a skilled doctor and psychologist, who appeared to be personable, friendly and likeable.

Luke shook his head. "Please tell me this is some sort of joke."

"No, it's not," she said. "He's the strangest person I've met in this job."

"Crazy?" asked Luke.

"Probably not," she said. "He seems completely rational, articulate, serious and in control. I can't imagine that someone who's insane could conduct himself as this man does."

"And you say he's a doctor," said Luke.

"Many times over, and not just in medicine, but in theology, law, and history," agreed Ruth. "Not only that, but he has some peculiar, and secret, relationship with David Hanes."

Luke explained David to Nicole, who said, "I wonder if Cepha helped David, at some point."

Ruth thought. "Well, I guess that makes as much sense as anything else," she shrugged. "I didn't feel free to ask about it, anyhow."

"Mom, are you aware that this sounds as goofy as hell?" asked Luke.

"Well, come and meet him with me," challenged Ruth. "See what you think, Luke."

The conversation continued for some time. At last, Nicole excused herself to the washroom.

"Luke," said his mother. "She is a spectacular young woman."

"I know," he smiled.

"Get her to marry you."

"What?" laughed Luke.

"If you want to avoid incurring my eternal wrath," said Ruth, "You will marry that girl as soon as possible."

"What makes you think she'd have me?"

"Don't be silly," scoffed Ruth. "She lights up like a candle when she's with you."

"Well, Cinnamon wants to try to have her marriage

annulled, rather than working on divorce," Luke said. "We'd have to wait until that's complete, or until she can arrange the divorce."

"Do you think that's a problem?" asked Ruth.

"Not as far as we can see," said Luke. "Her husband has vanished. He may be dead, for all we know."

Ruth nodded and sipped at a martini until her dinner arrived a few moments later.

Chapter Nine

It was a few days before the volleyball season would start. Practices were going well. It looked like the team could be good.

Nancy Barnes, the Westwood High School volleyball coach, rinsed off under a hot shower in the coaches' locker room, dead tired, but mad as well. Her stomach churned. She'd had an argument with some parent after girls' volleyball practice that afternoon.

The parent had come into the gym after the workout and conditioning session. She was convinced that her daughter was the victim of Nancy's ineptitude and unkindness.

"I don't understand why you don't value Heather more," said the parent. "She's the best player you have."

"I'm sorry to disagree," said Nancy, making a powerful effort not to tell the parent that she regarded the woman's daughter as a lazy slug who didn't deserve to be on the team. Struggling to be diplomatic, she said, "Please understand my position. Heather doesn't try hard in practice. She sulks and is rude not only to me but to her teammates. I'm just one or two more incidents from cutting her from the team. I cannot overlook her attitude, which, I must say, disrupts our effort and detracts from team morale."

"You don't understand how to handle her," the parent said. "You have to present Heather with choices."

Nancy, a ten-year veteran of the teaching profession,

thought that by this stage of her career she'd heard it all. This assertion, however, struck her as something new. She struggled to find words to respond. "What?" Nancy managed.

"Yes," said the mother with a look of contempt. "If you loved and understood the players on your team, you would find ways to accommodate differences in attitude and personality. You wouldn't just condemn. . ."

"Excuse me," said Nancy, recovering her wits. "I am the coach of the team. I make decisions about who plays and who doesn't based on class effort and grades, attitudes, work habits, efforts and team play, not just talent. I am not obligated to, nor will I, make separate rules to accommodate differences in students. On the contrary. They work within my parameters. Now if there's nothing else, you'll have to excuse me."

The parent started to say something but Nancy didn't hear. She turned and walked toward the locker room to hustle the students out.

When the locker room was clear, she checked lockers, and then went to the coaches' office. A few people sat there doing some paperwork. "What's wrong?" asked one of the other coaches. "You look like someone beat you up."

Nancy related the event with the parent. "Yeah, I've dealt with that mother. A total wacko," grunted another coach, a nice guy named Jason Cohen. "Don't let it ruin your evening."

"Not a chance," said Nancy. "Ron's taking me out to buy me a new car tonight. First, we're going to have dinner at Dino's."

"Yeah," said Jason. "Relax and enjoy yourself. Life is good."

Nancy called her husband, Ron, to let him know she was leaving. "I'll be home in about a half hour," she said. Jason offered to walk her to her car.

* * * * *

Two hours later, Ron Barnes called the police. His wife had called him at 5:30, to say she was on the way. She was overdue and she wasn't answering her cell phone.

"Maybe she stopped for some shopping?" asked the policeman.

"No. We planned to have dinner together at a local restaurant, and then go look for a new car for her."

"Did you call the restaurant?"

"Yes, over an hour ago. They know her. They said she hadn't been in. Yes, they told me they would have her call if she came in."

He gave them a description of her car, and the license plate number.

The police called him back in about an hour. They'd found her car in the high school parking lot. No, the officer had checked and no one was around except for the night custodial staff. The custodians had checked the locker rooms, then the rest of the building.

Ron's stomach fell with fear.

Two days went by, but Ron received no calls, no notes, or any communication from or about Nancy. The FBI had been alerted and were trying to trace Nancy Barnes' movements.

On the third day, Ron got a call from the state police. "This is Lieutenant Rusty Ivers. We think we've found your wife. Could you meet me at the medical examiner's office?" Rusty gave him directions.

Ron ran to his car and sped to the medical examiner's office. Lieutenant Ivers met him. They shook hands and Ivers tried to prepare him.

"Is this as bad as it sounds?" said Ron.

"Yes," Rusty told him. "The woman we found died in a fiery crash. Indeed, the fire burned the body almost beyond recognition."

Ron staggered a few steps and clutched at his stomach. "Oh my God," said Ron.

"This won't be easy, Mr. Barnes. It was a dreadful accident."

"Okay," said Ron. "Let's get it over with." He pulled out his handkerchief and wiped at his eyes. Then he pressed the handkerchief to his lips.

Ron Barnes saw the personal effects first. They had her purse, her rings, and a necklace.

"We found her body in a car. Another person died in the accident as well, a teacher named Jason Cohen. The fire burned the car to a cinder."

The officer led him to a window with a Venetian blind curtain. Ivers stood at his right side.

Rusty opened the blind. Ron held his breath. A body lay on a table, covered with a white sheet. An attendant pulled the sheet back. Ron bit back a scream.

Ron almost didn't recognize Nancy. The mental picture of her burned and charred body lying on the cold table would haunt him for the rest of his life. Ivers took his elbow as the tears which Ron had been fighting to hold back now burst forth.

"Yes, that's Nancy," he told the cop. Ivers closed the curtains.

"I'm so sorry," said Lieutenant Ivers. "Do you need a few moments?"

"Yes. Perhaps I could sit down. . ."

"Sure. Over here." Lieutenant Ivers pointed to a door that

stood open on the other side of the room.

The cop led him into a room. "I'm sorry, Mr. Barnes," he said again. The lieutenant showed him a chair, and then took out a notepad.

"Thanks for your kindness," said Ron. "I'm pretty shaken. You understand."

"Yeah, I know. I'd like to ask a couple of questions, if you can handle them now."

"Sure."

"Can I get you some water or coffee?"

"No, thank you. Let's just. . ." Ron broke off, again pressing the handkerchief to his lips.

"Okay," said Ivers.

"Let me ask you something first," said Ron. Rusty nodded. "Do you have a theory?"

"No," said Rusty. "And yes, we investigated your movements for the day she went missing."

"I see. You suspect the husband first, right?" asked Ron, his voice dull.

"Something like that," Rusty said with a shrug. "But you're in the clear, Mr. Barnes."

"I relieved to hear it," said Ron.

Rusty looked Ron in the eye. "I can't think of an easy way to ask this, Mr. Barnes. Do you have any reason to believe that your wife could have had a romantic involvement with Mr. Cohen?"

Ron fixed Rusty with a blank stare for several moments. Then he comprehended the question. "Oh. I get it. The man in the car. No, I have—No, none whatever. We saw Jason at faculty get-togethers, but. . ."

"On the surface, it seems like they were together," said Rusty. "We can't spot a reason for this accident. No skid marks on the road. The road hasn't been even moist for a couple of days. They shouldn't have gone off the road. No evidence of a heart attack in Mr. Cohen. He has an almost flawless driving record."

"Look," said Ron. "Here's all I know. Nancy called me at 6:30. She was on her way home. She and I were going out. I had dinner reservations for 7:00 at Dino's Restaurant, and then we were going to shop for a new car for her."

"Uh, huh," said Rusty. He wrote on the pad. "Mr. Barnes, I have a feeling this has nothing to do with a lover's nest thing. They were acquaintances in the P. E. department, but no one seems to feel that they were even close friends."

"Then why do you ask?"

"I'm sorry," said Rusty, and Ron nodded acceptance. "I know it's offensive. I just needed to see if you had any suspicions. . ."

"None whatever."

"Yeah. Let me be frank. I think someone murdered your wife, Mr. Barnes. I just can't figure out why people keep hurting coaches at Westwood High School." Rusty talked with Ron for a few more moments, then had one of his men drive him home and stay with him until Ron's parents could be summoned.

Two days later, Ron held his wife's memorial service. As she requested in her will, he had her body cremated.

Many teachers and students, including athletes who had worked with Nancy years before, attended. Her best friend gave a tearful eulogy in which she described Nancy as a dedicated, well liked and well respected member of the high school community. Her pastor spoke of her as a devoted wife, daughter and friend.

Rusty stood at the back of the church, moved to tears himself. This woman should not be in ashes. The circumstances convinced him that someone had murdered Nancy Barnes and Jason Cohen.

Later that day, Rusty met with the medical examiner that had performed the autopsy on Nancy. The autopsy struck Rusty as strange, too. The pathologist told Rusty that her liver was missing. Yes, the body was burned to a severe extent, but the doctor couldn't find any evidence that her liver had been in her body when she died. Jason's body had all its organs intact, on the other hand.

"You mean someone took her liver?" repeated Rusty, surprised and in disbelief.

"Yep," said the doctor. "For some reason, they wanted her liver, not her heart, eyes, or any other organs. Mr. Cohen's body showed no signs of surgery, but I'm very sure someone strangled him before the accident."

Rusty did a double take. "So I'm investigating a double homicide, not a traffic mishap?" The medical examiner nodded.

"Who steals someone's liver?" Rusty asked the pathologist.

The doctor shrugged. "Only one thing I can think of," he said. "It could have been removed for transplant."

"So someone used her as a donor?"

"Not by choice," said the doctor. "You only have one liver. You can't live without it."

"My God," said Rusty. "Someone murdered this woman for her liver?"

"Looks like a good guess."

"Where in the U. S. do they do that type of transplant surgery?"

"Too many places to list in a hurry," said the pathologist. "They have a substantial waiting list for donors."

"Jeez," said Rusty.

"Yeah. Remember Walter Payton contracted liver disease? Lots of people volunteered to donate livers. Of course, you can't do that."

"I remember when Walter died, of course," said Rusty. "My favorite Chicago Bear of all time."

"I'm a little older than you," said the pathologist. "I idolized a big guy named Doug Atkins. He played in the early sixties and the '63 Bears had one of the greatest pro defenses of all time. This guy wound up in the Hall of Fame as a Defensive end. University of Tennessee. 6-8, 280 pounds."

"Good, huh?" grinned Rusty.

"Yeah. He seemed bigger than 6-8. I swear, he'd just tackle the whole backfield and throw out people until he found the one with the ball. Some of the linemen who played against him swore that if they made Doug mad, he'd pick them up and throw them into the quarterback."

Rusty laughed, and left. He drove toward home, through for the day, happy to be seeing his lovely wife. Then he thought about the two teachers, now in ashes, and sobered.

Then it struck him. *Good grief. Could all these other incidents be a smoke screen? Set up by someone who wanted to steal a young woman's liver?*

He hugged Paula and kissed her. Then, he led her to the bedroom. A half hour later, he lay next to her, breathing hard. "Wow," she said. "What's that for?"

"Just in case you thought I didn't appreciate you," he said, kissing the tip of her nose. She giggled and snuggled into him.

He couldn't bring himself to tell her about the man on the other side of town who would never kiss his wife hello or goodbye again. The Cohen family had also lost a son and a brother. A tear leaked down Rusty's cheek in the dark of the bedroom.

Chapter Ten

Gil Westlake was the last one in the locker room at the high school, and he realized, that was pretty normal. He really didn't give a rip about going home.

He couldn't help some bitterness and it had been showing in his teaching. His boss, the Department Chairman, had called him in a couple of times to talk about his negative attitude toward his students. His treatment of several of them in routine discipline situations had bordered on abusive, and had certainly been uncalled for.

Well, it wasn't *his* fault, he decided. Of course he was angry. McKenna DiBiasi had blown him off and now had gotten serious about some other guy, so it looked like he had no chance of getting back with her. Yeah, he thought, but she was the right girl for him. And he was the right guy for her. He knew it and he didn't understand why she didn't.

He hadn't gone on a date since she'd dumped him at the football game. He hadn't even considered it.

Oh, well. He got up from his desk, put on his jacket—a letter jacket from his college, at that—and locked up the office. Doc Halladay, the trainer, had gone home, too. Cripes.

He walked out the door and a fist hit him in the stomach. The punch drove his breath away and he fell to his knees. Then someone hit him with a flurry of punches. He hovered just above the level of consciousness as three or four men dragged him to his feet and pulled him to a van. The side door stood open and the men lifted him inside.

A little man, with stunning green eyes, looked back at him. And, suddenly, Gil couldn't look away.

* * * * *

Dale Sadler slouched on the bar stool and contemplated his life. He felt great to be free again after two years of being married to that bitch Nicole. She'd never understood him. Never made an effort to understand him.

Then, the day he'd moved out, she'd left him penniless. She'd closed down the checking account, the savings account, and the Visa card. He'd had to borrow money from his parents, like when he'd been single. He sold the TV, the stereo and the furniture, but he hadn't gotten much for them. He snarled at his wife. He'd make her pay, he vowed.

He needed space, and freedom. He couldn't let a nagging wife handicap him, someone who lorded it over him.

He'd sneaked out that day with all their stuff and his car. Okay, so she'd made the payments on it, but dammit, he had every right to consider it his car. He'd driven it all the time when he'd been married. He felt entitled to it. He'd tried to sell it, but he couldn't because she had the title.

Dale had it all figured out now, however. All he had to do was figure out where she lived, and then go over there and swipe the title. He could forge her signature. Sure, that would be no problem. He'd been doing it for a long time, back before she'd gotten rid of the joint checking account and taken out one on her own. He snorted. She didn't trust him with money.

He became aware of someone standing next to him. He turned to see a somewhat unkempt man who now spoke to him. "You own that SUV in the lot?" asked the man, who looked like he slept in the suit he had on. Short, overweight, needing a shave.

"Yeah," said Dale, a bit annoyed at being interrupted. This didn't sound good. "What's it to you?"

"Well, I'm really sorry," said the man. "I banged into it. 'Fraid it's damaged. I called the cops, they're on the way."

Dale muttered a foul expletive and started for the door. He reached the parking lot and headed toward the Explorer but found the little man had grabbed his sleeve. "Listen," said the man. "Your name is Dale, right?"

Now Dale stopped. "How'd you know that?"

"Well," chuckled the man, "I've sort of been looking for you."

"You have?" said Dale, now getting suspicious.

The man handed him a card. Jack Earle, Private Investigations. Dale saw a phone number on it.

"What do you want?" asked Dale.

"Just the keys to the Explorer, thanks," said the man. "Then you can go back to your beer."

Dale became conscious that two large men had come to stand behind him. Now, he became scared. He went into his bravado bit and growled a filthy expletive. "I ain't giving you nothing," he said.

Jack Earle shrugged, and then nodded. Before Dale knew quite what had happened, the two large men had pinioned his arms behind him.

"Let me put that another way," said Jack Earle. "Perhaps you didn't understand. Give me the keys, now."

The beer-enhanced bravado gave way. "You got no right—"

Jack Earle stepped forward and felt at Dale's pockets. "Ah," he said, reaching into Dale's left front pocket and extracting a key ring. He pushed the Unlock button on the Ford's remote control and the locks flew up. He removed the keys and the remote and put the key ring back in Dale's pocket. Dale, meanwhile, continued his futile struggle with the big men.

"I'll be going now," said Mr. Earle. "So will my friends as soon as I've gone down the street a way, at which time they'll let you go. I imagine you're in some pain. However, let me make a suggestion. I found you without any difficulty. I can do it again, and the next time won't be quite as pleasant. The TV, the stereo, all that stuff you stole, y'know? Bring it by the office at the address on that business card in the next day or so, or we'll come looking for you. Here's an extra card in case you lose one."

He nodded and the men tightened up their grip on his arms and wrist. Tears came to his eyes. "Goodbye for now, Dale," said Mr. Earle. "I hope you take my advice about the stuff."

With that, Earle climbed into the SUV. Before he shut the door, Dale yelled. "Hey!"

"Yes?" said Earle with a smile.

"How'm I s'posa to get home?"

Earle smiled. "Goodnight, Dale." He shut the door and started the car.

Chapter Eleven

Clint awoke on Saturday morning to the phone ringing next to his bed. "Clint?" came a familiar voice. He knew the voice at once.

"Ross," he said, smiling and coming awake. "It's been a couple of years. How are you?" The two friends chatted and caught up.

Ross Burgess, his best friend from college, took a few moments to bring Clint up to date on his family, the girl he planned to marry, and inquired about Clint's life.

"I think I may have met the right girl last night," Clint smiled. "I went to a high school football game and met her there."

"Holy cow," laughed Ross. "You mean, love at first sight?"

"I never believed in it, but—"

"Are you free today? Or Tonight?" asked his friend.

"Well, I do have a date with McKenna tonight," began Clint.

"Why don't you bring her and we'll have dinner somewhere?" asked Ross. "I have something I want to show you."

"What is it?" asked Clint.

"You remember I'm working on my doctoral dissertation, right?" asked Ross.

"Sure I remember," said Clint. "In Archeology, right?" His friend assented. "I haven't heard how it's going, though."

"I'm through the course work and research," said his friend.

"I've been writing like crazy. In another couple of weeks I'll defend my dissertation and I'm done."

Clint congratulated his friend. "Then what?" asked Clint.

"I may go into the field," said his friend. "I think you might be interested in what I'm working on. My professor and I did a dig last summer near Old Panama City."

"Ah, yes," said Clint. "Henry Morgan's old stomping ground."

"Stomping ground indeed," Ross said. "He damn near destroyed the whole city in what, 1671?"

"Yeah, I'm pretty sure that's the date."

"Well, I've got something I want to show you," Ross returned. "I could use your gifts."

The friends talked a bit more and arranged to meet for dinner.

Chapter Twelve

McKenna came out on the back porch of her aunt and uncle's home with a cup of coffee. It was a beautiful autumn day, temperatures in the mid 80's, bright sun, a gentle wind.

"Hi, Honey," said her aunt. "Did you have fun last night?"

"I'll say," agreed McKenna. "I got home a bit after three. I'm seeing Clint this evening, too."

"Great," said Mickey Logan. "We're having dinner with Gail and Rick down the street."

"Oh, did you need me to babysit—" McKenna began.

"No, thanks," smiled Rand. "Joey's going to have a sleepover with their three boys. They're older than him, but they treat him well, they've got a Wii—well, he's thrilled to death."

"Good," said McKenna. "Clint's picking me up later and we're going to a movie he wants to see. Then I think we're going out to dinner."

"McKenna, what happened with Gil?" asked her uncle.

"I don't know for sure," said his niece, "but I'm not seeing him anymore." She explained about his proposition to take her to a sex motel. "I just don't love him," she concluded. "We had fun together, but—"

"You do love Clint?" asked Rand.

McKenna thought for a second. "It seems likely," she grinned. The doorbell rang and McKenna went into the house. She came out a few moments later with Clint. The group chatted for a bit until McKenna and Clint departed.

"Boy, wouldn't they be perfect for one another?" asked Logan.

"They sure would," said his wife. "What a striking couple."

A few moments after 6:30 that evening, Rick and Gail Benedetto arrived. Rick, a lieutenant on the local police force, looked like he might be in line for Captain on the force. He told the couple about what he'd been working on in the village.

The couples sat in the Logan living room, enjoying a cocktail while Joey ran down to their house and got settled in for the evening. The Benedettos were their neighbors and close friends in the neighborhood.

The doorbell rang. Then again. Then the door flew open as Logan reached for the handle.

"Where is she?" snarled Gil Westcott, his face red with anger.

Logan blocked Gil's entrance to the house. "Stop it, Gil. Stop it now." He smelled the liquor on Gil's breath and Mickey didn't like the situation at all. Gil, a big guy with a powerful build, could cause some real problems. Rick sidled up next to Logan.

"Get out of the way," snarled Gil. Mickey didn't budge. "You don't move, I kick your ass."

"Gil, McKenna left here already," said Logan. "She's out for the evening. Get yourself together. You're making a fool of yourself. Calm down."

"I'll wait here for her," said Gil.

"No, Gil, you won't," asserted Logan. "We're going out and you can't stay."

"All right, I warned you," nodded Gil and he threw a

roundhouse punch at Logan. Logan stepped back and the clumsy punch missed by a foot. Gil reeled off balance and almost fell. Rick grabbed his arm, twisted it behind him and held him tight. Logan grabbed his other arm and pinioned it as well. The two men turned the raging man and steered him out the front door, where they deposited him on the top step of the porch, struggling and cursing.

"Gil, damn it, stop struggling, will you?" said Logan. "We can't hold you forever."

Gil made a powerful effort to calm down and managed to get himself under control. "I came to see McKenna," he said, his speech slurred a little.

"You've made that clear, I think," said Rick. "But she's not here. She's out for the evening."

"But—" tried Gil, but he wasn't having a lot of success talking.

"Mickey, he can't drive," said Rick. "He's been drinking."

"I'm okay," protested Gil.

"Yeah, that's what you say, but I'm a cop and I say you aren't okay," said Rick. "You get behind the wheel and I'll have you thrown in the clink, understand?"

"Gil, I'm going to drive you home, okay?" said Logan, with a nod at Rick. Gil now began to cry, and Logan found himself feeling sorry for the younger man. Rick and Logan managed to raise Gil to his feet and get his car keys from him. They deposited him in the passenger seat of his car and Logan drove off, Rick and the two women following in Rick's car.

After a lengthy silence, Gil spoke in a faltering voice. "Mickey?"

"Yeah."

"I'm sorry," said Gil. "I really made an ass of myself."

"Yes, you sure did," Logan assented.

"Would you please apologize to Rand and your friends for me?"

"Of course I will."

Silence. Then, Gil asked, "Can you tell me something?"

"Sure," said Logan.

"How's McKenna?"

"She's fine, Gil."

"Er..." Gil stammered.

"Gil, look," said Logan. "I think she's nuts about this guy. I've known him a long time, and he's a fine man."

"Yeah," said Gil, the bitterness unmistakable.

"I don't blame you for being upset, Gil," said Logan. "But you're young, handsome, with a good job and a fine future. You'll be okay, and you'll find the right girl soon. I'm sure. I urge you to put everything in perspective, okay?"

Gil nodded. Then to Logan's surprise, a tear started down his cheek. "I thought I'd found the right girl," he said.

"Yeah," said Logan. "I'm sure you're in a lot of pain. Give yourself a chance to grieve, okay?"

In a few moments Logan parked in front of Gil's apartment. Rick parked behind them, and the two friends walked Gil to his apartment. Logan got him inside, tossed the car key ring in behind him and pulled the door shut.

"Thanks, Rick," said Logan as they drove away from the apartment building.

"Yeah," said Rick. "One day off and I have to go back to shagging drunks. Disgusting."

"Yeah, I'm sure it is."

"What's his deal?"

"Heartbroken, I think," said Logan. "He blew it with McKenna, knows it, and can't work it out on his own."

Then the four friends arrived at the restaurant and put aside the unpleasant episode. A couple of martinis helped.

Chapter Thirteen

McKenna and Clint sat at the bar of the restaurant where they would meet Clint's friend Ross. "What're you drinking?" asked Clint, when the waitress brought their cocktails.

"A Bahama Mama," smiled McKenna.

"Snort," said Clint.

McKenna giggled. "Did you just say the word 'Snort'?"

Clint shrugged. "Yeah," he said. "It's easier to say it than to make the sound."

"Ah," said McKenna. "And what are you imbibing, Mister Macho?"

"Red-Eye whiskey," sneered Clint. "In a dirty glass, see? A real man's drink."

Now McKenna laughed. Clint realized that he wanted to hear that laugh the rest of his life. He started to tell her that, but a huge hand gripped his shoulder. Clint grinned, turned and embraced his best friend from college. "Ross," he beamed. "Great to see you." He took the hand of Janet, Ross's fiancée, gave her a hug and introduced them to McKenna.

"Yeow!" said Ross. "What does she want with you?"

"I make her laugh, I think," shrugged Clint, and McKenna laughed with Ross and Janet.

"As a matter of fact, he uses bribery," teased McKenna. "He has to pay me to go out with him." McKenna and Janet smiled and exchanged greetings as the maitre d' came over to escort them to a table.

Once everyone was settled with menus and cocktails, the waitress came over and took their orders. Chitchat proceeded for a minute or two longer.

"Ross, it's great to see you," said Clint, "and even better to see Janet, but whassup?"

Ross opened his briefcase and extracted a bundle of papers. "I need to tell you how I got this," said Ross. "Then I'll tell you what I want you to do, okay?"

Clint shrugged.

"Okay," said Ross. "You remember Professor Clyde, my advisor at Weller?"

"Yeah, sure," Clint said.

"I took his classes in Anthropology and in Archeology, and stayed in touch over the years. McKenna, I told Clint, but I've just about finished my doctoral dissertation at The University of Chicago."

"Your doctorate?" said McKenna, impressed.

"Yeah, I just kept going once I graduated," said Ross. "Believe me, it's not as impressive as it sounds, really."

"Well, *I'm* impressed," said Janet. "I'm also very proud of him. We'll get married when he finishes."

"Yeah, that's great," said Clint, waving an impatient hand. McKenna told him to cool his jets. He nodded, but then said, "Tell the story, will you? I've been waiting to hear this all afternoon."

"Sure," chuckled Ross. "Well, last summer, Dr. Clyde e-mailed me to see if I wanted to go on a dig in Panama, not far from the old city. He had a line on some fantastic things."

"Wasn't the old city destroyed?" asked Clint.

"Yeah, for the most part," said Ross.

"Who destroyed it?" asked McKenna.

Ross looked at her. "Does the name Henry Morgan mean anything to you?" asked Ross.

"Sure, of course, the British terror of the Spanish Main," said McKenna.

"A dreadful person, a pirate without scruples or mercy," agreed Clint. "In Panama City, he killed until almost no one was left alive, and then plundered what was left."

"Yeah," said Ross. "Well, Dr. Clyde somehow found out that an ancient graveyard—now almost completely overgrown—still existed in the area around the old Cathedral. We thought we might take a look at the old place.

"So, we headed down there with a grant from the Panamanian government. As you will imagine, they'd like to recover what Morgan stole, if it still exists.

"We arrived and found several old graves, though most of the names were unintelligible with blurring and aging. The climate is pretty damp, you know—" everyone nodded "—and we didn't find much, and we didn't want to disturb any graves if we could avoid it."

"Right," said Clint.

"Anyway, our guide pointed us to the far edge of the old cemetery—and understand, now, that this place has been abandoned for three hundred years—and we found an unmarked grave, which was identifiable only by a slight depression in the sand," Ross related, and paused to take a sip of water. "The guide told us that he'd heard legends about an old grave, that it held the key to a treasure of amazing value."

Clint stole a glance at McKenna, who was sitting forward,

rapt with attention. "We dug there and found a stone coffin, with a seal of the church on it. When we opened the coffin, we found—"

But at that moment their dinners arrived. For a few moments they thanked the waitress, accepted some more wine, and began to dine.

At last, Clint could stand no more. "What did you find!" he stage whispered to Ross, who laughed.

"Okay," he said. "We realized we'd opened the grave of a priest, now almost completely desiccated, as you can imagine. He had been buried in his clothes, then his alb, and a chasuble."

"You mean the robes worn by Roman Catholic priests, right?" said McKenna.

Ross nodded. "They were in terrible shape, of course, but the priest clutched a book—well, not quite a book—in what was left of his hands. I don't know how we knew what to do, but all of us felt we needed to take the book with us."

"I think I understand," Janet said. "I've had some time to consider this, and I guess I'm okay with it."

"Yeah, in particular because of what the book was," said Ross. "Anyway, we saw no reason to take anything else, so we reburied the priest with appropriate bell, book and candle."

"Did you find out what the book was?" asked McKenna. "I mean, could you read it?"

"Yeah, it survived in pretty good shape considering its age," said Ross. "We began reading it and soon realized that we'd found a Gospel."

"A Gospel!" gasped McKenna.

"Yeah, it's apocryphal, of course, but fascinating reading," said Ross. "It reads like a novel."

"Did the writer credit it to an apostle?" asked Clint. McKenna arched an eyebrow. "Sorry. Most Gospels are attributed to one or more of Jesus' apostles. Besides the Canonical ones—Matthew, Mark, Luke and John—some have turned up over the years, like the Gospel of Thomas, another one called the Acts of Nicodemus and Pilate, the Gospel of the Hebrews, and a few others. Except for the ones included in the canon, they didn't survive well."

"Why didn't they make it into the Bible?" asked McKenna.

"They don't stand up to a number of tests, for one thing," said Clint. "Also some of them are preposterous."

"Yeah, this isn't canonical, for sure," said Ross. "It describes certain facts about Jesus, yes, but mostly it's a biography about the acts of one of his female followers."

"The gospels were, in some traditions, established at an early Council," said Clint. "Nobody knows for certain when and how the canon was established. It could have been the Council of Nicea in the fourth century."

"So what do you think you found?" asked McKenna.

"We discovered a book that has been, until now, completely unknown," he said. "It's entitled The Gospel of Rachel."

"Who?" said McKenna.

"Well, I can tell you her story," shrugged Ross. "Remember, of course, it's apocryphal, which means that by no means can it be characterized as infallible, nor could it be called useful for teaching. It gives us virtually no insight into the person of Jesus. Despite that, it does deal with something he did, told through the eyes of a witness to his crucifixion. As a result, it's worth investigating."

"Why do you think it has any credibility?" asked Clint.

"For one thing, the author wrote in Latin," said Ross. "Also, it stays true to the other gospels. It seems to extend our understanding of that time, and some things that happened." He began to tell the story.

* * * * *

Rachel stood by the side of the road, leaning on a pathetic crutch and dressed as usual in rags. Her parents were gone. Her brothers and sisters wanted no part of her. She was unclean.

Anyone, in fact, who had the disease that she did was unclean, according to The Law of the great prophet Moses. No one could stop her bleeding. Her period had come, as normal, one month. Then it didn't stop. It continued. She bled for a week. Then two weeks, agonizing in that it stopped for some hours, then began again.

Then, she had suffered for a year. Then, five years. Now, twelve.

Moses had said that this problem made her unclean. When the bleeding would stop, as it would for sometimes as long as a week or even a month, she would go to the priest for the ceremonial cleansing. He would bless her in the prescribed method.

Then the bleeding would begin again.

She'd heard all her life that Messiah—*Mesiach*—was coming. He would deliver all Israel from the fear of invasion, from the oppression of the Romans, from the Greek conquerors, and from their ancestral enemies such as the Philistines.

Maybe, she thought, *Mesiach* would be able to deliver her from this affliction.

People described Mesiach as ordinary in appearance. People told her that she wouldn't think him handsome. A working man, with calloused hands, he had worked as a carpenter for several years in the shop of his father in Nazareth.

Word had spread about him all over the region. Gentle, they said. Not a warrior. Yet he could be moved to anger, they said. He'd led an insurrection against the merchants in the temple.

That part of the story pleased her. She remembered that once, she had gone to the great temple in Jerusalem with her father as he offered a lamb from his flock. The priests had told him that the lamb's imperfections rendered it unfit for the sacrifice.

Her father had protested, calling this lamb the best of his little flock. He took pride in bringing the fruit of his labor.

The Levite priests refused to accept his lamb. They instead offered to sell him a perfect lamb. All he had to do was to trade his worthless lamb and so many shekels and they would give him another.

Her father, teeth gritted, had agreed.

The priests took the lamb and came back in a few moments with another lamb. Rachel inspected the little animal with care. She saw that this lamb was in no way better than the lamb her father had brought.

She looked into the crafty face of the priest and knew, then, the truth. Their lamb would be kept somewhere, and sold—maybe later today or tomorrow—to someone who brought another "imperfect" lamb.

So the Nazarene had driven these people out? That was fine with Rachel. She was happy he had done so.

She saw the crowd was coming, and in the center of the roiling group she spotted the man. He had his prayer shawl over his shoulders. *If only I can touch him*, she thought.

Then she stopped. *No. I cannot make this man unclean. If I touch him, he will need purification. No, I will touch the blue tzitzit- -*

* * * * *

"The what?" asked Clint.

"The prayer shawl, called the *Talit*, of a rabbi reminded Jewish believers of the Tabernacle," said Janet. "He would drape the *talit* on his head as he prayed."

"Yeshua—Jesus, that is— like other teachers of Galilee, would have worn a head-gear wound into a kind of turban called a *Sudar* covering his head and shoulders," said Ross. "Then he wore sandals and a special inner garment called a *Chaluq* that had to be worn by teachers or anyone who would read the Scriptures in public or perform any function in the synagogue. Perhaps he might have worn a rope fastened around the middle; finally, the Talit with the fringe."

"They called the fringe on the shawl *tzitzit*," said Janet. "The fringe was tied with 613 knots."

"Yes," said Ross. "One knot for each of the laws in the Torah."

"The prayer shawl could have been a heavy blanket-like outer garment that you would see bedouins wear today," said Janet. "Also the shawl could protect them from the elements."

"The tzitzit had one blue fringe," said Ross. "Most Hebrews like Rachel believed that the blue tzitzit possessed some magical power to heal. Religious people of the day believed that both the color blue as well as the knotting of the fringes possessed healing powers."

Clint understood, now. "So the woman touched. . ."

"The blue fringe of his shawl, yes," said Ross. "According to Hebrew Law, the prayer shawl could not be made unclean. She thought that if she touched the Lord himself, the touch would have rendered him unclean. And He, of course, could not be touched by sin—"

"Until He became sin itself," said McKenna, nodding. "At the cross."

"You understand," said Janet.

* * * * *

Rachel pressed forward. People recognized her and backed away in horror, not wanting the unclean woman to touch them.

The rabbi walked toward her, laughing about something with a beautiful woman walking next to him. He said her name. Miriam.

Rachel reached out and managed to clutch at the blue *tzitzit*.

Then, she couldn't let go. Time seemed to freeze, to stop running.

She fell into darkness, a deep pit of chaos and terror seized her. Then, as if someone opened a long sealed tomb, she saw the radiant light of purity shining as a mere speck in the distance. The light enlarged until she felt overwhelmed with warmth, peace, and a gentle touch of grace. The white, pure light surrounded her. Later, she would tell one of his followers that she felt herself cleansed of all filth and dirt and sin in one second.

Something else happened as well. Her mind and her spirit changed. In that moment, she knew that never in all her life would she ever be afraid again.

Then she found herself back in Judea, kneeling in the dust next to the carpenter from Nazareth. No more than a few seconds had passed, she realized. Despite the noise and commotion around her, she heard him say, "Who touched me?"

One of the men who followed him said, "Rabbi, you are surrounded by people pushing to get near to you, and you ask 'who touched me'?" The people nearby laughed.

The carpenter swung around and saw Rachel kneeling, weeping in the dust. He knelt before her and she felt his brown, deep eyes boring into her soul. All noise and commotion ceased as His kind hands brushed the hair from her eyes.

He knew. He knew she was unclean, yet he knelt, stroking her cheek. Now he embraced her. She wept and returned the hug.

"Daughter," he whispered. "You have been cleansed of all impurity now. Go, show yourself to the priest."

"Master," she said. "How did you know?"

"I felt the power leave me," he said. "I am glad it went to you, and I'm delighted that you came to me. Be sure, Rachel"—*he knows my name?* she thought—"that the Father loves you."

"Thank you, Master," she wept. "Thank you." Then the crowd with all its noise was back. People stood aghast to see the rabbi kneeling to embrace the woman.

"I have something for you to do, if you will agree to it," he said.

"Of course, Master," she said. He rose and helped her to her feet.

"Come, follow me," he said, with his kind expression. "We will talk together."

"How do you feel?" asked one of the women in the group.

"I am tired," she said. "But I have never felt better."

One of the men who followed the Nazarene gave her a small piece of bread. She devoured it, feeling real hunger now. Now he offered her his wineskin. She drank.

* * * * *

"Touching his shawl healed the woman Rachel?" said McKenna. "Surely not?"

"No, not touching the shawl. Her faith healed her," said Ross.

"What about the rest of that story?" said Clint.

Ross nodded. "As the Nazarene said, she had something to do."

"What?" said Clint.

"She's the one who obtained the shawl from one of the disciples. When Yeshua was taken away for trial, the disciple received the prayer shawl from his mother Miriam."

"Which disciple?" asked McKenna.

"That would have been John, who wrote the gospel bearing his name, and the three letters, and the book of Revelation."

"Then what happened?" asked McKenna. Ross smiled and picked up the story.

* * * * *

Many years after the crucifixion of the Nazarene, Rachel's fever to tell others about *Mesiach* had never faded. John received a sentence of exile on the island of Patmos. Rachel sneaked over to see him, and he entrusted the shawl to her. She returned to Ephesus.

Rachel took her prized possession and went aboard a ship bound for Rome to see one of the key figures in the church. Paul, once an accursed oppressor of the church, had become a great leader in the new faith. He languished in prison in Rome.

"You *want* to see that madman?" said the prison guard, his voice incredulous.

"Yes, I do," she asserted.

He took her though a series of doors to a dismal cell. The cell door clanked open and a guard inside stood up.

"Who's there?" asked Paul, his dim eyes not able to focus on her.

"It is I, Rachel," she said.

"Beloved friend," he smiled. "Please come in."

The guard gave the woman his chair and stood off to the side as the warden of the Roman prison shut the door behind her.

"It's all right," said Paul. He motioned to the guard. "Tertius, the Nazarene once healed Rachel."

"Please tell me the story," said Tertius, giving the woman a firm hug.

Rachel understood. Paul, with his astounding gift of evangelism, had converted this guard to The Way. His name, Tertius, indicated that he had been born into slavery. The name connoted that he was the third child born to a pair of slaves.

"I'd rejoice to tell you," said Rachel. "But I have come to enlist the aid of Paul."

"Help from me?" smiled Paul, his chains clanking as he shifted position on his bed.

"I must find a way to protect the master's shawl," she said. "I cannot keep it any longer. Yet it must not be lost."

Paul agreed. This shawl should become a treasure of the new Church.

Paul stood, and with Tertius chained to him, began to pace the cell. At last he said, "I cannot go myself, of course, but I think the shawl may be safe in Spain. Timothy plans to carry the work there—"

"The young man who accompanied you when you came to Jerusalem," she said. "I remember him."

"Not so young anymore," said Paul, smiling. "But yes, he is a wonderful man."

"How can I get it to him?"

"I believe that he will stay in Corinth until just after winter. Then, he'll come here. I look for him to arrive in time for the Passover. Can you stay here in Rome?"

"I have no reason not to stay," she said, "but I know no one..."

"You are welcome to stay at my home with my wife and children and me," interrupted Tertius. "You will be safe there."

So it was settled. Timothy arrived just before the feast of Passover, and visited with Paul. He remembered Rachel, and they spent a great deal of time together.

"Do you want to come with me to Spain?" he asked Rachel one night.

"I cannot finance such a trip. I have no money. . ." she began.

"The church at Corinth has sent us money for the journey," said Timothy. "I would be grateful for your help, as well."

Rachel was a few years older than Timothy, but Paul married them in his prison cell. They departed and took passage to Spain.

* * * * *

"So the shawl went to Spain?" asked McKenna.

"Yes, it seems so," said Ross. "It remained there in secret for many centuries, and an order of monks hid and preserved it."

"Then what happened?" said Clint.

"The Spanish Armada," said Ross.

"Ah, yes," said Clint.

McKenna looked up, surprised. She asked, "What's the connection?"

Ross turned to Clint, who nodded and picked up the story.

"To call King Philip a zealous Catholic would be an understatement," Clint said. "He came to believe that England had to be redeemed from what he regarded as the Protestant blight. Philip mustered so much confidence that God was on his side and that the Spanish would conquer England that he considered the success of the invasion all but a given. He went so far as to draft a man who had never been to sea in his life to be the admiral of the Spanish fleet."

"He chose someone who had no sea experience?" asked McKenna, sounding amazed.

Clint nodded. "Santa Cruz, the original choice for the fleet admiral, was respected and successful, but he died. So Philip chose a rich—and very successful—general named Medina Sidonia. The man tried as hard as he could to get out of the assignment. He pleaded that he had always been an army man, with no naval experience. His protests availed nothing. In fact, when he did go on board his ship, he got terribly seasick."

"Oh brother," sighed McKenna. "Like Lord Nelson for the British? Legend says that every time he went to sea he got violently seasick."

"Yes, but of course Horatio Nelson was a great sailor and a warrior," said Ross. "And unlike Sidonia, Nelson would recover from his seasickness in a few days. Sidonia apparently felt miserable the entire time he spent at sea."

"If you've never been seasick," said Janet with a wry smile, "you can't imagine the misery it entails."

"And after two years of battle after battle, the Armada went down in ignominious defeat," said Clint.

"Two years?" asked McKenna.

"Yeah," nodded Clint. "A lot of people think the assault of the Armada consisted of one battle, but really, the siege lasted for many months."

"Yuck," shuddered McKenna.

Clint resumed the story. "When the Spaniards learned of the defeat of the Armada, they assumed that England would be coming for them in no time."

"Rachel and Timothy hid the shawl with the Christian church they helped found in Spain," said Ross. "The church considered it a great treasure, of course. Fifteen or so centuries later, one of the men believed in this coming British invasion, and fled to the sea coast. He took the shawl with him."

"And he took a galleon to Panama," said Clint, nodding, "at the height of the Spice Wars with England."

"He arrived in Panama as—" said Ross, as he checked his notes—"*Catedral de Nuestra Senora de la Asuncion* was preparing to cast the statue of the Virgin to bless its sanctuary."

"Then," said Clint, grim-faced, "Sir Henry Morgan arrived."

"Right," affirmed Ross.

"What happened?" McKenna asked Clint.

"Sir Francis Drake had been there first, in 1573," said Clint. "He destroyed the fort at Nombre de Dios. He took a train of 190 pack mules and stole tons of gold and silver. So the Spaniards built two stone forts to repel invaders, one at Portobello and the other at the mouth of the Rio Chagres. That one was called Fuerte San Lorenzo.

"Nearly 100 years later, Sir Henry Morgan showed up. Of course, the Spaniards were terrified when they heard that a new pirate, Henry Morgan, had set out to conquer them. He overpowered Fuerte San Lorenzo and sailed up the Rio

Chagres. He ascended the river up to Venta De Cruces, and then marched overland to Panama City on the Pacific Coast."

Clint stopped and blushed, realizing that he'd been lecturing the group. They were smiling at him.

"I'm impressed," said Ross to McKenna. "This guy has some brains after all."

"Don't get carried away," said Clint, grinning. "I wrote papers about Morgan in college. Anyhow, the city wasn't fortified. It had impenetrable protection on three sides—swamps, marshes and the sea. The landside, though, had a bridge."

Clint looked at the others. "So when he attacked, the Spaniards for some unfathomable reason didn't wait for Morgan to cross the bridge, where he and his men would have been massacred. Instead they went out over the bridge to meet him. Morgan's men killed them to all but the last man, then sacked the town and burned it."

"Don't I remember that they even sacked the cathedral?" asked McKenna.

"Right, they burned it almost to the ground," Clint said. "They stole everything of value."

"Wasn't there some legend about a golden altar?" asked Ross.

"Yeah. It was located in the Iglesia y Convent de la Companie de Yeshua," said Clint. "The head priest, according to legend, painted it black."

"Was it solid gold?" asked McKenna.

"No, it was mahogany, carved in magnificent detail and covered with hammered gold," Clint said. "Anyhow, the priest—taking his life in his hands, in fact—told Morgan that the golden altar had been stolen by another pirate and this one was nothing but a cheap replacement. To which Morgan replied, 'I don't know why, but I think you're a bigger pirate than I am.' He didn't take the altar. Then, the legend continues, he even contributed to the cost of a more appropriate replacement altar."

"What a strange story," said McKenna, shaking her head.

"Then, Morgan and his men sacked the entire city. Later the city was moved south and west. The district of Casco Viejo is the site of old Panama City."

"Did any of the cathedral survive the attack?" asked McKenna.

"Not much. A wall or two still stands there. Also the bell tower at the back of the church which may have served double duty as a watch tower."

"What about the golden statue?"

"No one knows," said Ross.

Having finished their dinner, Ross explained he had an early meeting the next day, and he and Janet left the restaurant.

Chapter Fourteen

Ross and his fiancé had been gone for a couple of minutes when McKenna spoke up. "What do you make of this?" she asked.

Clint shook his head. "I haven't a clue. It seems that, for a Catholic nation, something as valuable as the shawl would be a national treasure, and that the people would take care of it."

"Anyway, the trail ends with Morgan's raid," said McKenna. "And no one knows what happened to his loot, right?"

"Thereby hangs a tale," Clint shrugged. "When Morgan went back to England, he was captured, tried and sentenced to hang as a bloody pirate."

"Sounds like the charges were inadequate," she said.

"No kidding," Clint agreed. "Then, a day or two later, the queen pardoned him, set him free, and made him the governor of Jamaica."

McKenna got it. "Okay," she nodded. "So he beyond question bribed the Queen, right?"

"Sure," he said. "But he didn't use the statue. That would also be a national treasure for England if he'd given her that. So he must have used money that he raped out of Panama, the gold, the silver."

"Couldn't he just have melted down the statue?" McKenna asked.

"Yeah, he could have," Clint nodded. "But that doesn't ring true, either. I don't know why I feel this way, but I don't think even Morgan would have desecrated that statue."

"In 1673 or '74, though, the church of England was in ascendancy, right?" McKenna asked. Clint shrugged. "Would they have cared about a statue of Mary?"

At that moment a man appeared next to their table.

"Yes, sir?" asked Clint.

"Excuse me," said the man. He had the faintest trace of a foreign accent. "Would your name be Clint?"

Clint started in surprise. "Well, yes it is," he said. "Do I know you, Sir?"

"No, we haven't met," said the man. "I see you have finished dinner. Would you consider having dessert and coffee with us?"

He pointed to a large table. A couple sat there, and a woman who was somewhat older. "Please," said the man.

Clint turned to McKenna, who shrugged. "Sure," she said. "We'd be pleased."

Clint retrieved his credit card and dropped a tip on the table. They rose and followed the man to his table.

"Miss Nicole, Dr. Frey, and Ruth, I want you to meet McKenna and Clint," said the man.

Clint and Luke shook hands, and he greeted the two women. Then he and McKenna sat down with the other couples. An awkward silence ensued. "Yes?" said Clint.

"I don't know," said the man. "Can I do something for you?"

"What is your name, sir?" asked McKenna.

"My name is Cepha, though that isn't real important now," he said. "I was sent to Clint and Nicole."

"By whom?" asked Clint.

"I don't know," Cepha said.

"Ah," said McKenna. "Nicole, may I know your last name?"

"Sadler," Nicole responded. "Though not for long. I'm divorcing my husband and I do plan to change it."

"Your maiden name?" asked McKenna.

"Fixx," she said.

"Are you Casey's sister?" McKenna asked.

"Well, yes I am," said Nicole.

McKenna sat back. "I'm his daughter," she said.

"Daughter!" said Nicole.

"Yes," said McKenna. "He married my mother, who divorced the man I considered my father, who is currently doing 15 to life in Stateville."

The whole group turned and looked at Cepha.

"How did you know who Clint was?" asked Ruth.

"I don't know if I can tell you," said Cepha. "No, I wouldn't mind telling you, but it is complicated." He smiled.

"How complicated?" asked Clint.

"I don't know where you are in your personal faith," said Cepha. "Let it go for a few moments, anyhow."

Luke spoke up. "McKenna and Clint," he said. "Do you know anything about the Wandering Jew?"

"Yeah, I guess," said Clint. "I read Chaucer, McDonald, Keats."

"What would you say if I told you this is the man?" said Luke, indicating Cepha.

Clint and McKenna couldn't say anything. They could only stare. "How do you do?" said the man.

Chapter Fifteen

Clint and McKenna drove away from the restaurant, both of them bewildered by the evening.

"Well, he is a nice man," said McKenna.

"I don't know how much of this to believe," Clint said. "The Wandering Jew? In the Chicago area?"

"He explained that," said McKenna. "The Voice told him to come here."

"But why?" asked Clint. "Why me? What do I have to offer?"

"Talk about a loaded question," she said. "But there's Nicole, as well."

"What makes her special?"

McKenna thought for a few seconds. "You do have a few things in common," she said.

"Like what?"

"Someone she loved, or tried to love, abandoned her, hurt her feelings and made her feel like someone with absolutely no value."

"And you think that happened to me?"

"Why don't you want me to meet your parents?" she countered.

Clint thought it over. "I take your point," he said. "But I have a feeling that something bigger is involved."

"Like what?" she smiled.

"I don't believe in coincidence," said Clint. "Ross was

talking about a legend just before Cepha showed up. You were talking about how Cepha is a legend. I get the feeling we're part of something important."

"You and me?"

"Why not? You're a famous treasure hunter. You've dealt with mysteries, the occult—"

"What occult?"

"Haven't you dealt with the occult?"

McKenna stared at her hands for a moment. "Not exactly," she said at last.

"Oh." They grew silent. "But you have found buried treasure."

"Well, I was part of a couple of teams who found treasure, yes," she said. "My Grandpa and my Dad and I found Blackbeard's treasure in North Carolina. My friend Steven Levin and I went with Mickey and Rand to White Island, New Hampshire and we found the treasure of Sandy Gordon."

"So—ah—you're pretty rich, huh?"

"I guess you could say that," she said. She pulled a ring from her finger. "I kept this as a remembrance of finding Gordon's treasure."

The beautiful solid gold ring surrounded an exquisite emerald. "It's beautiful," he said. "What do you know about it?"

"Nothing," she shrugged. "I'm sure it's pirate plunder. I haven't a clue to the name of the person who owned it. I wear it to remember whoever it was that had it stolen from her nearly 300 years ago."

"You know..." he said.

"What?"

"What do you want with me?"

She laughed at the abrupt shift in the conversation. "A famous football hero, Phi Beta Kappa, and you have to ask?"

"Thank you," he said. "But I don't have a family like you do."

McKenna turned and looked at him. "You don't have a family?"

He took a second to gather his thoughts. "I have a mother and a father," he said. "I also have a brother and a sister."

She fixed him with an intent stare. "What's going on here?"

Clint pulled the car into Mickey Logan's driveway. He stared out the windshield. He couldn't quite bring himself to answer.

"Clint, I asked you a question," whispered McKenna.

At last he said, "Look, here's my problem," he said. "If I tell you what's going on, I'm pretty sure you won't want to see me anymore."

"What on earth—"

"That's what always happens."

"It's something you're ashamed of, then?"

"Well, yes, it is. My family has never wanted much to do with me. Something major happened years ago, but my family is still ashamed of me for it. Not that they ever really wanted me around."

She took his hands and nodded to encourage him. "Okay. Then you need to tell me about it."

Clint, his stomach hollow, reached for his water bottle in the car's cup holder. "Okay, then." He took a sip of water. He began, but he didn't look up much during the story. He told the girl he wanted to spend the rest of his life with about the thing in his life he was the most ashamed of.

The story came out in bursts. His freshman year in College. The success as a quarterback. The fraternity. Raising hell most nights. Finals. Suspension. "So then," he said. "I go home to my parents' house. I don't have anywhere else to go. I don't have a job, I don't know what I'm going to do. They tell me I can move into the basement—"

"Clint," she interrupted. "Are you aware that you're talking in the present tense?"

"I am?" he said. "I'm not aware of it."

"You have been for a little while. This situation traumatized you, didn't it?"

"Yes, it did," he said. "It came close to destroying me."

She took his hand. "Okay. Finish the story. But remember, it's already happened. It isn't happening now."

He swallowed. He remembered his friend Ross Burgess telling him to remind himself from time to time that it had happened in the past. "Ross told me the same thing," he said. "I forget sometimes. Give me a second." He repeated his own name, and hers, and where they were. He grabbed her hand and held it to his cheek for a second. "Where was I?"

"You went home. . ."

"Right. Well, I did pretty well at the community college. I got straight A's. . ." he paused.

"You're doing fine," she said, smiling to reassure him.

He told her the details about how the fraternity tossed him out and he found himself without a place to live on campus. "So I couldn't figure out what to do." He told her about her uncle Mickey's help when Clint found himself at his wit's end, near defeat, thinking about suicide—

"Suicide!" she said.

"Yeah. For a while the Old Women kept trying to talk me into it. . ." he broke off. He looked up at her. "You know about them, don't you."

"Yes, they're always waiting, aren't they," she said. "They come for me sometimes, too."

"I'm sorry," he mumbled. "Anyhow, I left home for good when I enrolled at Weller. I never got any more help from my parents. They never came to my games, to graduation, to the football banquets or anything. They've never called, never written—" he paused. A moment or two passed. "So, now you know the story."

She said nothing for some time, just staring at him.

"I see," he said, his voice hollow. "It's worse than I thought it would be. Okay. Let me walk you to the door." He let go of her hand to reach for the door handle.

She spoke, her voice puzzled. "Why do I have to go home now?"

"Well, you don't, but it's just that I figured—" then he couldn't go on. He choked, sure that this was the last time he would ever see her.

"I don't want to go home yet," she asserted.

Clint looked up, surprised. "You don't?"

"Of course not. Don't be silly. We need to finish this conversation."

"I . . .er . . ." he stammered.

She confronted him at once. "Did you cheat again in college?"

"No. Never," he said, shaking his head for emphasis. "I made sure I couldn't."

"Are you lying to me now?"

"Of course not."

"Are you going to lie to me in the future?"

"No. I'll never lie to you."

"Then why," she said, drawing out the words, "should I hold a mistake against you when you already paid hard and heavy for it? The fraternity rejected you. Your parents and family rejected you and continue to reject you. That's more than enough. You need someone to love you."

He began to speak. Then, he looked into the deep sapphire blue eyes. He said, "I just thought—" It began to dawn on him. She wasn't outraged. She could overlook the biggest screw-up of his life. "You don't care about what I did?"

"Of course I care," she said. "But I care about who you've become now, not who you were several years ago. Not one cell in your body is the same as when you did that. You're kind and loving and you've always been a perfect gentleman with me."

"But..." he couldn't find any words.

"Did you think," she said, choosing her words, "that I couldn't deal with one screw-up in your life?"

"I don't know. I couldn't. . ." he murmured.

"Look," said McKenna. "Did you ever do something stupid when you were a child?"

"I did. Sure. Lots of things."

"I did, too. Remember what Paul wrote?

"When I was a child, I spoke as a child, I understood as a child, I thought as a child: but when I became a man, I put away childish things".

"First Corinthians 13," said Clint. "I know, but..."

"I could regard everything I laid my hand to as a flop if I wanted to," returned McKenna. "Do you want to hear about those things, too?"

He hesitated for a second or two. "Thank you," he said.

"For what?"

"For not—for –" She reached out and took his hand. He drew her hand to his mouth for a brief kiss.

"They beat you up," she said. "People who should've tried to help you, stand with you, re-build your self-concept and self-confidence, betrayed you. The fraternity. The university. Your parents, worst of all."

"I deserved it," he said.

"You deserved to be punished, not humiliated," she said. "You were castigated, and now you're done with that part of your life."

"But. . ."

"Let it go," she asserted. "Let it all go. That episode of your life ended years ago. You acknowledged that you screwed up, you were punished for it, and it's over forever. It changed you and the way you see life. Now you're different. Let's go on from here."

"There is something else, though."

"What?"

"The real reason my parents don't like me is that I can do something no one else can," he said. "I have the ability to see what people are thinking."

"Uh, huh," said McKenna.

She said this as if he'd confessed a minor consideration, as if no one would give such an insignificant ability any consideration. He looked up in surprise. "You don't believe me, do you."

"Why wouldn't I believe you?" she asked. "You just gave me your word that you wouldn't lie to me."

"But. . ."

"People call that ability the Cymreig," she said. "It's rare. I suspect you've never met anyone else who could do it."

"You know about this...talent?"

"Yeah," she said. "My mom has it too. So does Mickey."

"Your mom?" he managed, open-mouthed.

"Sure. I've seen her use it many times."

"I don't use it very often," he said. "I try not to."

"It's a part of who you are," she smiled. "It's a gift, not a curse."

"Has your mom used it on you?"

"I guess so, but she's never beaten me up with it."

"Will you marry me?" he asked, the abrupt question out of his mouth before he knew what he was saying.

"Sure," she said. "I think that's a good idea."

Then she came to his arms and the kiss continued for some time. At last they drew back and McKenna smiled at him, stroking his face with her long, gentle fingers.

"When do we tell everyone?" asked Clint.

McKenna shrugged. "I guess the sooner the better. I think we ought to go to see my parents as soon as we can. They live in Palatine, so maybe tomorrow on the way home from the Botanic Gardens?"

"Perfect," said Clint.

"I'll call and tell them we want to come to dinner."

* * * * *

The next morning, Sunday, McKenna came upstairs at about ten. For her to sleep past six A. M. was rare, but she had never slept better.

My goodness, she thought. *I'm in love. So this is what it feels like.*

She called her mother, who said she'd be thrilled to have them come for dinner. McKenna poured a cup of coffee and looked outside, where she saw a beautiful late summer day. "I've known him for three dates, and we're getting married," she said aloud. Then she knew that wasn't quite right. She'd known him her whole life, somehow. Of course he'd asked her to marry him.

She walked out onto the back deck of Mickey's house and found her aunt and uncle eating a coffee cake with some butter. She steeled herself not to tell Mickey and Rand that she accepted Clint's proposal last night.

"You're up," smiled Rand.

"Sure," she said. "Does that surprise you?"

"What time did you get in?" asked Mickey.

"I don't know," she admitted. "I know it was after midnight."

They nodded. McKenna knew them well enough to know that something had upset them.

"Okay," she said. "Tell me what happened."

Mickey looked at Rand and scratched his eyebrow. "McKenna, Gil barged in here last night."

"He came here?" McKenna gasped, as if she hadn't heard.

"Well, yeah," said Mickey. "He wanted to wait until you got home. Rick and I had to drive him home."

"So he showed up drunk, too?" said McKenna. "Not just violent?"

Rand and Mickey nodded. "He fought with me, too," said Mickey. "It didn't last long. One punch which didn't connect, then Rick and I restrained him."

McKenna's mouth fell open a little, and she had a hard time

talking for a few moments. "He tried to hit you?"

"He missed. Rick and I grabbed his arm, spun him around, and then we sat with him until he calmed down."

Rand put in, "McKenna, he broke down and cried. We had to drive him home."

"Let me make sure I understand," she said. "He drove here drunk and violent, right?"

"Yes. Now, I don't know..." Rand began, but her niece had pivoted and gone back into the house. She grabbed her purse and stormed to her car.

* * * * *

An hour later, Mickey and Rand looked up as McKenna walked out onto the deck.

"It's okay," she told them. "You'll never see Gil again. I'm so sorry that he came here and upset you. I..." she broke off and choked up.

Her aunt and uncle rose and hugged her. McKenna stared for a moment at the yard. Then she began to cry. Mickey and Rand held her.

When the crying stopped, McKenna remembered her real news for her beloved aunt and uncle. For the next half hour McKenna told them about her evening with Clint.

"This already looks pretty serious then," said Mickey.

"Yeah, I think so," said McKenna. "I feel like we've known each other all our lives."

"I understand how you feel," said Rand. At that moment, they heard the doorbell.

"That's Clint, I imagine," McKenna said. "I'll be right back." She hurried into the house.

Five minutes or so elapsed until McKenna brought Clint out

to the back deck. They began to visit, and McKenna ran back into the house to get a sweater and her purse.

"Where are you guys going today?" asked Mickey.

"Oh, I thought I'd take McKenna to The Hyatt in Deerfield for brunch," said Clint. "Then, I want to go to The Botanic Gardens. They have a display of electric trains there."

"Ah," said Mickey.

"Electric trains, huh?" said Rand.

"Yeah. We're talking about the large trains, not like HO or the Lionel." He held up his hands to show the size.

"Huge. Yeah," said Mickey, trying to be polite.

"Yeah. McKenna said she was excited about it, so. . ."

McKenna burst through the door, kissed Rand and Mickey, took Clint's arm. They set out.

"That's funny," Rand said to her husband as the car pulled away down the street.

"What's that?" grinned Mickey, amused.

"A new aspect of McKenna's personality. An interest in electric trains." They laughed together.

"Yeah," said Mickey. "She's becoming well rounded. Great, huh?"

"They certainly seem happy together."

Chapter Sixteen

Within two months Nicole felt okay, her confidence restored. She received her master's in business administration a month thereafter. Her family—Mickey and Rand with their son Joey, Cinnamon and her boyfriend—came to and celebrated her graduation. The family was again intact.

The best part of the whole experience was that Luke Frey continued to see her almost every day. She felt herself falling in love with him and enjoyed the feeling.

The kissing became more and more intimate. When they were alone, his gentle caresses filled her with warmth and joy. She wanted to make love to him many times. When she'd graduated with her M.B.A., Nicole requested and received a transfer to her company's office in the western suburbs of Chicago. She moved into an apartment near her brother Mickey in Geneva, a suburb west of the city. She was about twenty minutes from Luke's house.

In late June, she sat at dinner at Luke's house in DeKalb, not far from Northern Illinois University where Luke worked. Nicole watched Luke bustle around, serving her a special dinner he'd prepared, pouring wine, and fussing over her. After dessert she gave him a long look.

"What's that for?" he asked.

"What's what for?"

"The look," he said. "You're up to something."

She leaned back, crossed her legs and folded her hands in

her lap. She wore a short summer dress she knew he liked, smiling as she dressed to please the man she'd come to love.

"You're the one who's up to something," she said. "What's on your mind?"

"Same as any other time I'm with you," he said. "Sex."

"Other than that, let's say," Nicole giggled.

"You ought to know better," he said. "Men never think of anything except sex and food. Everything else is a corollary to that."

"Okay," she said. "I'll give you my news. Then you give me yours."

"You've finalized the divorce," he said.

"You knew already?"

"I didn't know for sure," he said. "But I had to talk to Cinnamon on Monday. She told me she thought we'd hear something this week."

She sighed. "Yeah, it's over," she nodded. "Jack, her investigator, found Dale and my car. I also got back my TV, my stereo, and some other stuff. I haven't gotten my little pearl necklace back. I'm afraid it's gone forever. I haven't seen Dale, though."

"Just as well," he sniffed. "Not seeing that bum, I mean."

She agreed. "I'm guessing he has gone to, like California or Florida, or maybe Canada." He nodded. "I just have to sign the papers. I thought maybe you and I could run over there on Monday."

"Great. Does that mean we can start dancing in the streets?"

"Dancing in the streets?"

"Figure of speech, you big Ding Dong."

"What's your news?" she grinned.

"I wouldn't call it exactly news."

"No?"

"Come on in the living room."

She followed him into the living room. He had her sit on the couch. He stood over her for a few moments.

"What?" she said.

"I have to force myself not to stare at you all the time," he said. "I just like to indulge myself sometimes."

She giggled and waved a hand in a feeble gesture of modesty. "Okay, what do you want?"

To her surprise, he knelt in front of her. "Run your hand between the cushions," he said. "Right about there." He pointed. Puzzled, she did as he said.

"A little box," she said, drawing it out. "What. . ." her voice trailed off as she realized what it was.

"Open it," he said.

She did. A beautiful ring with an exquisite diamond sparkled up at her.

She sat unable to speak as he withdrew it from the box and slipped it on her finger. It fit pretty well.

"Nicole. I know that you've just come out of a crummy marriage. This may be way too premature. I apologize if so. But I'm asking you on my knees to marry me. As soon as you can. As soon as it feels right. If you need a week, a month, a year, two years, it's okay. But please say that you will. I'm miserable when you aren't around. If I don't see you for a few days, I feel. . ."

He broke off, seeing the tears on her cheeks. "What? Are you angry with me? Did I offend you?"

She fumbled for a Kleenex, blew her nose and wiped away

her tears. "No, you didn't offend me. I've wanted you to ask me that question since I first met you," she said.

"That makes us even. I've wanted to ask that question since I met you. So?"

She took his face into her hands and kissed him.

Chapter Seventeen

The next day, McKenna and Clint came for dinner at the home of Casey and Anna Fixx. Casey and Anna were delighted to meet Clint and the plans for a wedding thrilled them even more.

Casey and Anna held a party the next weekend to celebrate and introduce their friends and family to Clint. McKenna and Clint decided to marry in June, only a few weeks away, after school was out for the summer.

Ruth Frey came to the party with her son Luke and his fiancée Nicole, and to his obvious delight, brought along Cepha, who had become her fast friend.

"Mom," said Luke when he had a moment alone with her, "isn't Cepha supposed to stay in the same place only for a little while? Doesn't he have to leave?"

"I have talked to him about it," said Ruth. "It seems that he's allowed to stay if he's doing something to help others. That's how he was able to go to medical school, to college, and so on."

"He seems to be having quite an impact on the shelter," asked Luke.

"I think so," she said. "Every time I visit he's busy doing medical work, but he also does janitorial work, like mopping the floors, washing dishes, and so on. The administrator at the facility, Joan, has told me that he's become invaluable, because he also is an accomplished psychiatrist in addition to his general medical skills."

The news surprised Luke a little. Then he shrugged. "He apparently decided at some point to make the most of the time he has," he said. "And she, in essence, gets this assistance for free..."

"Yes, I think that's what's going on, I mean, the reason he's allowed to stay."

The party was going well, but Anna nodded at Mickey and Clint and asked them to come into her study with her.

They shut the door and sat in silence for a few seconds. At last Anna said, "Clint, you have the Cymreig, don't you?"

"The what?" asked Clint.

"The same ability Mickey and I have," said the woman who would become his mother-in-law. Clint didn't know what to say.

"McKenna said something about that the other night," he remembered. "I didn't know what to call it."

"Clint," said Mickey, "Did your parents reject you? Treat you as if you meant nothing to them? Ridicule and belittle you?"

"Well, yes," Clint said. "McKenna wanted me to bring her to meet them, so I called them. I spoke to both of them, though they weren't pleased to hear from me. They said they wouldn't be home, no matter when we came."

"I don't regard that as much of a surprise, to be frank," said Anna.

"Right," said Mickey. "Other than Nicole I never hear from my family, and I know you don't either, Anna."

"Yes, that's true," she said. "My parents died before I graduated from college, and I haven't spoken to my stepsisters in years. My grandfather, though, lives with us and he has the gift too."

"What does this mean?" Clint asked.

"We have descended from the Old Ones in Ireland," said Anna. "The correct term is Faerae," she added.

"As in *The Faerae Queen* by Spenser?" asked Clint. Anna nodded.

"People think we are mythological," smiled Mickey. "And really, what we do seems like magic, but it's more a type of profound hypnotism."

Clint nodded. "Are we the only ones?"

Anna shook her head. "No, as I say, my grandfather and Luke's mother share the gift as well. We seem to attract one another. I don't know how."

She nodded to Mickey, who left the room and returned with Ruth and Grandpa O'Neill, who seated themselves on the couch opposite the desk in Anna's office.

"Thank you, all of you," Anna said. "I'm hoping we can do something to help, as you know."

"Help who?" asked Clint.

"Cepha," said Ruth Frey.

"What could we do?" asked Mickey. "Isn't he under a curse?"

"Yes," said Anna.

"But you think maybe we can help?" said Grandpa O'Neill.

"What?" asked Clint.

"Ruth, why don't you tell them what happened yesterday?" said Anna.

"I told Cepha about Nicole marrying Luke," said Ruth. "He was thrilled for them. He said something about Clint marrying McKenna, and he was also pleased."

"Yes?" said Mickey.

"Here's what's happening," said Ruth. "Several nights ago, Clint and McKenna met one of Clint's friends, an archeologist who has done some significant work in Panama. In one dig, he found what appears to be a lost Gospel."

"Surely it is not canonical," said Anna.

"No, but it is a story of Jesus, to be sure," said Clint. "The main thrust of the Gospel concerns the life of a woman named Rachel who became the keeper of the Talit belonging to Jesus. She went to Ephesus after his death, then to Patmos, where the Romans imprisoned the Apostle John, and then to Rome. From there she married Paul's associate Timothy, and then went with him to Spain, where she died."

"And what happened to the Shawl?" asked Mickey Logan.

"An order of monks preserved it," said Clint. "A monk took it to Panama for safe-keeping at the time of the Spanish Armada, around the time of the last two or three decades of the seventeenth century."

"Are you sure it vanished?" said Anna.

"Well, I can't find any mention of it after 1671, when Henry Morgan invaded and laid waste to the city," admitted Clint. "However..."

He rubbed his chin, thinking. "Yes?" said Anna.

"I read a photocopy of this Gospel that my friend Ross gave me last night," said Clint. "The author wrote it in Latin, except for one thing."

The group waited. "A margin note on the gospel, handwritten in Spanish, said 'We hid it inside the Virgin,'" Clint noted. "Oh brother," he muttered.

"What might that mean?" asked Anna's grandpa.

"It just occurred to me," said Clint. "I think it might mean that they hid the Talit in the statue of the Virgin Mary that Morgan stole from the Cathedral." The group stared at him.

"But this helps us not at all," said Ruth. "That statue never made it back to Spain, nor to England. It's been lost for centuries also."

Clint looked at her for a moment. "Could it be at all possible that Cepha was there?"

"You mean at the Sack of Panama?" asked Ruth. She thought.

"If this is indeed the Wandering Jew," said Mickey, "then he shows up at the site of an awful lot of horrid tragedies."

"What do you mean?" asked Anna.

Mickey reached down and opened his briefcase. "I've been doing a little scholarly research on the Wandering Jew. I found some pictures of some tragedies of the last century." He pulled out a few pictures and laid them on Anna's desk. "Look," he said. He pointed to a man standing next to the gangplank of a ship.

"It does look like him," admitted Ruth. "What ship is that?"

"A ship on its maiden voyage," Mickey said. "The pride and joy of the White Star Line, making its maiden voyage—"

"Omigod," said Clint. He looked at Mickey. *Titanic.*" Mickey nodded.

"Could this be his, what, great-grandfather?" asked Clint.

"I thought so at first," said Mickey. "But look at the next picture."

A battleship lay on its side in the background. Smoke rose around it. A man stood on the pier, looking out at the wreckage.

"Pearl Harbor?" said Anna.

"Yeah, that's the *Arizona*. She's about to go down with her guys trapped below decks."

"Okay."

"Now look at the next picture."

The next picture was a blowup of the man who was standing on the dock watching the *Arizona* in its death throes. The resolution wasn't good, but. . .

"The same guy?" asked Clint.

"Looks just like him, doesn't it?" said Mickey

"Jeez. It can't be," said Mickey. "He doesn't seem to have aged at all. But what, around thirty years have elapsed since the first one where we see him standing by the *Titanic*?"

"Now this one," said Mickey Logan. The photo showed starving inmates of the Dachau death camp. Mickey pointed to the man in the top bunk.

Clint whistled. "Good grief—"

"Yeah, keep going. The next one is a picture of the collapse of the World Trade Center. Look at the guy. . ."

"I see him," said Clint. "Still hasn't changed at all."

"That's not the end, either. I found pictures of all kinds of disasters. I think I can pick this guy out of a lot of these pictures. Hurricane Andrew, the shootings at Columbine, an earthquake in the early eighties in Ecuador..."

"You mean," said Anna, "that disaster seems to follow him around."

"Not always," said Mickey. "I wouldn't say that. But he sure shows up a lot."

"How about if we talk to him?" asked Anna.

"Why not let me and McKenna do it?" said Clint. "She can be pretty persuasive."

"I should be there too," said Ruth.

"I don't disagree," said Clint. At this moment, someone knocked on the door.

"Come in," said Anna. McKenna came in.

"Hey," she said. "What's with you guys? You're missing the party—" she saw the serious expressions on their faces. "Is something up?"

"Sit down, Honey," said Anna.

Chapter Eighteen

Later that night, the group of McKenna and Clint, Luke and Nicole, and Ruth with Cepha returned to Ruth's home. Nicole made Ruth sit down while she bustled around serving sandwiches, pouring coffee, soda and lemonade and making sure everyone was comfortable. Luke helped her, smiling at the energy of his fiancée.

"Thank you for allowing me to come this afternoon," said Cepha. "I am seldom invited to parties."

"You were a welcome guest," said Ruth.

"You certainly were," said McKenna with a smile.

"I think I ought to return to the shelter shortly," he said. "May I ask one of you to drive me?"

"We will," said Nicole. "We live not far from there."

"We need to ask you something," said Clint.

"Yes," said McKenna. "Something unpleasant."

Cepha looked around at the faces watching him. "You all know about this?" he surmised.

Five heads nodded. He sighed.

"Cepha," said Clint. "Were you present at the Sack of Panama?"

He looked thunderstruck. "I did not expect that question," he said. He sat in silence.

"Cepha?" prodded Ruth.

Cepha stared at them. "What can you tell us about Sir Henry Morgan?" asked Luke.

Cepha's eyebrows shot up. "I. . ." he tried. "You mean the knight who invaded and destroyed Panama?"

"Yes," said Ruth.

"I remember that he saved his life with a curious gift to the king of England. He went from being a wanted criminal to being the governor of Jamaica."

"What else?" asked Luke.

Cepha shrugged. "He had the reputation of being a brilliant seaman and military tactician, of course. He stole a fortune in gold from South America—"

"But," said Clint, "you remember him, don't you?"

Cepha didn't respond at first. When he spoke, he kept his eyes riveted on his hands. "So much death. Destruction. The visitation of evil." He wiped at his eyes with the back of his hand.

"You saw the destruction of Panama, didn't you?" said McKenna, her voice full of compassion.

"Yes," whispered Cepha. "I could do nothing to stop them. I could do nothing to help the people he kept killing, and killing, and the burning, the conflagration. . ."

"You followed him back to his ship?" asked Luke.

"Oh yes. I should have stayed and helped re-build, but I didn't. He stole all the horses and pack animals the people of the town owned. Then, when they reached the ship, the sailors butchered the oxen for ship's food and set the horses free. I imagine they died in the swamps."

"Do you remember the statue?" asked Luke.

"Yes, of course," said Cepha. It appeared to Clint that the memory upset him. "I have nightmares of the sacking of the cathedral. Morgan's men disassembled the statue for transport.

Even so, it had to be dragged on a sledge by two oxen. I believe it was solid gold."

"Do you know what happened to it?"

Cepha shook his head, unwilling to discuss it. "Gold comes from the earth. Men rape it from the ground and transform it into pleasing forms. Two people pledge their love to one another by wearing rings made from it. And men kill other men in the fever the metal inflames."

"Yes, that's true, of course," said Ruth. "But I believe we could do some good with this statue, Cepha."

"How?" said Cepha. "The Devil used Gold to construct his palace of Pandemonium. Hundreds of thousands of Indians in this country and in South America died because of the European greed for gold. No," he affirmed, "the world is better if the statue remains hidden in the earth."

"Is that why you've never recovered it?" asked Nicole.

"That's part of it to be sure," he agreed. "But also, what should I do with it? Melt it down, sell it? Why? What use would I have for it? To whom would I give it? You are the first people in centuries who have befriended me."

"Does it surprise you that people want to be friends with you?" asked McKenna.

Cepha studied her copper red hair for a few moments. "You do not have the Cymreig, daughter," he said.

"No, I don't," said McKenna. "But my mother does, and so does the man I'm marrying." She took Clint's hand. "Not only that, I have found two other pirate treasures: That of Blackbeard and that of Sandy Gordon. We have done good things with the treasures. In both cases we set free people who were bound to earth by their fears and doubts."

"I've read about you and your treasure hunting," Cepha nodded. "What does that have to do with me?"

"Do you know what was placed inside the statue?" asked Ruth.

Cepha looked puzzled. He stammered for a few seconds. "But nothing is inside the statue," he said. "It is solid gold."

"Not all the statue is solid gold, Cepha," said Ruth. "The artist built a compartment in it."

"What?" said Cepha. The others could see he was taken aback. "You are serious? Someone hid something inside of it?"

"Yes," said Luke. "We are all but certain of it. The object inside may explain why the pirates were so terrified, in fact. If we are correct, we might be able to help you."

Cepha gazed from person to person. Clint saw that his interest had been peaked. "Would you tell me about this object?"

"That night in the garden. What did you see the Nazarene wearing?" asked Clint.

Again the question caught Cepha off guard. He stammered for a second, collecting his thoughts. "I will trust you that the question has relevance," he said. "I see him bathed in a white light: moonlight, I think. It grew cold that night, I remember. He wore a reddish cloak. He'd put his white prayer shawl over his head."

"Did you see the shawl the next day when he was being dragged to the cross?"

Cepha again hesitated for a second, examining his memories. "No, I didn't. I'm certain that he didn't have it on. I guess I assumed that it had fallen off when they whipped him. . ." then, tears choked him as they always did when he thought of that day. For a moment, he couldn't go on.

"It didn't fall off, we're sure of that," said Ruth. "We believe that he managed to give it to someone who in turn gave it to the disciple named Rachel. You remember her?"

"Yes, Rachel had the bleeding problem," muttered Cepha. "I don't recall everything that ever happened to me, but I can never forget a moment of those days. Rachel's face remains vivid in my memory. She became one of his followers."

"Yes, she developed into a loyal and brave disciple. We believe that Rachel took the *talit* to Spain," said Ruth. She placed a gentle hand on Cepha's shoulder, which he covered with his hand. "Then, hundreds of years later, someone took it to Panama where the goldsmith sealed it into the golden statue of the Virgin."

Cepha gazed at them in silence, his mouth working. At last he spoke in a voice so soft they had to make an effort to hear it. "Why do you think the *talit* would help me?"

Clint cleared his throat. "Do you remember Jairus?"

"Yes," said Cepha.

"Could you tell us how you remember the story?"

Cepha nodded.

* * * * *

Jairus, one of the synagogue rulers, forced his way through the crowd and knelt at the rabbi's feet. Jairus wiped at the tears of worry and stress that streaked his cheeks and tried hard to speak. Yeshua saw at once that the man kneeling before him seemed dumbfounded with grief.

Yeshua knelt and laid his hand on the man's shoulder. "Tell me," he said.

"Master," Jairus said, speaking with great difficulty. "Our daughter is dying. She had a fever. The fever became a cough.

She can't breathe. She is suffocating, Master."

"I am so sorry, Sir," said Yeshua. "Why have you come to me?"

"Good Master," said Jairus. "Please come with me to my house."

Yeshua nodded. "Yes, of course I will. Lead the way."

Jairus rose to his feet, then turned and started off with the crowd following. Yeshua paused to talk to a woman who had touched his *talit*. He knelt and embraced the woman.

Jairus, dumbstruck, almost screamed. He knew this woman named Rachel. For twelve years she had walked through the streets of Kaphar Nahum crying "Unclean! Unclean!" Now Jairus watched as the Nazarene hugged her.

Jairus knew what the embrace of an unclean woman entailed. The Nazarene had put himself in a state of ritual uncleanliness. Yeshua would have to wait until nightfall to purify himself. Jairus knew his daughter couldn't survive that long.

As the Nazarene rose, two men from Jairus' household came to Jairus. He turned and looked at them.

"Yes?" he asked, his face white.

"Sir," said one of them. "Your daughter just died."

Jairus couldn't speak with the horror that clutched at him. He uttered a hoarse, strangled croak that would have been a scream if he could have managed anything else. The pain drove him to his knees as his grief overwhelmed him.

"Sir, don't trouble the Master anymore," said his servants. "He can do nothing."

Again Yeshua knelt next to Jairus. "No," he said and embraced Jairus' shoulder. "You mustn't give into the grief. Don't be afraid, sir. Try to believe."

Jairus turned and looked into the rabbi's eyes. In that moment, the courage returned to his heart. He wiped at his eyes with a cloth and blew his nose into the cloth.

Yeshua rose and helped Jairus to his feet. He spoke in a quiet tone, soothing Jairus with kind words. Jairus again led the way to his home.

In less than ten minutes, they arrived at the house. They heard the din of the professional mourners, who had showed up already, wailing and weeping.

"Would you summon your wife, Sir?" Yeshua asked Jairus, raising his voice to be heard over the racket. Jairus waved to his wife, who stood in a corner of a room draped in a shawl. She excused herself from her mother who sat next to her, holding her and comforting her.

The wailing quieted as the people in the room realized that the rabbi from Nazareth stood among them in the room. Yeshua waited until they grew silent. Then he spoke. "Why are you wailing like this? We do not require your services. The little girl has not died; she is only sleeping."

The words stunned the room. Then, one person began to laugh. Then another and another. In moments the whole house came alive with derisive mockery directed at the Nazarene madman.

"Ask them to leave," Yeshua told Jairus. Jairus spoke to the mourners and they started to depart. When they were gone, Yeshua embraced Jairus and his wife.

"Take me to her, Sir," he told Jairus. His wife motioned to a room at the back of the house.

Yeshua took the husband and wife along with his disciples James, Andrew and Peter into the room with him.

Jairus' child lay on her back, pale and cold in the clay-like sleep of death. Yeshua gazed at her for a moment while Jairus and his wife clutched at him. He disengaged from them and walked to the bed where the girl lay. He removed the *talit* from his shoulders. He tied the child's wrists with the *tzitzit* and draped the shawl over the child. "You are mistaken," he smiled at the parents. "The child has not died; she is only sleeping."

Yeshua said, *"Talitha Kuom."* Now, he took her hand. Jairus and his wife gasped. Rabbis did not touch a dead body. For Yeshua to do so astonished them.

Now, as Jairus watched, his little girl sighed. He saw her chest rise and fall. She gave one cough, than another. Her eyes opened and she turned. Her eyes fell first on Yeshua. Her face became radiant with joy. "Master," she said.

He smiled at her and hugged her. He removed the *Talit*. "My friends," he said to the parents. "Give her something to eat."

* * * * *

"Can you translate the phrase that Yeshua said over her?" McKenna asked Cepha.

"Yes," he nodded.

"The New International Bible translates it, 'little girl, I say to you, get up.'"

"That's close," admitted Cepha. "But it would be more accurate to say, 'little girl in my *talit*, wake up.' Talitha is a compound word: *talit*, meaning 'prayer shawl', and *ha*, which means 'little girl.'"

"What about the prayer shawl makes it so important?" asked Luke.

Cepha shrugged. "It has to do with Hebrew ritual as spelled out in the *Mishnah*."

"The what?" asked McKenna.

"The *Mishnah* is the section of *Torah* which sets down what were once oral laws," Cepha said. "The woman Rachel had suffered from bleeding for twelve years. The Law required her to proclaim herself 'unclean, unclean' as she walked through the town of Capernaum."

"I understand," Luke nodded.

"Christians believe that Yeshua could not be touched by sin," said Cepha. "In this case, when he embraced her, he became unclean in a ritual sense, according to the Mishnah. He would have to wash himself at sundown to become clean again."

"I'm confused. Do you mean Yeshua became unclean?" asked McKenna.

"Only in the ritual sense, McKenna," Cepha smiled. "When he imputed his purity to Rachel, and then to the little girl, he took their impurity on himself."

"Oh, my," said McKenna. "Then both of these events, Rachel and the little girl, foreshadow the cross, don't they?"

"Yes," said Cepha. "On the other hand, the woman—"

"Rachel," said Nicole.

Cepha turned and looked at her. "By the way, how do you know her name? The stories and Gospels of Jesus don't record it anywhere."

"Don't I have it right?" asked Nicole.

"Well, yes, but. . ." Cepha paused. He looked confused. He shrugged and resumed. "Anyhow, the defilement by blood could now prevent Yeshua from going to his house. But Yeshua saw the bigger good in the healing. He went to the house anyway."

"He thought the little girl was more important than the Law?" asked Luke.

"Not quite. It was more that the exigency of her death overrode his devotion to the law. But he bound her hands with the *tzitzit* and then covered her with the shawl."

"So," said Clint, "the agency—Am I saying that right?—of the shawl brought the twelve-year-old girl back to life."

"The same shawl that helped the woman who had been unclean for twelve years," said McKenna. "Twelve years in both cases. The same length of time. I'd never thought of that."

"The *talit*, of course, couldn't be made unclean," said Cepha. "The garment couldn't be defiled because the garment was greater than her defilement."

"Are you saying, then, that Yeshua responded to an emergency that took precedence over the Law?" asked Luke.

Cepha thought. "I hadn't put it in those terms, I guess."

"It sounds similar to when he asked the people, who among them would not save a farm animal which had fallen into a well on a Sabbath?" asked McKenna.

Cepha nodded. "Yes. In this case, he showed that his power exceeded the defilement."

"Then could his power go out to you if you put on his *talit*?"

Cepha thought. "I don't know. In both cases, the *talit* became the agency through which power went out to heal. . ."

"Would it be worth a try?" asked Nicole.

"I don't know," began Cepha. "Yeshua hasn't returned, as he promised…"

"But we may be living in the right time, mightn't we?" asked McKenna.

"What do you mean?" asked Cepha.

"Do you remember what it says in Hosea?" she asked.

Cepha looked at her and quoted. *"Come, let us return to the Lord. He has torn us to pieces but he will heal us; he has injured us but he will bind up our wounds. After two days he will revive us; on the third day he will restore us that we may live in his presence."*

"On the third day?" said Nicole.

"Yes. In Biblical terms we're living in the third day if we start counting with the destruction of Israel and the temple in A. D. 70," said Cepha. "Israel has wandered for centuries, but now they have returned to the land."

"Two thousand years," said Luke. "Two days have gone by." McKenna looked at him, curious. "Remember, in the Bible, I think it's Second Peter, it says 'A day is like a thousand years.'"

"He minored in theology," said Nicole to McKenna.

"Ah," said McKenna.

"That quote comes from the psaltery. It's found in Psalm 90," muttered Cepha. The four friends could see his mind working.

At last he said, "Very well. I can't deny that you have a point. It hadn't ever occurred to me to think of the Nazarene's shawl. But power did go from him through the *talit* to someone, yes."

"When can you go?" asked McKenna.

"I can go anytime," he said, a rueful expression on his face. "I would like to be out of this cold, as well."

"My parents and Nicole's brother and sister-in-law will sponsor the trip," said McKenna. "They asked us to regard the gifts as wedding presents."

The friends chatted with Cepha for some time. He agreed to

come on the expedition, on the grounds that he could return to the shelter when he concluded. "For the first time in ages, I have felt free to stay somewhere," he explained with a smile at Ruth. McKenna and Nicole exchanged glances, their eyebrows raised.

They dropped Cepha at the shelter and drove together to Mickey Logan's house in Geneva, not far from the shelter. Rand and Mickey sat with them in the living room.

"We're going to get married on Saturday in the afternoon," said McKenna. "Would you two please come?"

"Of course we will," said Nicole, and Luke nodded. "We're getting married at ten, so we'll have no trouble getting there for the ceremony."

"So it's good that we're getting married, huh?" said Luke to Nicole, who grinned.

"I suppose," she said. "Do they have such a thing as the Mann act in the Caribbean? We don't want to break the law, you know."

"I want to have a proper honeymoon, though," said Luke.

"Luke," said McKenna, with a grin. "Think about it. A treasure hunt on a desert island in the Caribbean? What more could you want?"

"Privacy," said Luke. The group laughed.

Chapter Nineteen

Three nights later, Luke dropped Nicole at Mickey Logan's house and gunned the Trans Am down North Avenue on his way to his house in DeKalb. He'd lived there since he'd accepted his professorship at Northern Illinois University.

He'd been tempted to sell the place when he split with Sharon. The memories that went with the place were not pleasant. Still he had held onto it. The home, convenient to the university, was a lovely Colonial in a pleasant neighborhood that had lots of young families and plenty of kids. He felt out of place as a bachelor in the community.

Then he'd brought Nicole over. He felt the young woman's radiance filling the lonely places in the house, even the bedroom. The ache and pain of the split-up with Sharon eased and then vanished as Nicole walked around the place. He could feel her taking claim of it.

Luke listened to her plans to change the carpets, paint the place, wallpaper the bathroom and re-do the landscaping. He smiled and agreed to each suggestion, understanding that his fiancée had begun not only redoing the house, but working to make it hers. He suggested that they buy new furniture. In particular, they needed a new bed and linens.

The new bed waited for them now in the master bedroom, covered with new linens, blankets, pillows and a bedspread. They decided not to use the stuff until they married.

Luke smiled to himself as he remembered the joyful smile on

the face of the young woman he loved as she saw her plans for her house coming together. Bitterness and despair had fled from him in the love she showed him.

Tomorrow morning, he would marry the woman who had brightened and helped to restore his life. Cinnamon's judge friend would perform the ceremony at ten o'clock. They would proceed to Clint and McKenna's reception, then to the hotel for a special wedding night celebration together.

Luke pulled the Trans-Am into the driveway and noticed a small Honda parked in front of the house. He remembered his uncle Ted. Ted's next door neighbor had insisted on parking an old rusty Oldsmobile, about the size of a dump truck and every bit as attractive, in front of Ted's house. One day Uncle Ted couldn't take it anymore and walked next door.

"Why do you park that car in front of my house?" he asked. "Why don't you park it in front of your own house?"

"I can't park it in front of my house," the neighbor said.

"Why on earth not?" asked Uncle Ted.

"If I do, it blocks my view," the neighbor explained, trying to be patient.

"Oh," said Ted.

The story made Luke grin. That didn't surprise him. He smiled most of the time, now.

He walked in his front door and noticed that the kitchen light burning. *That's odd*, thought Luke. *I don't remember leaving the light on.*

Now, he saw that the door to the master bedroom lay open and a weak light—perhaps one of the bedside table lights—was on. Again he felt surprised. That emotion faded and he began to get scared.

He took out his cell phone as he looked around the first floor of the house. The wall safe in the study was closed and locked. His desk hadn't been disturbed.

He went into the kitchen. Everything looked okay at first. Then—

Luke, though not much of a drinker, loved an occasional glass of good scotch. Once on a vacation with Sharon in Mexico, he splurged and bought an half gallon bottle of Johnny Walker Blue Label Scotch, one of the best single malt scotches in the world. Though the cost had been unbelievable even in a duty free store, he permitted himself a small glass of it on occasion.

Like the night he'd proposed to Nicole and she'd accepted. In celebration he'd poured them each a shot of the expensive whiskey. She'd never tasted anything like it, loved it and asked for more.

"Not a chance," he said. "No way."

"Why, you cheap, penurious. . ." she began, teasing.

"You can have some Black Label, or some Glenfidditch. How about that?"

"Harumph," she snorted.

He laughed. "Isn't that what Winnie-the-Pooh and Piglet dug the trap to catch?"

"Certainly not," she sniffed. "That was a heffalump. Everyone knows that. Now pour me some more of that scotch or face the consequences."

"Oh, all right," he chuckled. "One more."

Now he stood in his kitchen and saw his bottle of Blue Label sitting on the counter. He knew it hadn't been out when he left home that morning.

Luke was becoming more and more alarmed. He opened the

hall closet, picked up a baseball bat and went upstairs.

He tiptoed down the hall to the master bedroom and stepped through the door.

"Hello," said the woman who was lying in his bed. She drew back the covers. She was naked.

"Sharon," he said. "What the hell. . ."

"It's good to see you, Luke," said his ex-wife. "It's been a long time."

"How did you get in here?"

"I still have a key. You haven't changed the locks."

"I never thought you'd keep the keys, much less use them."

"Well, I'm back," she said. "Come here." She held up her arms. "I poured us some Blue Label to celebrate."

* * * * *

Nicole, groggy, realized that she heard her cell phone ringing. It had been ringing for several moments. She'd been asleep. She fumbled for the phone.

"Yes."

"Hi, Honey. It's me."

"Luke, what in the name of. . ."

"Please come to the house now. As soon as you can."

"You have to be kidding," she moaned. "It's after midnight. We're getting married in a few hours."

"Honey, I need you here. Please trust me and come."

"Okay. I'll be there in a half hour." Nicole swung her legs out of bed. She cast a longing glance at her pillow. She sighed and hummed a few bars of *Love is a Many Splendored Thing.*

* * * * *

Nicole saw the Honda sitting in front of Luke's place. *Where'd that car come from?* She wondered. Puzzled, she shut off the Explorer and walked to the door. She knocked, then turned the knob and went in. Luke stood against the bookshelf on the far side of the room.

"Okay. What do you want?" she asked, stifling a yawn. Then she saw that Luke looked dreadful. His face was drawn and haggard, his eyes dull. "What on earth—?" she asked.

Luke turned and pointed to a chair next to the fireplace. A beautiful woman sat there, staring at her, her expression stone.

"So," said the woman. "You've been filling my bed with this child? The one who has destroyed my house with this execrable bad taste?"

"Who are you?" asked Nicole. "What are you doing here?" She saw that the woman was wearing one of Luke's robes. This woman hadn't tied the robe shut. Nicole saw she was naked beneath the robe.

"I'm Sharon Frey, Little Girl," said the woman, sneering the words, as if she were speaking to a three-year-old. "And I'm home. So you see, for you to be here with my husband in the middle of the night is not only inappropriate but even scandalous."

Nicole felt the spark of anger start to burn hot. She refused to yield to it. Luke needed her to be strong. "If you are Sharon," said Nicole, keeping her voice even with an effort, "then what I see is the woman who carried on an affair with another man for several years and who then blamed and humiliated the man I'm marrying. Please put your clothes on and leave my house at once."

Sharon's eyes blazed. She rose, the robe falling open. Nicole noted that she had a well-sculpted and beautiful body that suggested many hours in a gym.

Sharon stormed across the room and stood before Nicole. Nicole didn't back away an inch.

"How dare you speak to me like that?" Sharon demanded.

"Luke," said Nicole, not breaking eye contact for an instant with Sharon.

"Yes," he murmured.

"Does she have any legal right to be here?"

"None whatever."

"Right," said Nicole. She spoke again to Sharon. "This man will become my husband in a few hours. We're going to be married at ten o'clock. You are no longer married to him and have no right to be in this house. Again I say: please get dressed and leave at once."

"How *dare* you speak to me like that, you little. . ." began Sharon, and started to slap at Nicole with her right hand.

Nicole reacted at once. She threw up her left hand and blocked the slap. At the same time she took one step with her left foot and slammed her right fist into Sharon's stomach just below the sternum.

Sharon gasped as the punch drove her breath away. She bent over and clutched at her stomach with her left hand.

Now Nicole shifted her weight and swung her left fist in an uppercut to Sharon's jaw. Sharon's teeth smacked together with a "pop" that resounded through the house. She started to reel backwards as Nicole took one step with her left foot and slugged Sharon below her left eye, staggering a little with the force of the punch.

Sharon landed hard on her back. The impact knocked the rest of the wind out of her. She wheezed and tried to stand, but slumped backwards and began to cry, gasping for air. The fight had come to an end.

"Where are her clothes?" asked Nicole.

"The—uh—the master bedroom," said Luke, dumbfounded.

"Get her some ice in a plastic bag. I'll get her clothes." Nicole pivoted and marched up the steps to the master bedroom. She found Sharon's clothes draped over the new chair. She gathered them up and slung Sharon's purse and coat over her arm.

She came back to the living room. Sharon, still dazed, sat on the floor. Luke had filled a plastic bag with ice which Sharon applied to her eye.

Nicole dumped clothes, purse and coat on the floor before Sharon. She tossed Sharon's car keys to her fiancé. "Get the keys to our house off of that key ring," she demanded. While Luke complied, Nicole demanded to know if she had any more keys to the house. Sharon, still dazed and clearly intimidated, shook her head no.

"Luke and I will go to the guest bedroom," Nicole scowled. "You have five minutes from right now to dress and leave my house. If you aren't gone by then, I'll call the police and have you arrested for trespassing. I assure you I'll press charges. Until the police get here, though, I'll give you a beating that'll make this one look like bunny kisses. Now get out. If we notice anything missing I'll have you arrested for burglary."

Nicole turned and led Luke down the hall to the first floor guest bedroom. She turned back to the living room and yelled, "Four minutes." She shut the door behind her and crossed to the couch. "Come and sit down." He did. She embraced him and felt him trembling a little.

Two minutes later, they heard the front door slam. Pictures rattled on the walls from the force. A few moments later, they heard the Honda parked in the street start up.

"Go and make sure that she's gone, that she didn't just go in the kitchen or something," she told Luke. "Then, set the deadbolts."

He came back and found her still waiting. "Do you have your alarm watch?" she said, trying to be gentle.

"Yeah, I do. . ." said Luke.

"Set it for 7:00 A. M., okay?"

"Why?"

"We have a lot to do. First thing in the morning, you have to wash my new sheets and get them back on the bed in the master suite. While they're washing you have to change the locks on the doors. Yes, I know I took the keys, but we can't be sure she doesn't have copies. I sure don't want that woman in this house again. Then you have to make sure the judge plans to marry us. Meanwhile I'll run home to change and pick up my suitcase and get my hair done. I'll come back. Then we'll get married. Then we'll go to Clint and McKenna's wedding and reception. Then we head to the Hyatt Regency, find our room, and get this marriage rolling."

Luke's smile had been building as she spoke. Now he chuckled. "You've got this all figured out, huh?"

"Any objections?"

"No," said Luke. "Not on your life. I wouldn't have the nerve."

"Good idea."

He laughed and said, "Something else."

"Mmm-hmm?"

"I'm afraid you've made a rather bad enemy of the Witch of the West."

"Uh-huh. I'm sure I have."

"Can I ask you something?"

"How long will it take? I'd like to get *some* sleep before my wedding."

"Where did you learn to fight like that?"

"Oh," she said. "I don't know how to fight. That's the only fight I've ever been in."

He chuckled. "What?"

She gave a nervous giggle. "It's stage choreography. My brother Mickey came in as a guest lecturer and ran a workshop on stage combat for our drama club when I was in high school. We all learned how to stage fight, where no one gets hurt, even touched. I've never tried to hit someone. Mickey said I did it well at the time, though."

"You did *real* well this time. Jeez."

"Thank you. At least I didn't break my hand. I think."

Luke cuddled her and she held him as he relaxed and fell asleep.

That was good. She had to be strong for him in the face of his ex-wife who had come close to destroying him.

It was also good that he didn't see the tears on her cheeks. She'd never been so scared.

Chapter Twenty

Anna and Casey had planned a beautiful and memorable wedding ceremony for their daughter. McKenna's aunts and a couple of friends served as her attendants. Clint's football buddies and a guy from work stood with him, and Ross served as his best man.

As expected, Clint's family didn't come, though McKenna called and begged them to be part of it. They gave a curt refusal and asked McKenna not to call again. To Clint's delight, Coach Miller and his wife Ruth drove over from Weller College and stood in for his parents. Coach Robbins, his high school mentor, sat with his wife in the pew next to the Millers.

Casey and Anna both walked McKenna down the aisle and gave her away. McKenna took his arm as the congregation sat down. "Where'd you get the necklace?" asked Clint in an undertone. McKenna wore a magnificent emerald necklace.

"An heirloom," whispered McKenna. "It's been in my family for ages. My mom gave it to me this morning."

"It's gorgeous," he said, and she smiled. "So that's the something old?"

"Yes."

"What about the something blue, the something new, and so forth?"

"You can't see those things now, Goofy," she said.

"You look beautiful."

"You look the way I always knew you would."

"Is that good?"

The conversation was rolling along and might have continued for some time, but the pastor of McKenna's church cleared his throat to attract their attention. To their embarrassment, they realized that the church had grown silent behind them. They heard laughter. "Sorry to interrupt," he whispered. They giggled. "Would this be a convenient time for you two to get married?"

"Yes," they said in unison.

A young man entered the church and stood at the back. He moved into a pew and watched the ceremony. He stood in the shadows as the wedding party left the church. No one noticed him. He took out a cell phone after the last person left and speed dialed a number. "This is Gil," he said. "He's not here. I'll move on to the reception." If anyone in the wedding party had seen him, they would have been puzzled to see an absolute mask of fury on his face.

* * * * *

Casey and Anna hosted the Wedding Reception at a lovely country club. Anna and Casey joined their daughter and her new husband in the greeting line, welcoming guests in the lobby of the country club. Nicole and Luke walked in, both of them grinning ear to ear. Right behind them they saw Ruth walking with her arm linked with Cepha, then Mickey and Rand Logan. Anna studied the glow of happiness surrounding Nicole. She asked, "Did you just get married?"

"Yes," said Nicole. "At ten o'clock this morning." Anna let out a little scream of delight. She and Casey offered congratulations as Ruth embraced her son and her new daughter-in-law.

Casey Fixx took his wine glass and walked to the microphone. He tapped the edge of a glass. "Ladies and gentlemen," he said. "We're here to celebrate the wedding of McKenna and Clint." The audience applauded, delighted. In keeping with the local custom, several people clinked the side of their water glasses with their spoons. McKenna and Clint responded by kissing. The audience applauded again.

"However," said Casey, "I'm delighted to announce that this wedding is not the only one we'll be celebrating today. We have another pair of people in the room who were just married today, as well."

"Oh, no," groaned Luke. Nicole elbowed him.

"Therefore," said Casey, "let me point out the man and woman standing by the door. They were just married this morning. It's a terrific honor to introduce, for the first time anywhere, Dr. and Mrs. Luke Frey. Will you please greet them?" He pointed at Luke and Nicole who were standing by the door. Almost blind with embarrassment, Luke and Nicole came forward blushing to the applause of the entire group. They were greeted by Clint and McKenna, then Cinnamon and her boyfriend Durango and the rest of the Fixx clan.

The reception continued into the evening. The last guests departed at about ten o'clock. At last, Nicole and Luke had a chance to talk with McKenna and Clint.

"Are you guys ready to go?" asked McKenna.

"Yes," said Nicole. "We're all packed and our bags stowed in the trunk of my new car."

"New car?" asked Clint.

"Yes, my wedding present from my husband. It's a 1963 Corvette Sting Ray. He had it rebuilt it for me."

"Oh my," said McKenna, impressed.

"We both have the next two weeks off," Nicole said. "We're going to the Hyatt tonight, and we'll be ready to go first thing in the morning."

"Well, maybe not *first* thing," said Luke. Nicole turned a violent red and whacked his arm.

"Agreed," said Clint.

"Sex maniacs," said Nicole.

"What?" said Luke, looking wounded. "We have to eat breakfast, don't we?" Both Nicole and McKenna whacked him, and Clint laughed at his friend.

"Mom and Dad are having brunch at the house at nine o'clock tomorrow morning so we can open wedding gifts. About twenty people are coming," said McKenna. "So we can leave around noon from there, if that's okay with you. You can park the Corvette at Mom and Dad's house."

"Are we all set with reservations?" asked Luke.

"Mom and Dad gave me the tickets today," said McKenna. "The limousine will pick us up at 11:30 in the morning. We leave O'Hare about two in the afternoon and fly to San Juan, Puerto Rico. Then we fly from San Juan to Tortolla, arriving at about 9:40. We stay in Tortolla overnight. In the morning we meet Liane, who's secured us a big cabin cruiser to go to Fallen Jerusalem."

"Fallen Jerusalem?" asked Luke.

"That's the name of the island. Cepha says we'll understand why it's named that when we see it. We showed him a map. He's sure they hid the treasure on the island called Fallen Jerusalem. It's about ½ mile south of Virgin Gorda, one of the bigger islands."

"So," asked Nicole, "are we going to camp out over there?"

"No," said Clint. "It's dangerous to anchor overnight in those waters. We'll stay up in the harbor in Virgin Gorda. We're renting a boat that sleeps eight, so we ought to be comfortable."

"Well, it doesn't sound too bad at all," said Luke.

"Of course it doesn't," hissed his new wife, and both women whacked Luke again. "Keep it up," Nicole asserted, "and you're going to find yourself sleeping on the deck. By yourself."

Luke promised to behave, chuckling.

"Are you going to pick up Cepha, or are we?" asked McKenna.

"Mom's going to bring him in the morning," said Luke. "He's excited to come to the brunch. I don't think he's been to many parties."

"Your mom seems to be having—er—quite an effect on him, huh?" noted McKenna.

Luke thought about that for a second, rubbing his lips with a forefinger. "Hmm. You're right, McKenna. He seems to enjoy being around her a great deal, too." Four pairs of eyebrows raised at the same time.

Chapter Twenty-One

Clint and McKenna drove toward their hotel for their wedding night.

"Are you nervous?" she said.

"About what?" he asked.

"About. . .well, about tonight."

"No, I don't think so. I know how to get to the hotel. I've stayed in them before. Don't worry."

"I didn't mean that, you big dope," she said, giggling.

"I think we'll learn together, don't you?"

"I think we're going to learn a lot together in the next, what, 65 or so years?"

"All I know," said Clint, "is that I'm with the only girl in the world I want to learn with."

She took his hand and raised it to her lips. "Can you hurry up a little bit?"

"I'll try," he agreed.

* * * * *

McKenna and Clint worked hard the next morning not to betray their impatience to get going. They were careful to dodge the questions about where they were going on their honeymoon.

Luke and Nicole showed up about ten o'clock. Ruth Frey escorted an embarrassed Cepha into the group. She and Anna took him in hand so that he would feel welcome and at home. To the surprise of both women, they saw his eyes tear.

"What is it?" Ruth asked the man who had become not only a professional colleague but a valued friend.

"I am not welcome at parties as a rule," he said. "I am so grateful for your help." Anna smiled and nodded.

Cepha spotted Nicole in a corner, chatting with a guest. She met his eye and nodded. "Hmm. Excuse me. I need to speak to Nicole for a few moments in private." He crossed over to her. She stood and they walked down the hallway.

"What's that about?" Clint asked McKenna.

"No idea," said McKenna, puzzled.

Paula and Rusty Ivers were guests at the party, as well. Rusty asked Clint and Luke to step outside with him for a moment.

"Clint, you know about these accidents at Westwood, don't you?" he asked when he pulled the door shut behind them.

"What accidents?" said Luke as Clint nodded.

Rusty took a few moments to explain about the assault on the cross country coach, the swim coach's heart attack, Mel Robbins' auto accident, the assault on Gil Westlake, as well as the murder of a volleyball coach and another P. E. teacher.

"A murder?" said Luke. "Someone killed a couple of coaches?" Rusty shrugged and asserted that the police were sure the two teachers had been murdered.

"What happened with Gil?" asked Mickey, and Rusty explained that the police had found him in the parking lot at Westwood, beaten badly and semi-conscious. The police had taken him to the hospital overnight.

"Jeez," said Mickey.

Rusty agreed and went on. "The volleyball coach had a fight with a parent the afternoon that she disappeared. We interviewed the parent, but she has an ironclad alibi. She was home with her family," said Rusty. "There doesn't seem to be much doubt that she's in the clear."

"I bet she's brokenhearted about the coach," said Luke, with a humorless smile.

"Yeah, right," said Rusty. "She said that she's sorry about her, but now the school will be free to hire a teacher and coach who cares about kids." Clint and Luke snorted with contempt.

"Why would anyone kill the coach?" asked Clint. "I didn't know her, though she was on the faculty when I went to school there."

"They stole her liver," shrugged Rusty.

"Why would they do that?" asked Clint. Rusty explained the medical examiner's theory that her liver had been stolen for transplant. Clint swore under his breath, shaking his head.

"Rusty," said Luke, "it sounds like a gang of parents have some sort of plot, like a conspiracy to kill or hurt coaches at the high school, am I right?"

"I know that the community has some true nutcases, that's for sure," said Rusty. "I spoke to the trainer about that. He sees the parents at all the events, of course."

"I bet he's got some stories," said Clint. "From what I hear, the assertion that they treat coaches like hell would live in Understatement Hall of Fame."

Rusty shook his head. "No doubt," he agreed. "The trainer, a guy named Barsanti, told me that in one game a year ago, Mr. Robbins' team had the ball on the other team's five-yard line, just before the end of the first half. First down and they're losing by a touchdown. Westwood runs four plays and doesn't score. The other team's parents are cheering, and Westwood's fans are booing. The half ends and the teams run off the field.

"Some of the Westwood parents were screaming profanities, several others were yelling at Coach Robbins, 'Why didn't you kick a field goal? Get some points, at least.'

"They don't realize that the kid who kicks the field goals couldn't do it. Someone kicked him in the head about half way through the quarter, and Coach Robbins had to take him out of the game. The kid was delirious, and didn't know if he was in Green Bay or Westwood Stadium."

"Yeah, I've seen guys knocked goofy in games," said Clint.

Rusty continued, "The trainer walked over to the stands and explained it to the parents. They didn't let up. Mr. Robbins should have had a backup kicker, they said."

"Oh for Pete's sake," said Luke.

"Yeah," agreed Rusty.

"I can't believe I'm hearing this," said Clint. "I played for Coach Robbins. He couldn't have treated me any better. He treated more like a father than my own father *ever* treated me."

"I hear that from a lot of people," said Rusty.

"So why are you telling us this?" asked Luke.

"I know where you're going and why," said Rusty. "Mickey and Rand sought me out to ask if I thought it was safe for you to go."

"Why?" asked Clint, surprised.

"I'm pretty sure that the parents weren't behind all of the attacks, perhaps most of them, at least the murder."

"Why?"

"Because something strange happened with the murder."

"What?" asked Luke.

"I don't want to tell you everything, not because I don't trust you, but because we are investigating and want to have some identifiers for the real criminals. Let me just say that I think that someone else has set up a smokescreen and is using these incidents to cover another purpose. I'm pretty sure the volleyball coach was at the center of it."

"What does that have to do with us?" said Luke. "We don't work at Westwood, never have."

"No, but Clint went to high school there, McKenna did her student teaching there, teaches English now and helps coach track, and Mickey used to teach there," said Rusty.

"You think we're in danger?" asked Luke.

"Luke, I just don't know," Rusty admitted. "I can't figure the real purpose of the accidents, or why someone would hurt coaches. I don't know if it relates to what you guys want to do. Just be sure to keep your eyes open, okay?"

"You can bet that neither one of us intends to put the women we love in danger, Rusty," said Luke.

"I'm sure that's the case," said Rusty. "I can see how much you guys love those two. I identify with your feelings."

"Yes," said Luke. "I've seen how you feel about your wife, too."

"Don't take any chances or unnecessary risks, please. Also. . ."

He paused. "What?" said Clint.

"The guy you're going with. Most people think of Cepha as just a legend," said Rusty. "Of course, now we know that he isn't a myth."

"Yes?" said Luke.

"If you're familiar with the legend, then you know that wherever he goes, death and disaster tend to follow him," said Rusty.

Luke and Clint nodded. "We've studied the legend. We know," said Luke.

"Okay, Rusty," said Clint. "I appreciate your concern. I promise we'll be careful."

The group rejoined the party. Bagels and several varieties of cream cheese sat on the dining room table, along with pitchers of juice and carafes of coffee.

"Clint," said McKenna, her hand against her chest, eyes cast heavenward, her voice melodramatic. "Thank goodness you're safe."

"Oh for heaven's sake," he sighed.

"What?" she said. "At any moment I expected to receive a ransom demand."

"I wasn't gone that long, for gosh sakes," snickered Clint.

"Come on, we're going to open gifts," said McKenna, impatient to get going. "Better than Christmas."

"You bet," he said. "I get real excited about mixmasters."

McKenna giggled and backhanded his arm. "It isn't just stuff like that. We'll also be getting our china and crystal and silver."

"Whoopee," he grunted. "Give me meat and potatoes on a tin plate, according to the Geneva Convention. I'll be happy."

"Right," she said. "I forgot. Mr. Macho, right?"

"Right," he growled.

"We'll also get a whole bunch of cash, I imagine," she smiled.

"Oh," he said. "In that case, Yahoo!" She laughed and grabbed his arm.

Chapter Twenty-Two

Mickey watched in amusement as his friend Rusty bustled around the dining room and kitchen, helping Mickey and Rand clean away the debris from the bridal breakfast. The couples, smiling and excited about their honeymoon, had just left in the limousine with Cepha.

Rusty insisted that Paula sit and watch. "Rusty," she said, amused at him. "I'm pregnant, not disabled. You do know the difference, right?" Everyone laughed, but Rusty remained adamant.

He and Mickey worked together in the kitchen. "Well, I warned them, like I promised," he said, loading the dishwasher.

"Thanks, I appreciate it," said Mickey. "I sure hope they'll be okay."

"Ah, they're terrific. I think—" Rusty's pager blipped and he looked at it. "Excuse me, Mickey," he said, then pulled out his cell phone and punched in the number. "Lieutenant Ivers," he said. He listened for a second. "Okay. Hang on." He turned to Mickey. "Do you know where Pete Morley lives?"

Mickey nodded, puzzled. Rusty again spoke into the phone. "We'll go right over there." He hung up. He turned to Mickey. "Somebody shot up Pete's house last night." Mickey's jaw dropped. "Lots of damage. No one was hurt."

Rand came into the kitchen as Rusty hung up. When she heard the news she insisted on packing up some sandwiches for the Morleys.

* * * * *

Logan and Rusty pulled up in front of Pete's house about a half hour later. Pete's wife, Michelle, stood in the living room, crying and terrified.

"Mickey," said Michelle, hugging him. "How nice to see you again."

Pete shook hands with his friend. "Yeah," said Pete. "Like you say at funerals, sorry it's under these circumstances, pal."

Rusty and Logan talked with them, but they had no idea whatever about what would cause someone to shoot out their picture windows. No, no one else in the neighborhood had been vandalized.

After a few moments, Rusty went off to consult with the police. They were chatting with neighbors to see if anyone had heard or seen anything. He came back in and reported that so far no one had any sort of information.

Several cups of coffee later, Pete reflected with his old friend. "You know, Mickey," he said. "In all my teaching and coaching I've tried to model life skills and behaviors for my students. To be attacked like this…" his voice trailed off.

"Yeah, I know," said Mickey. Logan and Rusty insisted that Pete and Michelle eat some of Rand's sandwiches. A bit of food made them feel better.

Pete sat on his sofa, cradling a styrofoam cup of coffee in his hands. He gazed at his shattered picture window. At last he said, "Several years ago, four of our students went for a weekend to a cabin in northwest Wisconsin. One of their parents bought them a couple or three cases of beer. I know, of course you're right, the parents were morons. What kind of idiot supplies alcohol to a high school kid?

"Anyhow, on Saturday night the temperatures dropped below zero," he went on. "Nevertheless, two of the kids decided to take the snowmobile out on the lake for a spin close to midnight. They were pretty drunk and they didn't know their way around very well. They drove the snowmobile too close to open water. The machine went through the ice into the river." His eyes misted. He took a bite of a ham and cheddar sandwich and chewed for a few moments.

"One of the kids made it back to the bank," Pete went on at last. "Soaking wet, all but frozen solid, close to hypothermic. He had the presence of mind to know he couldn't go back for his friend. He started to look for the path." Pete took a swallow of hot coffee.

"Then he rallied himself," Pete went on. "Somehow, he found the right path. He climbed up it. He stumbled, fell, and couldn't go on. The other two kids heard him yelling, thank God. They went out and helped him indoors, called for an ambulance, and saved his life. The body of the other boy, the driver of the snowmobile, wasn't recovered until some days later." He choked up at this point and his wife leaned over and embraced him.

"I saw the survivor in the hospital," said Pete, brushing at his tears. Mickey could see how this story still touched him to his heart. "He had been nearly hypothermic, frostbitten. Thank God he didn't lose any fingers or toes. He told me that his body had just wanted lie down and sleep during that whole walk, which must have taken him forty-five minutes. Then he would realize that death hid behind that sleep, just waiting for him to drift off. He knew he'd never wake up. He told me..." Pete broke off. Tears choked him again for a few moments. Logan also put his arm around his friend's shoulders.

When Pete regained his composure, he said, "He told me that he heard the voices of our line coach Bill Wyatt and me in his head. He said we kept telling him that he had to keep going. He couldn't give up just because things got tough. Quitting was too easy." He wept again, looking around at the wreckage of his living room.

"I'll never forget it. In this life people don't often get to save someone's life. That was the proudest, most important moment of my teaching career. Something I said had a real impact on someone. Now this," he said with a grimace, waving his arm at his smashed windows and door. He asserted, "Well, if they wanted to scare me off, they're full of it. I'm not quitting."

An insurance adjuster came in and began making arrangements for cleanup and glass replacement. Pete and Michelle needed to give him their full attention. Logan and Rusty said good-bye and went back to Logan's home.

"Rusty," said Logan. "Who's doing this?"

"I don't know. Pete lost what, two games this season with the football team? Led the team into the quarterfinals of the state playoffs?" asked Rusty. Logan affirmed it with a nod. "The team was terrific. Well disciplined, good spirits. . ."

"There's more to this than idiot parents harming a coach," said Mickey.

"I've got a hunch I'm following up on," Rusty said. "We'll see what happens."

PART TWO

The Road to Tyburn

Chapter Twenty-Three

He struggled just to remember that his name was Stallings. Yes, that was it.

The dream would begin again any second, Stallings knew. He lived it over and over. Or maybe he'd only lived it once. Or maybe it had been two million times.

The dream always turned into a nightmare which terrified him to the pit of his soul. The worst part of the nightmare, though, was that by no amount of willpower could he ever make himself wake up from it. It kept going and going, showing the nightmare landscape of his life since just before he'd been sent to Newgate.

The dream scared him of course, but he was always *cold* as well. It was always dark, no trace of light anywhere. The smells were always the same.

Not for the first time, he wondered if he was dead. *Yet, if I was dead*, he reasoned, *I would be in hell. Hell is supposed to be hot, is it not?* He asked no one in particular. There was no one to ask. He was always alone, too.

Time meant nothing. A few minutes might have gone by since he'd been in here. Or ten years. Or two hundred. Or more.

To his horror, the dream started again. As always it began with the fight. He'd gone out on a Friday night to the London Pub called The Hanged Man. A grisly name, of course, but then it wasn't too far from the nightmare of the triple tree of Tyburn, where every day people were hanged, strangling and dancing in terror at the end of a rope, closing off their lives in disgrace, ignominy, fright, suspended, struggling against the final plunge into darkness.

Was I hanged, after all? Stallings asked himself. He shrugged the idea away. No, he couldn't have been.

In the dream, Tripworth challenged him during in a game of cards, where Stallings had, of course, been cheating. He'd always gotten away with cheating before, and considered himself quite proficient at it.

Stallings remembered that he felt terrible about being caught. Not about being in the wrong. It was only wrong to cheat if someone caught you doing it.

Tripworth and Stallings used their fists first, and Stallings could hear the cheers of the onlookers. He found himself winning the fight against the enraged opponent, who was about his size but slower. When Stallings hit him on the temple, Tripworth reeled backward and fell hard on his backside. Tripworth reached into his trouser pocket and produced a knife. Tripworth stood and came for him. Stallings, unarmed, backed away in terror.

Tripworth slashed back and forth at him, stabbing up with the blade, trying to kill him. Stallings, now, came to realize that he could die in this fight. He stumbled against a chair, then picked it up to knock the knife away. Someone handed Stallings a thin knife, long and terrible. Tripworth lunged and slashed Stallings on the left arm. The cut was deep and would be painful. But Stallings entangled him in the legs of the chair. Tripworth lost his balance as Stallings yanked. Stallings came up with his knife. The point of the blade entered the gut just above the belt. Tripworth's momentum pulled the blade up to the chest. Tripworth died in seconds.

The constable took him to Newgate, the ghastly criminal prison. The court rejected his pleas of self-defense. The judge with the black cap condemned him at Assizes, pronouncing the familiar words: *"Hosmer Stallings. You are sentenced to be taken hence to the prison in which you were last confined and from there to a place where you will be hanged by the neck until dead and may The Lord have mercy upon your soul"*.

The wardens dragged him, dazed with horror and sick misery, to his cell which stank of urine, excrement, sweat and terror. A prisoner who didn't die during his incarceration—and many did—had three ways to get out of Newgate: released, hanged, or transported. He dreamed in gruesome detail the horror of those days until his execution.

At midnight before he had to face the hangman, a bell rang. It was the death knell at St. Pulcher's, the church nearest to Newgate. Stallings heard the bellman pronounce the traditional exhortation:

> All you that in the condemned hole do lie,
> Prepare you, for tomorrow you shall die;
> Watch all and pray; The hour is drawing near,
> That you before the Almighty must appear.
> Examine well yourselves; in time repent,
> That you may not to eternal flames be sent.
> And when St. Pulcher's Bell in the morning tolls,
> The Lord above have mercy on your souls.

When the terrible morning came, the bell of St. Pulcher's Church—or, as the prisoners called it, Saint Sepulcher—tolled at

8:00 A. M. as always. Groans of terror rose from the prisoners in the condemned pit.

Five men, three women, and one boy, an accomplished pickpocket even at the age of fourteen, trooped to the Chapel where some of them, including Stallings, received the sacrament. He received the sacramental host on his tongue and let it dissolve in the wine. *Oh God,* he prayed—as he would several dozen times in the next several minutes—*O God, please don't send me to Hell.*

The constables now brought the condemned into Stone Hall. One by one, the guards knocked off their wrist manacles and leg irons and draped the condemned in their rough-weaved hempen cloth shrouds. The guards roped their hands together in front of them.

The guards herded them downstairs. The constables dragged those who couldn't walk, unconscious with fear in many cases, to the four waiting carts for the ignominious journey through the streets to Tyburn and the waiting ropes. Once they were seated and tied to the carts, the hideous journey began: along Lombard Street, the High Holborn Road, and then the road to Tyburn.

The carts stopped, as was customary, at The Crown Inn where the condemned received a glass of cheap wine called Canary. The wine was supposed to steady their hearts. In some cases, the prisoners were so overcome with fear that they couldn't hold the glass. Stallings fell into this group. He hadn't been able to eat or sleep for three days, and just managed to drink water.

Then the procession started up again, and people at the side of the road thrust nosegays into their hands to help overcome the stench of sweat and accumulated filth in the carts.

They arrived at Tyburn Hill. As they came up the hill, they saw Jack Ketch, the hangman, lounging, lying on top of the gallows, smoking his pipe. *"Oh my, think I'm going to die,"* chanted the waiting crowd.

The hangman was not the real Jack Ketch, of course. Jack Ketch, who died in 1686, served in exemplary fashion as one of King Charles the Second's executioners. He became famous through the way he performed his duties during the tumults of the 1680's. All the Tyburn hangmen since Ketch, though, had been known by that name. By custom, the assistant to the hangman would be appointed to the office when the executioner went mad, as many did, or quit, as few did, or died. *"Oh my, think I'm going to die,"* the crowd chanted.

The boy was the first. Ketch looped the rope around his neck, then pulled the white nightcap over the boy's face. The boy wailed in terror, crying for his mother. The crowd laughed and mocked the child as Ketch roped the women to the gallows. Then the men. Stallings realized that he was the last, the honor saved for the most vicious of the criminals. He was the only killer in the group today. The rest were petty thieves or other ne'er-do-wells.

Ketch stood before him and glared at Stallings with contempt. The hangman's eyes were anthracite, and the red lips drew back in a horrid grin, revealing, to Stallings' horrified eyes, pointed teeth. Stallings all but fainted with fear as the hangman pulled the hairy hemp rope over his head. *"Oh my, think I'm going to die."*

Ketch adjusted the rope at the back of his neck so that Stallings would strangle. He jerked the rope so tight that

Stallings struggled to breathe. Then Ketch started to pull the white night cap over his eyes. The crowd booed. They wanted to see Stallings' face as he strangled to death.

Ketch stepped back and looked around the crowd. He made a motion to put the cap onto Stallings, and again the crowd booed. Ketch swept an elegant bow of surrender to the crowd's will and walked away. The crowd cheered.

"Oh my, think I'm going to die."

The performance had reached its climax. The mocking chant died away and silence fell. The anticipation grew. The crowd knew that the hangman paused the proceedings on purpose. The Tyburn executioners liked to draw out the drama.

The hideous scene was a dramatic tableau. Over the years, more than 50,000 people died at the Tyburn gallows.

The victims would fall perhaps a foot, not enough to break their necks. The dance of death would please the people in the grandstand, who liked to see them dance with terror and spasmodic jerks. The audience at Tyburn often brought picnic lunches.

Stallings prayed that he would fall hard enough that his neck would break. He prayed that he would just go into darkness, and sleep, with no dreams, no terror like at night. He prayed that the sermons he had heard about Hell were lies told to frighten little children.

Again he prayed: *Into your hands, O Lord, I commit my spirit. .*

The crack of a whip interrupted. The horses harnessed to the first of the four carts galloped away. The large crowd cheered as the ropes yanked three people out of the cart. A minute later, Ketch whipped away the second cart. More cheers. Then, the third.

As Ketch reached the fourth cart, a man came forward and handed Ketch a parchment. He seized Stallings, who gave a moan of terror at the touch.

The man loosened the rope around Stallings' neck and pulled it away. The crowd jeered with disappointment. He pulled Stallings down and untied Stallings' hands.

Stallings collapsed forward into the stinking, unspeakable muck below the gallows. The man grabbed the shroud and pulled him aside. Ketch, with a sneer, swung his whip at the horses pulling the final cart. The two men who had stood on either side of Stallings screamed in terror, then fell, their legs jerking, their necks stretching.

The eight victims swung back and forth, all of them jerking. Their bodies would remain for an hour. Then they'd be cut down to be tossed into a mass grave or sold to hospitals for dissection.

One spectator standing next to Stallings pointed to the boy struggling on the other side of the tree. He laughed to his friend that he liked it when boys died at Tyburn.

Stallings, in a desperate terror still, not daring to speak, watched the carts roll away. He looked at his rescuer. He couldn't speak. He could still feel the hairy touch of the hempen rope around his neck.

The man spoke to him, not without kindness: "It is not death."

Stallings turned and began to retch. Nothing came up, since he had not eaten. The man handed Stallings a flask. Stallings' hands trembled as he took a deep drink of the hot liquor. He felt it burn him as it descended his throat. Some feeling crept back into his limbs, and he was soon able to stand. Then the man took his arm and led him stumbling to a dogcart which would take them both back to Newgate prison. The crowd booed as he drove away in the dogcart.

Stallings' heart sank. He concluded that the man would take him back into the death cell, perhaps to die tomorrow or the next day. The man took hold of Stallings' arm and almost had to drag him to the prison bath. A couple of guards cut away his filthy clothes, sluiced him with icy water and scrubbed away the muck with brushes and lye soap. They put him in cleaner clothes and took him to the warden's chamber.

In the warden's chamber sat a man wearing a powdered wig and estimable clothes. This man and the warden chatted with amiable cheeriness. For his part, Stallings heard little except the word "Transportation."

The men grew quiet. He looked up and saw that the warden and the assistant were staring at him, waiting for a response. He could say nothing. He managed a nod of acquiescence.

The warden pronounced Stalling's new sentence: ten years of indentured servitude in the Carolina colonies. His life was forfeit if he violated any aspect of his parole, including returning to England before his sentence was up. Stallings told them he understood.

The ship sailed that day, with Stallings crammed into the stinking hold, filled with stinking humanity. All the prisoners sat crammed together, miserable in their own filth but grateful to be there and not at the end of one of Jack Ketch's ropes.

The journey was one of horror, starvation and seasickness, but he managed to stumble ashore to meet the man who had purchased his service as one would purchase a slave. It was indeed the man he had met at Tyburn who had rescued him from the rope. He told Stallings to begin today working with his specialty, making and laying bricks. That skill had saved him.

The Carolina colony struck Stallings as beautiful, and the climate more temperate than what Stallings had come to accept in Britain. Five years went by in a short and happy time. Stallings' Dream touched on that period only in brief flashes.

One day the master called him to the front parlor in his home. In the parlor stood a guest, a very tall, well-dressed man. Stallings heard the name Morgan.

Stallings looked at the man who was at least for a time his master. Morgan's eyes were those of a demon and terrified Stallings. He'd seen eyes like those before, on the hangman of Tyburn.

Stallings learned that this gentleman required his services for some days, perhaps a month or two, aboard a ship. Stallings, holding his hat in front of him, nodded. His life was forfeit if he returned to England, the master reminded him. The stranger would bring him back here after a brief voyage.

Over the next few days, Stallings molded and fired a large number of rough bricks. Several men loaded them into longboats and hauled them out to Morgan's vessel *Satisfaction*.

When Stallings came aboard, the voyage had already lasted over a year. During his first moments with them, Stallings realized that he had been indentured to a pirate.

The ship sailed south to the eastern side of Panama and continued up the Rio Negre as far as the ship could go. Morgan saw that Stallings had no skill as a warrior. Stallings stayed aboard for several days while Morgan's men sacked the hapless town of Panama City.

Morgan returned with tons of gold and silver on the backs of oxen and horses. Stallings watched as several large men butchered the oxen. The pirates released the pack horses.

The ship sailed back up the river and onto the Caribbean Sea. As Morgan's ship crossed the Caribbean to head back to England, Stallings noted that the tension on the ship had risen to the point of becoming uncomfortable. He learned that the captain had decided to put something ashore.

In a few days, the ship anchored off a small, rocky island that from a distance resembled a destroyed city. Stallings thought he could make out buildings, roads, and other landmarks. However, the buildings proved to be nothing more than fallen boulders. The captain summoned Stallings to his quarters and told him he would go ashore in the morning. He would use his bricks to build a treasure vault on the island. Stallings knuckled his forehead in acquiescence.

The next morning, some volunteer sailors rowed Stallings ashore with the bricks he'd made before coming on board the ship. Five men came with him as well as the horrifying Captain. They began to dig, as Stallings began to mix his mortar. He fashioned a vault of large bricks. When he had completed the vault, it was about eight feet long and wide and six feet deep. When the men filled in the sand around the vault, Stallings stuffed oakum into the cracks and then mortared over them. Then he layered mortar over the entire vault. The foreman assured Morgan that the chamber was waterproof.

The captain returned to the ship as Stallings and several of the men fitted a huge steel door over the vault. The captain came ashore again, this time with a large chest. The sailors rigged a tripod and lowered the chest in. Then, to Stallings's awestruck eyes, a life sized gold statue of the Virgin, which the pirates had disassembled.

Stallings stood by the side of the pit, ready to seal the vault. The Captain asked him to look into the pit one last time. As he did, a thin rope encircled his throat, and consciousness fled. The crew threw his body into the brick-lined pit to serve as the guardian of the chest. His consciousness returned in the pit, which had been sealed. Then the dreams began.

Then something interrupted his dream. He heard something and looked up, but of course he could see nothing in the utter blackness of the vault. He realized that he heard the sounds of someone opening his crypt. He waited.

Chapter Twenty-Four

McKenna found a Tortolla cab driver at the airport to take them to their hotel. The couples enjoyed a late night dinner and then spent the night at a hotel called The Jolly Roger.

After breakfast, Luke and Clint met Liane, the boat broker, at the Turtle Bay dock. She gave them the keys to a power catamaran known as *The Pussy Galore*. Nicole and McKenna shopped for provisions and bottled water which Cepha helped them load aboard the boat.

After the two couples stowed their luggage into their cabins, Luke started the engines and headed the *Pussy Galore* east across the narrow bay toward Fallen Jerusalem. "What's with the name of the boat?" McKenna asked Clint as they came onto the bridge with Nicole and Luke.

"Got me," Clint shrugged.

"Oh, come on," said Luke. "Haven't you ever read Ian Fleming?"

"Who?" asked Nicole.

Luke sighed. "Philistines," he said. "Ian Fleming wrote the James Bond series of books. Pussy Galore was the villainess slash heroine of *Goldfinger*."

"Oh yeah," said Clint. "I saw the movie. Honor Blackman played the part."

Again Luke sighed. "But you didn't read the book, I suppose. Alas."

"You know, Luke," said his wife. "You really have to be

careful. Be sure you put on lots of sunscreen."

"Me?" said Luke. "Why me?"

"Well, I think Nicole has a point," said Clint.

"Which is?" said Luke.

"Your legs, Dear, in those shorts," returned his wife. "The Glare is blinding."

The friends laughed together at the teasing, and Luke assured them that he saw himself as no better or worse than any of them. Clint looked out. "There," he said, pointing. "There's Fallen Jerusalem." McKenna climbed down to point out the island to Cepha. He stood and looked.

"Yes," said Cepha. "Yes, I recognize it."

McKenna observed that the Island of Fallen Jerusalem approached from the west looked about as hospitable as an abandoned quarry. "It isn't much," agreed Cepha. "No one has ever wanted to live here. It's now a national park for the British Virgin Islands. The beach is beautiful, but. . ." he grew silent, staring at the deck. His hands trembled.

McKenna took his arm. "What happened?" she asked. "You were fine, then all of a sudden—"

"I've seen so much destruction, so much death," he interrupted. "I could name terrible tragedies that I've witnessed. None of them give me any joy when I return to the scene. On the contrary."

"What happened here?" asked Nicole.

Cepha told the story of the burial of the treasure. "Five men went ashore, including me. We took bricks and mortar. We hoisted it up the side of the hill. Oh, yes, it took several trips. One of the men in the group had worked as a mason. I remember him being crude, vulgar, and reclusive. I never spoke much with him, but I gathered that he had been deported to Carolina because of . . ."

He paused, and cleared his throat. When he didn't continue, Nicole said, "Because of?"

"I'm pretty sure that he was a murderer," said Cepha. "I don't know how he escaped the gallows. On the other hand, I remember him being quite a skilled stone mason."

"A mason. That's why the bricks and mortar, huh?" asked Luke. "They constructed something, I suppose a vault, to hold the treasure. I guess I figured that they just dug a hole in the sand."

"Not in this case," said Cepha. "Morgan had him build a vault for the treasure. I don't think Morgan ever intended to return to recover this treasure. In fact, I think that he was as frightened of what we buried as anyone."

"Frightened Sir Henry Morgan, the scourge of the Spanish Main?" said Clint. "The treasure could do that?"

"I don't know," said Cepha. "I do know that he wouldn't go near the statue. Most of the men tried to avoid it. They were afraid of it."

"Why didn't they just melt it down into ingots?" asked Clint.

Cepha shook his head. "I don't know. I remember thinking when I saw the statue that they would. But they never did."

"Huh," said McKenna. .

"Morgan tried to get volunteers to go ashore with – what was his name? – I think it could have been Stallings. When he couldn't find any, Morgan assigned five of us, myself included. Morgan himself wasn't thrilled to go ashore, I'm sure."

"What happened when you came ashore?" asked Nicole.

"We excavated a pit, about 6 feet deep, and about 8 feet wide and long. Stallings used the bricks to construct a vault, and we laid an iron slab with a trap door over the top of the vault."

"An iron slab?" asked Clint. "It must have weighed a ton."

"Yes, it did. Morgan had it cast somewhere in the Indies, I know. We had a hard time dragging it up the hill and putting it in place."

"I can imagine," said Nicole.

"Then you set the treasure inside, I suppose," said Luke.

"Yes. Then Morgan told Stallings to look inside once again. The bosun's mate strangled Stallings with a length of cord. He and Morgan dropped Stallings' body through the trap door into the vault. I sealed the metal door. We laid oak planks over the top of the vault, and then covered it over with sand."

"So the bosun's mate murdered the architect of the vault?" asked Clint.

"Yes. Most people felt this Stallings amounted to no great loss to the ship."

"Why him and not you or the others?" asked McKenna.

Cepha thought for a moment. "I don't know for sure. The whole crew had developed such a traumatic fear of the statue that Morgan assumed that none of us would go back to recover the statue. His assumption was correct. Just being here makes me feel afraid."

"Didn't pirates have a superstition about leaving one man to guard the vault?" asked McKenna.

Cepha nodded and said, "In this case he left a dead man."

"Strange," said McKenna.

They anchored the boat and waded ashore in the delightful waters of the British Virgin Islands. "How about if we do some snorkeling while we're here?" said Luke. "We can rent some equipment in Tortolla, come back here..."

"Sounds like fun," said Nicole. "Let's see what happens ashore."

As they walked across the white sand of the beach, McKenna and Nicole noticed that the face of their friend Cepha had turned dead white. Nicole took his arm. "What is it?" she asked.

He shook his head. "I forgot the feeling of terror that comes with being near this statue," he said.

"Does this scare you?" asked McKenna, concerned. "Can we help? Should we stop?"

"Keep going," he said. "I'll try to keep up." He pointed to a large flat rock on their right. In front of it, several cacti grew. No one else was on the island, but they walked as if they were being hunted.

Cepha, though, choked on every step of the walk to the rock. Tears streamed down his cheeks. His face had turned the color of a manila folder. "Stop," said McKenna. "Can you do this?"

"I'm sorry," said Cepha. "I'm feeling the terror of what's in the vault, as I sensed it that day. I'm dragging all of you down with me. I'm not being fair to you."

"Do you want to go back to the boat?" asked Luke. "Or should we take you back to Tortolla?"

Cepha shook his head and motioned upward, making it clear that he wanted to keep going. "Are you sure?" said Clint. "I imagine we can. . ."

"No, please," said Cepha. "I'm sorry. I think I need to be here. Please keep going."

They arrived at the flat rock. Now Cepha turned back to face the sea. He looked up the hill toward a pillar of rock. He walked a few steps and fell to his knees. McKenna saw that he continued to weep with fear.

"Cepha," said Nicole. "Please, let's go back. It's not worth it."

"Yes, it is," said Cepha. "Something important is about to happen, I know it."

Luke and Clint walked in the direction he pointed and stopped a few feet from a large cactus. "Yes," whispered Cepha.

Luke and Clint dug down a few feet in the sand. Luke jabbed his spade and all heard a loud clunk as the spade struck something. "What did you hit?" asked McKenna.

"Wood, I think," said Clint. He threw several shovelfuls away.

"Yes," whispered Cepha. "That would be the oak planks we laid over the top of the vault." He lay trembling in the sand several feet from the excavation, curled into a fetal position. McKenna and Nicole knelt next to him, embracing him as best they could.

Now, the men cleared away the top and saw that the planks formed a platform about eight feet long and as many wide. "Take them up," whispered Cepha. "There's a trap door in the center."

Using pry bars, the men managed to break away some of the rotten wood in the center. McKenna and Nicole hauled the old oak bits aside. The planks came up in pieces. Now the two men saw a metal trap door.

"I can't believe that Morgan constructed this vault so well," said Luke.

"He assumed no one would ever go in again," said Cepha.

"Should we stop?" asked McKenna.

"No," said Cepha, shaking his head with some violence. "No, please, open it."

Clint hit the old, flimsy lock with a pick. It shattered. A pry bar broke away the old hasp.

"Now, pull up the door," said Cepha.

Moving the door proved to be difficult, however. At last, though, the rusty seals gave way. Luke and Clint managed to get their wrecking bars underneath the door. They threw their weight on the bars and pushed.

With a metallic groan, the door lifted an inch. McKenna shoved a plank into the opening. The men repositioned the bars and pushed again. This time it moved a little more. Again the women inserted a plank.

At the next push, the door gave way. It fell back and clanged hard against the brick. Clint and Luke reeled backwards and fell into the sand.

Cepha stood. "Get back," he said. "All of you. Be quick."

They heard the strident command in his voice and backed away as Cepha rose to his feet and walked to the opening.

A hand extended out of the pit. "What the hell?" muttered Luke. "How could. . ."

"Shhh," said McKenna, clutching at Clint, scared but unable to look away.

Cepha bent down and took the hand. He pulled, and a wiry man, no more than five feet tall, climbed out of the pit.

The man blinked and shielded his eyes, trying to adjust to the light. "Cepha," he said. "Where are the others? Where is Morgan?" He looked out to sea. "Where is *Satisfaction*?" he demanded.

"Morgan died," said Cepha. "The ship's destroyed. Hello, Stallings."

"I have been trapped in that vault," said Stallings, his accent so severe that the group could understand him only with the greatest effort. "I could have suffocated. I am surprised I did not, in fact."

"Yes," said Cepha. "I know."

"You know?" said Stallings. "You knew I was in there and you did not come to help me? We are shipmates, you—"

"No longer," interrupted Cepha. Stallings blinked, his eyes wide with bewilderment. "These are my friends. They brought me to help rescue you. Come away." Stallings turned and surveyed the group, muttering unintelligible words. He stared in amazement at two tall, beautiful young women dressed in two piece swim suits covered by tee shirts, knotted at the waist. He'd never seen women dressed with such immodesty.

"This is impossible," whispered Nicole to McKenna, recovering her wits but cold with terror.

"No," whispered McKenna. "This spirit—yeah, I'm sure that's what he is—has been bound here, trapped in the earth by fear and hatred." She spoke up to address their friend. "Stallings is the reason we came, isn't he, Cepha?"

"Yes, I think so," returned Cepha.

"You came to help me?" said Stallings.

"Yes," said Cepha. "You have suffered more than you should have. You never should have been condemned. Imprisoned, yes. Punished, yes. But not tormented for all eternity." Cepha nodded to Luke and Clint.

McKenna and Clint lowered themselves into the vault, which was about six feet deep. They saw Stallings's bones lying in a ghastly pile. The bones turned to dust as Clint pushed them aside. Now, they saw the statue, piled in pieces. They tied a rope around one of the arms. Luke and Cepha hoisted the golden limb out of the pit. Then they pulled up the other arm. The legs. The torso.

At last, Clint secured the rope around the head with its delicate features. He and McKenna helped the others lift it out.

"Cepha," he yelled up. "There's a chest here, too."

"Leave it for the moment, Clint," said Cepha. "Come out."

Luke gave McKenna a hand out of the pit, then Clint. Clint saw the statue lying in rough order on the ground.

"Can we re-assemble it?" asked Nicole.

"I think not," said McKenna. "Let's leave that to a goldsmith in Panama."

"What do you mean?" said Clint.

"We have to return this to the cathedral in Panama City," asserted McKenna. "We don't have a right to keep it."

Clint looked at the lovely statue, sighed, and agreed. "I guess it wouldn't do us any good. We couldn't let anyone to melt down a treasure like this."

Cepha knelt by the statue, hands still trembling, inspecting the statue. He ran his fingers along the back of the torso.

"She's beautiful, isn't she?" said Nicole, looking at the head of the statue.

"Yes," said Luke. "She's exquisite. It looks like the artist used a native girl as his model."

"Here," said Cepha.

The friends knelt and saw a minute crack in the back of the statue. Cepha ran his finger along the edge and found, buried in the folds of the cloak, a small latch. "My God, what beautiful and intricate workmanship," said McKenna.

Cepha took a small screwdriver from his pocket and tripped the latch. Then he inserted the blade and lifted. The small compartment opened. Cepha started to reach inside, but drew back. His face went dead white and he took a few steps back. "Cepha," said McKenna. "Should I pull it out for you?"

"Please," he whispered. "I can't."

McKenna withdrew a packet of waterproof canvas. With care, she opened it and held the ancient shawl up. "My God," she said, falling to her knees. "It looks new."

"Yes," said Luke. "The gold would have destroyed any mildew or other crud. Also the air stays so dry here."

The cloth, indeed in remarkable repair, had been woven from exquisite wool, white with blue stripes and white wool fringe.

Stallings had drawn back in fear. "What is that?" he said.

"It's what we're afraid of," said Cepha. He stood, face drawn with fear. He reached for the shawl. Then he held up a hand. "No," he said. "No, I can wait. Here, Stallings. You have suffered long enough. Wrap yourself in it. It will heal you."

Stallings, kneeling and shaking with fear, managed to nod. Luke took one of his elbows and Clint the other, supporting him. Stallings looked from man to man, then bowed his head, trembling with fear. Nicole draped the shawl over Stallings' head.

A change came over the man almost at once and he fell to his knees. "Oh my God," he said. "Please, no. Yes. Yes. I cheated, I lost my temper, and I stabbed him. Of course I did it. I killed him. Yes, I deserved the pain. I deserved the cross, not you." He wrapped himself in the cloth as if trying to warm himself.

He knelt in the sand, his face contorted with pain. He looked up, and his face began to glow. "I am sorry," he whimpered. "I didn't mean. . ."

Now his body glowed, and McKenna remembered how the accounts in the Bible talked about people glowing with a light that was whiter than white. *He's being transfigured*, she thought.

"Mother," said Stallings. "Mother, help me. Help me please. . ." His voice grew soft, then indistinguishable. Stallings faded as the light faded. They heard him manage to breathe out, "Into your hands, O Lord, I commit…"

Then Stallings vanished. The prayer shawl fell across Luke's arm.

The group stood in silence. "Good grief," said Luke, thunderstruck. Nicole took his arm, trembling a little at what they'd seen.

"He's all right, isn't he," McKenna asked Cepha.

"Yes," said Cepha. "He's healed."

"Cepha," said McKenna. "Now you."

"No," said Cepha. He stepped backwards and tripped over a shovel. He sprawled in the sand. He began to crab walk backwards in the hot sand, his voice hoarse with fear. "No, take it away. Please. Take it away." McKenna and Nicole knelt next to him. They embraced the man whom they had befriended.

"Don't be afraid," McKenna told him. "We're right here with you, I promise."

"Yes," said Nicole. "We'll stay with you."

Luke came forward and lifted the shawl. Cepha, white with fear, let the two women and Clint help him to his feet. Weeping with dread, he breathed deep, and then stood straight. He nodded, and then bowed his head. Luke and Clint draped the shawl over him. Cepha closed his eyes—

* * * * *

Cepha opened his eyes. Yet, he realized, that was not his

name here. Rather, his name once more had become Malchus for the first time in many centuries. He looked around and realized that he no longer stood under a clear Virgin Islands sky. Instead, on a cloudy, dark day in Jerusalem, he stood at the side of the road, looking at the procession coming toward him. A man stumbled under the weight of a cross. *The whole cross*, thought Malchus, *not just the crossbar*. The typical condemned criminal left the jail tied to the crossbar known as the *patibulum*. This Nazarene had been forced to walk to the place of execution carrying and dragging the instrument of his death.

Malchus saw the Nazarene who had healed his ear staggering under the weight of the cross, trudging toward him. The man's torn and disfigured face shocked Malchus. The torturers had hit him across the face with the whip. The crown of thorns on the Nazarene's head tore jagged valleys from his cheekbones to the top of his head. *He can't see*, thought Malchus. *They're pushing him, blind, to his death.*

Now the Nazarene drew next to him. Yeshua lost his balance and fell.

Malchus didn't draw back. He stepped forward and caught the huge cross before it fell on the Nazarene. A Roman whip slashed him across the back, but he held the cross upright.

The weight of the cross left Malchus dumbfounded. *This is too heavy for one man to drag*, thought Malchus. Again the soldier hit him with his whip. He paid no attention. He extended a hand and pulled the Nazarene to his feet.

The Nazarene turned to him and managed a weak smile, his teeth—many of them broken— showing. "Thank you, Malchus," he said.

He sees me, **thought Malchus.** *He is blind with his own blood, yet he sees me.* **"Let me help you, Master," he said to the Nazarene. "I will carry the cross to the place of the skull for you. Please, sir, I am sorry." The Nazarene smiled a bit wider and nodded. "I didn't know," said Malchus, weeping in the pain of his regret. He took his robe and wiped at the blood that covered the man's face. "Please let me help you."**

"No, not me," said the Nazarene. "I will help you now. Go back to the Island. Help the young people there. They are in danger. I will see you soon and you shall always be with me, Malchus."

"Here, you," yelled a Roman soldier. A man stepped from the crowd. He put his shoulder under the cross and heaved. Malchus held the arm of the Nazarene so he wouldn't fall. The Nazarene smiled at him. Malchus again took the sleeve of his robe and wiped the face of the Nazarene. He looked deep into the one clear eye of the Nazarene. The Nazarene smiled . .

And Malchus fell, spiraling, helpless, out of control. He landed hard and opened his eyes. He found himself lying prostrate again in the sand of the island called Fallen Jerusalem. Two handsome, strong young men helped him to his feet. Two beautiful young women stood before him, concerned and scared.

They are worried about me, thought Malchus. *Me. No one has worried about me in centuries. No one has . . .*

"Cepha," said the girl named McKenna, stepping forward to embrace him.

She knows who I am, thought Malchus. *Yet she embraces me.* Tears fell as he put his arms around the young women.

"Cepha," said Nicole, embracing him. "Come back."

"He forgave me," said Malchus. "I'm alive again."

"Yes, of course you are," said Nicole. She kissed his cheek.

"You don't understand," said Malchus. "I mean, I'm alive. I can feel and sense and . . ."

"Yes?" said McKenna.

"I can say I'm sorry. I am. I'm sorry you came all this way"

"No," said McKenna. "No, don't apologize. We have been honored to help."

"Did something happen to you?" asked Luke. "Your eyes went blank, and you said some words in a language we didn't know"

"Hebrew," said Malchus. He nodded. "Yes," he said. "He took me back to that day." He tried for a few moments to explain what had happened. " He, . . . the Master . . . let me apologize."

"So you're . . . uh . . . all right?" said Clint.

"Yes, thank you," said Malchus. "I thought I had been summoned to the Fox River Valley to help you, Clint and Nicole. It turns out you came here to help me."

"Cepha--" began Luke.

"Not Cepha," he said. "No longer. I am no longer the Wandering Jew. No, I am Malchus again. Look." He pulled back his hair and showed them. A scar showed where the ear had been severed.

"Malchus," affirmed the group. The two young men shook his hand and the young women hugged him.

Chapter Twenty-Five

The next couple of days were complicated, but Luke, with a firm head for business, steered the proceedings. He and Clint retained a local lawyer and established their claim to the treasure in the pit, which was substantial. The government of the British Virgin Islands would keep about a third of the value of the treasure, but the ancient doubloons and silver coins, as well as the jewelry, would provide far more wealth than either couple would ever need.

A minister of antiquities from Panama came to take possession of the golden statue. He stood with tears on his face, and it was clear that the beauty of the artifact stunned him. He wrung their hands and thanked them for returning the national treasure.

"I must insist," the minister told them in a trembling voice, "that when we again dedicate the statue in the Cathedral that the five of you and your guests will promise to come as *our* guests. This goes beyond..." Emotion overcame him as he stroked the head of the beautiful Madonna.

Cepha walked around the island of Tortolla, breathing fresh clean air and rejoicing in his new freedom for about a day. Then he said, "I am in the way with you. I want to return to home."

"Home?" smiled McKenna.

"Yes," he said. "I think I am going to settle for a while near your mother, Luke. I am in need of some rest after wandering for so long."

Luke took him to the airport and Cepha caught the first of several planes that would take him back to the Chicago area. "Well, he's off," said Luke when he returned to the boat.

"Do you think he intends to marry your mom?" grinned his wife.

"I don't know," he said, rubbing his chin. "I know he likes her. Whether it's romantic, I don't know. . ."

"Well, duh!" exclaimed McKenna and Nicole at the same moment.

Luke chuckled. "Okay, I guess it could be romantic," he agreed.

The two couples spent the rest of their week together, snorkeling, fishing, cruising in the islands, sunning and relaxing. At night they would anchor and go ashore for exquisite seafood dinners. On their last night in the islands, Luke and Nicole lay together in their cabin, listening to the gentle lap of the ocean against the side of the beautiful motorboat.

"Did you have a good time?" said Nicole.

"Just now?" he said. "Yes, I had a terrific time."

"I didn't mean just the last 45 minutes or so," giggled Nicole. "I meant this week."

"Yes, I did," he said. "This has been the best week of my life."

Nicole switched on a small light and crossed to her dresser. "I wanted to show you this," she said. "It's one of the things I kept out of the treasure for myself." She took a string of pearls and hooked them around her neck.

"Look," she said, indicating the string of antique pearls, all of them tiny. "It's like the one my ex stole from me."

"Wow," he said.

"I was talking about the pearls around my neck, dear," she giggled. "Raise your eyes a bit higher."

"Sorry," he said. "It's hard for me to focus on your neck." She laughed, kissed him and returned to lie next to him.

She put a finger against his lips in a few moments. "What?" he managed.

"Listen," she smiled. "You can just hear Clint and McKenna making love."

"Inspiring," he agreed, and embraced her.

Chapter Twenty-Six

The day was cloudy and threatening as the American Airlines jet from San Juan, Puerto Rico, landed at O'Hare Airport late in the afternoon. Clint turned to his wife and saw a little tear on her cheek.

"Something wrong?" he asked.

"You only get one honeymoon, you know," she smiled. "And mine just ended."

"On the contrary," he said. "I'd say the honeymoon is just beginning."

She gave him one of the smiles he'd come to love so much and looked across the aisle at Luke and Nicole, who were just waking up from a nap that began shortly after the plane took off.

"I wonder if Cepha—" began McKenna.

"Malchus, you mean," smiled Clint.

"—Right, Malchus—if he already proposed to Ruth," McKenna chuckled.

"I wouldn't be surprised," her husband shrugged.

"Meanwhile, you and I have a mission," she said.

"What's that?" he said.

"You've heard me speak about my friend Stephen Levin," she said. "I called him, you know."

"And?"

"He can store the shawl in a proper environment," she said. "He has access to an organization that will preserve it, work to authenticate it, and all that stuff. You know, we don't have much to substantiate its real identity as it stands now."

"When do you want to take the shawl to New York?"

"Soon," McKenna shrugged. "But I think that we might want to take it to a few churches in our area and talk about it, don't you?" He nodded, eager to go about it.

They chatted until they deplaned at the terminal and made their way to a waiting cab. McKenna and Clint had a smiling, and even tearful parting with the two people who had become their closest friends. They agreed that they would see each other for dinner at a restaurant that weekend.

* * * * *

Malchus lay on his back and knew he was dying. He didn't feel afraid, not angry, but he did feel regretful. He'd met someone with whom he felt he could live out his life, but now he had to die.

He thought of the irony. Just before he'd met these people who'd come to mean so much to him, he'd tried to kill himself by jumping off a bridge. It hadn't worked, of course. It never did. Now he was going to be murdered, and he didn't want it.

These people who had captured him believed that they could heal someone—they hadn't told him who—by transferring his blood into someone else, someone who was terminal. They took a measure of blood from him each day and transferred it into someone in the next room.

He'd asked the nurses who were working on him why they wanted his blood, but they were vague. After a while, he'd figured it out: they believed that he was the Wandering Jew, immortal and indestructible, whose blood could heal someone else.

Malchus lay in silence. If they killed him, he would be in the arms of Jesus, he knew. He couldn't be scared about that. But he did find that he felt sorry for the people who were doing this to him.

They'd known he was coming, he felt sure. Someone had been spying on him and on the activities of his treasure hunting group in the Virgin Islands. They'd followed him to the airport in Tortolla, then Puerto Rico, and seized him as he deplaned at O'Hare Airport.

But they hadn't wanted the treasure. Fallen Jerusalem had always been an abandoned island, no one went there, anchored there, or anything. They would have had no difficulty overpowering the four young people and taking whatever they wanted.

They wanted him. They wanted to drain his blood and put it into someone else. Of course it wouldn't work. But who would that be? Why would someone else want the dreary immortality that had been his for millennia?

A tear formed in his eye as his thoughts turned to Ruth, who had cared about him, encouraged him, brought him into her family, made him part of celebrations. Then the two couples who had come with him to Fallen Jerusalem. They had been concerned about him: they had worried about him, celebrated with him, enjoyed being with him.

Now, he had a future. He'd found himself with people who cared about him, and he had received forgiveness, and his life had begun heading in the right direction at last.

But now, in a contemptible irony, he was going to die. Furthermore, his death would be meaningless. The person who was receiving his blood would not benefit. Malchus realized that all his knowledge would be lost, as well. All the good he could do with his healing gifts, his knowledge of the world, his insights—all would vanish with his death.

In an abrupt moment of insight, he got it: he didn't want to die because he wouldn't be able to share what he could do. His whole life had been focused on him and on his needs to the exclusion of all else, until he came to Geneva thinking he'd been sent to help Nicole and Clint, but who, he now realized, had helped him.

Now he understood. The meaning of life did not mean that people lived to serve him. He'd heard the Master say on several occasions that to have real life, a person had to be the servant of all. That, Malchus realized, was the reason Malchus loved helping the pathetic people in the shelter. Making beds. Washing the floors. Cleaning up after a sick person whose life had no meaning other than the daily horror of living. Slogging out a barn for a farmer in Quebec. He knew why he felt terrible at the tragedies he'd witnessed and survived, unable to do anything to stop the horror, grieving for centuries over the dreadful scenes he'd lived through.

His medical skills, acquired over the years, refined, honed in surgical suites, in remote African and Asian villages, during plagues and famine and pestilences—all of it would be gone in a day or two. He was sure he couldn't survive more than that at the rate they were removing his blood.

One man came into his room. "My name is Spalding," he said. "I am a doctor."

Malchus looked at him, his eyes not focusing well. "Yes, Doctor," he said.

"You are a doctor also," said Spalding.

"Yes," Malchus said.

"The transfusions are not working," said Spalding.

"Yes, I am not surprised," said Malchus. Spalding's

eyebrows went up.

"Your blood should be healing him," said Spalding.

"Why do think that?" smiled Malchus.

"Because you are the Wandering Jew," said Spaulding. "You have lived for two millennia. You cannot die."

"And you think my blood caused that?" Malchus said, his smile widening a bit.

Spalding controlled himself with a struggle. "This man is important," he said, his voice just a bit lower than a growl.

"Important to you, perhaps," said Malchus.

"To many people," Spalding said. "He is our leader."

Malchus thought. "What is his name?" he asked.

"Webster," returned the man.

"Petras Webster?" asked Malchus.

Spalding nodded. "He wants to see you," said the doctor.

"Shall I come now?"

Spalding hesitated. "Come," he said. Malchus turned his head and looked at the man who stood there. He was a physician, and to all evidence, competent and careful.

But he was evil. He intended to let Malchus die in order to—

Malchus, his head throbbing, managed to sit up. Then, stand. He had to lean on the doctor as the man led him down the hall.

The leader of the group—and it seemed to be a cult—lay in a hospital bed, cranked up a little bit. He turned his head and saw Malchus.

"Are you the wandering Jew?" he croaked.

"Yes," said Malchus. "May I please examine you?"

"You are a doctor?" asked the man. Malchus nodded.

"I have extensive training, yes, in medicine," said Malchus.

"Are you the leader of this group?" He walked forward, put on a stethoscope and pulled back the covers.

"My name is Webster," said the man in the bed. "Yes, I am the leader."

Malchus noticed at once a blood soaked bandage as he listened to the man's heart, and lungs.

Then, the Wandering Jew understood. "You're dying of liver failure," he said. "You've had a transplant, and it failed."

"Yes," croaked Webster. "I need your blood to heal me."

"It won't work," said Malchus.

The man looked hard at him. "Why not?" he asked.

"Because I'm not immortal, Webster," said the Wandering Jew. "I'm going to die. Look at me. You've been taking my blood, and it isn't helping you, and it's killing me. My body can't make the blood as fast as your people are taking it."

"No," said Webster. "You've lived for millennia."

"But it's over, Webster," said Malchus. "The Curse ended on the Island."

The room fell silent for some minutes. "I may be able to help, however, Webster."

"What?"

"Let me bring my young friends here," the Wandering Jew said. "I think they can help."

"And what do you get for it?" said Webster.

"I've already gotten it," said Malchus. "More than you can imagine, my friend."

"What do you mean?" said Webster.

"You don't have to die in guilt and horror, Webster."

Webster managed to nod a little.

Chapter Twenty-Seven

The two couples shared a cab from O'Hare to Casey and Anna's house, picked up their cars and headed for home. McKenna and Clint unloaded their bags, set them by the front door of his apartment, and let themselves in.

"Oh brother," sighed McKenna. "Laundry by the suitcaseful. Welcome home."

"I'll help you," Clint smiled.

"You may not get the chance," said a voice to their left. McKenna gave a gasp of surprise as they whirled.

"Gil?" she said.

"Hi, McKenna," he said, without the least warmth. He pointed a pistol. "Now, put your hands up, both of you."

"What for?" asked Clint. "We're not carrying weapons. We just got off an airplane. What do you want?"

"You're coming with me," Gil said. "And you're going to bring the treasure with you."

"We don't have any treasure with us," said McKenna.

"We want that cloak thing," said Gil.

"Jesus' prayer shawl?" asked McKenna. "But…"

"Enough talking," said Gil. He motioned with the pistol and McKenna opened a suitcase they had purchased on Tortolla. They'd placed the shawl in a plastic wrap to protect it. Gil took it, put it under his arm and waved the gun again. "Get going," he said. "Out the door and down to the car. Now."

The group went to McKenna's car and got in, Gil sitting in

the back.

"Where are we going?" asked Clint.

"To your buddy Luke's house," said Gil. "Get going."

Clint turned in the seat. "I don't know how to get there," he said.

"I do," scowled Gil. "I'll direct you."

A half hour later, the car pulled up in front of Luke's house. They saw Nicole's Explorer in the driveway and the Corvette on the street. No other cars were in evidence.

Clint parked the car, got out and came around to McKenna's side. He opened the door for her. She stood and he made eye contact with her.

Clint went into her mind. In the next moment they stood together on Fallen Jerusalem again.

"Do you have any idea what's going on?" he asked her.

She shook her head. "Not a clue," she said. "It must have to do with the cloak, but I can't imagine why they want it."

"I can stun this guy," he said.

McKenna shook her head. "No," she said. "Luke and Nicole may be in danger. I'd suggest we let this play out for a while."

Clint nodded. "Let's go back."

In the next moment they stood together on the parkway of Luke's house again and Gil climbed out of the car, carrying the prayer shawl. He kept his hand in his jacket pocket and pointed toward the door. Clint put his arm around McKenna and they walked together into the house.

Luke sat in a kitchen chair, his arms bound behind him. He spotted them and grimaced. "Clint. Nicole," he said. "I'm so sorry you're involved in this. They grabbed me and Nicole when we came in the house. They're holding Nicole hostage."

They heard a door open and Nicole staggered in, her face bloody and her hair messed. Luke groaned and tried to rise, but he was tied too securely.

A beautiful woman shoved Nicole and she staggered forward. Clint caught her before she fell and embraced her. Nicole was weeping.

"Thanks," she said. "She beat me. Two of her men held me. What amazing bravery."

"Did you get the cloak?" asked a man from the landing. Gil went to him and held it out.

"I think that one is a doctor," said Nicole. "He's taking care of someone up there, but I don't know who."

"You four," said the doctor. "Up here." One man untied Luke, who went at once to Nicole and embraced her.

"I'm okay, Luke," she said. "Don't worry."

"No, don't worry," snarled Sharon. "I'll get rid of her soon. Then we can be together again."

Luke would have lashed out, but Gil held up a gun. "Save your strength," he said. "Move."

Clint led the way up the steps and into the back bedroom. To his surprise, he found himself in a hospital room. A small man lay in the hospital bed, pale and wan.

"Ah," said Clint. "I get it now."

The little man turned and looked at him. "Did you bring the cloak?"

"Yes," said Clint. "I don't think it's going to help though, Petras."

"You know him?" asked Luke.

Clint and McKenna nodded. "Let me introduce you to Petras Webster," Clint said. "The Spiritual Head of the group."

"What group?" asked Luke.

"They call themselves the Beholders," said McKenna. "I've heard of them, too." Clint took the shawl and walked toward the bed.

"Right," said one of the men. "He is ill."

"With a terminal liver problem, I'd guess," said Luke.

The people seemed to be surprised. "How would you know?" asked one of the men.

"You set up that poor volleyball coach and took her liver, didn't you," said Luke. "Then you killed her and that other guy, her coach friend. She was a blood relative of Webster, isn't that right?"

"His niece," said one of the men. "Though she didn't realize it. We recruited Gil here and he. . .staged. . .some very convenient accidents, also."

"Luke," said Ruth Frey, entering the room.

"Mom," said Luke. "I didn't know you were here."

"I met Malchus at the plane," she said. "Two of them jumped into the car at the airport. They forced us to come here."

"Hello, dear ones," said a voice from the door.

"Malchus," said Nicole. "Are you all right?"

"No," he said. "They've been transferring my blood into Webster. It isn't helping."

Clint and McKenna turned to stare at the cult members. "His blood," said McKenna. "What on earth for?"

"You know his real identity," Sharon Frey. "The world knows him as the Wandering Jew. He can't be hurt, killed, or incapacitated. So, we've taken his blood and transferred it into the Leader."

"But you don't understand—" said McKenna. Clint squeezed

her elbow to make her be quiet.

"Don't understand what?" said one of the men.

Malchus spoke up quickly. "I'm afraid I suggested the shawl, Clint," he said. "Please believe me. I didn't dream they'd kidnap you and bring you into this. Please forgive me."

"What do you want from us?" said Nicole, with a sideways glance at Luke.

"We can't let you go and tell everyone who this is," said the leader, who the others called Armstrong, pointing at Webster.

"Why?" said Nicole.

"Because we're going to keep him around," said Armstrong. "So we will be eliminating you."

"Ah," said Nicole.

Clint caught Ruth's eye. He went into her mind.

Clint: How bad is this?

Ruth: They're serious. They thought Malchus's blood would help this Webster.

Clint: They're crazy.

Ruth: Yes, they are. The two with pistols seem to be the leaders. One claims to be a doctor. He's been draining the blood out of Malchus.

Clint: Did Malchus tell you what happened to him on the island?

Ruth: Yes. He seems to have changed.

Clint: He says he has, yes. Anyway he doesn't seem to be the same now as when we left, that's for sure.

Ruth: I can see a great change in him. But he doesn't seem afraid.

Clint: Has he fought this?

Ruth: No. He seems resigned. Not afraid. He's wanted to

die for centuries, you know. This could do it.

Clint: Shall we Paik them?

Ruth: We could Paik two or three of them. However others have surrounded the house, watching what's happening. If we just leave, they'll start shooting.

Clint: Have they hurt you?

Ruth: No, but they aren't making us comfortable, either. They live on potato chips and cola, from what I can see. Gack.

Clint: We can't let them kill Malchus.

Ruth: No, of course not. But we can't get rid of all of them.

Clint: Could we bring in the others? I mean Mickey, Anna, Grandpa...

Ruth: That's a good idea. Let's see what happens with the cloak, though.

Clint had never seen Webster, a small man with red hair and green eyes. He was just alert enough to turn his head. His eyes opened wide when they lighted on Clint but he didn't speak. He struggled to lock eyes with Clint, but Clint stepped back into the hall. The sight of Webster jolted Clint. *Does he have the Cymreig?* he asked himself.

A nurse sat next to the bed. An armed guard sat by the door. He went to the man with the gun and paiked him. He saw as much as he could in a great hurry, and then planted the idea in Randolph's mind that he was hungry.

Randolph took sandwich orders. Randolph walked back to the living room and Clint followed. When Randolph shrugged into a coat and went to a car, Clint released the Cymreig.

"Did you use the Cymreig?" asked McKenna.

"Yes. I make six guards, two in each of three houses."

"Have you been with Mom and Mickey?" she asked.

"Hey," said Gil. "Shut up over there. . ." Clint turned and looked at him.

* * * * *

Gil found himself in a forest, hiding behind a tree. He looked around him, hoping to find a place to hide.

He'd seen it happen. Before his eyes, McKenna's husband had transformed. As the full moon rose above the horizon, the guy named Clint had raised his head and begun to howl. Clint's face distorted, fur appeared on the backs of his hands and his shirt tore away.

Gil turned and ran from the house into the woods. He heard the howl of the werewolf screaming through the cold night air.

Now he remembered. He had his gun. He could shoot the werewolf.

No, he thought. Of course that wouldn't work. Everyone knew that you needed to shoot the werewolf with a silver bullet.

Now he heard the growl. Not ten feet from him. The werewolf turned to him with the hideous glare of green wolf eyes.

Gil knew. He had to hide. He scrabbled back against the wall—

* * * * *

Gil fell silent, staring at Clint, his face wreathed with terror.

McKenna grinned. "What did you do to him?" she whispered.

"Not much," smirked her husband. "He thinks I'm a werewolf. Right now he's caught in a feedback loop trying to think of where he's going to get a silver bullet."

Then, Mickey Logan stood in the middle of the room. Sharon Frey screamed. A guard ran out from the bedroom. "How the hell. . ." he began. Clint gathered his feet under him to spring.

"Hi, everyone," said Mickey. "Get down." He stepped to the side of the room. The guard fired his gun. The bullet ripped into the wall behind Mickey. Clint took two steps and launched himself into the guard's knees. The guard screamed as the crackback block destroyed his knee ligaments.

McKenna followed her husband and took the guard's gun. Sharon and Gil, stunned by what was happening, were slow to react. Luke dove for Gil, knocking his gun aside. As Gil stood, Ruth locked eyes with him. Gil collapsed, shaking with terror, holding up his hands to ward off an unseen assailant.

Mickey looked into the eyes of Crowley, the doctor. In the next moment, the doctor fell back, cowering in the corner of the room.

Nicole leaped to her feet and charged, shrieking. She hit Sharon with a flurry of punches to the face and the stomach that left Sharon dazed and gasping for air. Luke, stunned by his wife's fury, could only watch Nicole batter his ex-wife for a few moments. Then he crossed to her and wrapped his arms around Nicole's waist. "Stop, honey," he murmured. "She's no threat."

Nicole screamed profanities, swinging wild punches as her husband embraced her. At length she stopped struggling and began to cry. She embraced him until she calmed down. Then she helped her husband bind his ex-wife, who lay stunned at their feet.

The fight ended in moments. "I'll come back in a moment," said Mickey Logan. He vanished.

"What on earth?" said Crowley. Clint jerked Crowley's coat

off him and bound his hands behind him with the sleeves. Crowley didn't fight it. He stood in dumb silence, too dazed by what had happened .

"Luke," said Clint. "Call in the cavalry. Tell them to be here in five minutes."

Luke nodded and crossed to an antique writing desk. He pulled open a drawer and removed his cell phone.

Malchus lay on the couch, pale and weak. "You used the Cymreig," he said.

"Yes," said Clint.

Clint and Ruth walked into the backroom. They crossed to Webster's bed. The nurse tried to obstruct them, but Ruth Paiked her. The woman stood aside, smiling and welcoming them.

"Okay, McKenna," Clint yelled.

McKenna came into the room in the next moment. "Do you have it?" asked Clint.

"Yes," said McKenna, and held out the prayer shawl.

Clint took Ruth's hand.

Anna and Mickey now appeared in the bedroom.

The look of worry on the faces of his mother-in-law and Mickey surprised Clint. "What's up?" asked Clint.

"This situation is far worse than it looks," Anna whispered. "Try not to be afraid."

Mickey looked at the faces of each of the people in the room. They nodded.

Mickey walked to McKenna. He took the prayer shawl and draped it over his arm.

The bedroom disappeared. The group found themselves standing on top of a small hill, staring at a structure. Three large wooden beams stood embedded in the ground, packed hard with stone. Three beams of oak joined the standards across the top. Five nooses hung from the crossbeams.

Clint knew where he was. "Tyburn," he said. "We've come to the old gallows on Tyburn Hill."

"Yes," said Mickey. "I recognize the drawings. I sense the terror, the despair, the pathway to hell that so many walked."

"On June 23, 1649, 24 prisoners – 23 men and one woman – were hanged simultaneously, having been conveyed there in eight carts," noted Clint. "The Tree stood in the middle of the roadway. It was a major landmark in west London and was supposed to present a very obvious symbol of the law to travelers. After executions, the bodies would be buried nearby or in later times removed for dissection for doctors and medical students."

"They are still here," said Anna. "I mean, those who died in those ropes."

"I sense them too," said Mickey.

A light—yet not a light, a glowing presence—stood just inside the gallows.

Cold green fires burned. "We have to go in there?" Clint asked.

"Yes," answered Mickey. His voice sounded calm and unafraid. "Come."

He led them forward. Green fires burned but gave off no light. Mickey walked under one of the crossbars, pushing aside a rope…

And found himself in a ghastly nightmare.

Chapter Twenty-Eight

Cold. Despair. Depression. Anger. Guilt. Sadness. Gossip. Thievery. Murder. Terror.

The Snake waited for them in the midst of the hellish area, surrounded by wisps of smoke that moved back and forth. The man named Webster lay on the ground before him.

"People of the Cymreig," the Snake hissed. "Why have you come?"

"We have come to take back the man named Webster," said Anna. "You have owned him long enough, Snake."

Now Clint understood. "So I get it now," he said. "I see the reason for the treasure hunt, the search for the shawl, everything. Webster has the Cymreig. Somehow, the Snake took over Webster and perverted the power of the Cymreig to imprison the people who now serve him."

"Yes," said Mickey. "Including Luke's wife Sharon, who joined them to deal with the guilt she felt because of her adultery and abysmal treatment of Luke."

"And Gil, too?" said McKenna. Clint put an arm around her.

"Yes," said Mickey. "The Snake, working through Webster, forced Gil to hurt people, steal and murder."

The Snake turned and looked at him. "The Knight," he said. "Gareth."

"Yes," said Mickey.

"Yes," said Clint. "Me, too."

"Viviane, also," the Snake hissed, looking from Ruth to

Anna, and then to McKenna.

"You cannot defeat us, Snake. You know it. You have no power over us. Give up Webster," insisted Mickey.

"How will you fight me?" sneered the Snake, weaving from side to side.

Mickey held up the Prayer Shawl. The Snake froze.

"Clint," said Mickey.

Clint reached out and took the prayer shawl from Mickey. He started to walk toward Webster, but a hand clutched his.

"No," said McKenna. "We'll do it together."

Clint turned to Mickey, his eyebrows raised. "Yes," said Mickey. "Together."

Clint drew himself up and walked toward Webster. As they approached, The Snake hissed dreadful imprecations and threats. But it didn't move, either.

"Are you afraid?" whispered McKenna.

"Of course I am," he said. "But I won't walk away from this."

Now the three old women appeared, standing over Webster. They snarled what sounded like vile curses in a language he couldn't understand. McKenna clutched his arm.

He felt a hand on his shoulder and turned his head. Mickey grinned at him. "We'll stand right with you," he affirmed. Anna took his other hand.

Clint knelt. The screaming reached a cacophony. Mickey stood at Webster's head and lifted his shoulders. Clint wrapped the Shawl around Webster's shoulders.

Webster writhed and began to scream with pain. Then his face shone with a sapphire blue glow. He began to relax.

The Old Women's screaming of rage turned to wails of pain

and terror. As Clint watched, they turned to a green mist. Then the mist dissipated. A powerful wind blew, beginning to clear away the stench of wickedness, possession, and terror.

"Be gone, Snake," said Mickey, and his voice rang with authority throughout the area. The Tyburn triple tree shimmered and disappeared. "You cannot have Webster. Restore him to sanity. I command it."

Webster opened his mouth. A green wisp of smoke emerged from Webster's mouth. It rose and moved toward the Snake. The Snake opened its mouth. The wisp of smoke entered his mouth. . .

Then, the group stood again in Ruth Frey's bedroom.

Webster lay on the bed, breathing with difficulty, writhing in terrible pain.

He opened his eyes and scanned the group. "Mickey," he gasped.

"Yes, Petras," said Mickey.

"Where am I?"

"You are safe, now."

"Mickey," said Webster. "The Snake—"

"It's gone," said Mickey. "It vanished when we confronted it with the Master's Prayer Shawl."

"Thank you," said Webster. "I couldn't stop him. He kept forcing me to—"

"I know, yes, Petras. Now release those whom you imprison. You won't need their help anymore."

"You're right, I won't," said Webster. His eyes went blank. Then a vestige of life returned to him. "I'm going to die now, am I not?" he asked.

"Yes," said Mickey. "You are. Be at peace, Petras."

Webster nodded, as if Mickey had just told him that the weather would be cloudy tomorrow.

"Who saved me?" he asked, his breath coming in gasps.

"This young man," said Mickey, indicating Clint, "and his wife," he added, pointing to McKenna.

"Thank you," Webster said, looking from McKenna to Clint.

"It's all right," said Clint.

"Yes," said McKenna. "Be at peace."

Webster's head lolled to the side. He sighed. Then, his spirit departed.

Anna and Mickey turned to Clint and McKenna. "Come to the house as soon as you can, Clint," said Anna. "Good work."

"We'll be back in a few moments," said Mickey, and then Clint and McKenna stood alone in the room.

Two nurses blinked at them. "What's going on here?" One of them asked.

Clint pointed to the bed. "I think your patient has gone beyond your help," he said. "You can go. Be at peace."

Chapter Twenty-Nine

The police summoned an ambulance. The ambulance attendants took Webster's body to the office of the medical examiner.

The police led Gil and Sharon as well as the other cult members away in handcuffs.

"What's going to happen to them?" Mickey asked Rusty, as the police loaded the cult members into patrol wagons.

"They have to face some stiff consequences. I think Gil will be tried for manslaughter or murder, the doctor and Randolph for first degree murder and most of the others will face conspiracy charges as well. It's hard to say for sure. The D. A. will have to decide."

"Behaviors always have consequences," said Mickey.

Malchus emerged from the bedroom, carrying the shawl. Luke helped Nicole to her feet from the chair where she'd been sitting and Malchus draped the shawl over her shoulders. She relaxed and Luke led her back to the chair. She clutched the cloth around her, enjoying the warmth.

"Nicole, I need to examine you," he said, and he looked worried.

"I'm okay, Malchus," she protested.

"Let me take a look," he insisted. "Come on in the back room."

Fifteen minutes later, Malchus returned with Nicole who looked happy. "No signs of broken bones," he told Clint. "The bruises are gone now." He took the shawl from Nicole's shoulder, folded it with reverence, and handed it to McKenna.

"Is the. . ." McKenna stuttered as she tried to ask the question. She tried again. "Is her baby in any danger?" she asked.

"No," said Malchus. "I don't think so. Still," he said to Nicole, "you'll want to get to your obstetrician as soon as possible—"

"What!" exclaimed Ruth.

"Wait a minute," Luke interrupted. "Did you say . . ."

"I think it happened the night you gave me the ring," Nicole said. "And the Blue Label Scotch. Remember we almost had a fight before you relented and gave me a little more? You cheapskate."

"You mean—you're—er—"

Nicole looked around at the rest of the grinning people, who beamed congratulations at her. She blushed. "Well, we weren't taking any precautions that night, you remember."

"You mean—er—we're going to be a father?"

"No," said Nicole. "*I'm* going to be a mother. *Ruth* is going to be a grandmother. *You're* going to be a father. The rest of our friends are going to be Godparents." The group laughed.

That evening, Rusty's wife Paula arrived at Ruth's house. Anna and Casey Fixx arrived with Mickey and Rand a short while later. The group sat in the living room. Mickey had tears of joy in his eyes as his sister revealed that she was going to have a baby, and couldn't stop hugging her.

"So Gil was behind the accidents at Westwood?" asked Anna.

"Yeah. They tossed him into the lock-up at Kane County Jail. The Judge ordered him held without bail," said Rusty. "He's been singing like a magpie."

"Rusty, we keep talking about this," said Paula, teasing. "You keep screwing up your clichés."

"Yeah," he said, looking rueful. "I don't have much talent for similes. If that's what I just used."

"That's a simile, all right," said Paula.

"How did he manage all those accidents?" Mickey asked.

"He hired kids, mostly punks at the high school, to help him out with this accident stuff. The little rodents weren't hard to find. We've hauled them in. They fingered Gil as the guy who put them up to the assaults."

"He hired people to hurt coaches?" asked Rand, disbelieving. "Why?"

"It seems he wanted to be the head football coach at Westwood. At first I think he planned to just get rid of the head coach, Mel Robbins. Then he decided that he should make the accident look like a group of disgruntled parents were behind it, so he staged a couple of other accidents."

"He did all this—hurt and scared all those people—so that the school would make him the head football coach?" asked McKenna, face red with anger and embarrassment. Clint took her hand.

"That's what he says," confirmed Rusty. "He never had the college football career to which he felt entitled and never got a lot of recognition. He figured the Westwood job would be a stepping stone to a good college program."

"But how. . ." Mickey started to ask.

"Remember when we went to see Mel at the end of the summer? He told us that the team this year could really be good."

"Yeah, I do remember," said Mickey.

"And he sure got the talent thing right. That team did a terrific job, you know. Gil thought that if he stepped in and coached the kids to a great record, he could get a gig at, say, a Big Ten school."

"Then the school loused everything up by hiring Pete instead of him, right?" asked McKenna.

"Yeah. Gil planned this for a couple of years, ever since he saw the group as freshmen. He realized then that the group of kids were exceptional and could generate a spectacular season or two for him.

"I don't know how much he has now, but he started with a kitty of five thousand dollars."

"He saved up to hurt people?" asked McKenna, stunned.

Rusty nodded and continued, "Gil paid a kid named Maxwell from the swim team $200 to put stuff in the coffee of the swimming coach. I don't know what it is. Gil told us that if you mix a couple of household chemicals, you can simulate a heart attack.

"He told that kid they were playing a big joke. When the kid—who would never be accused of being real bright, as you can guess—saw the coach almost die, he got too scared to say anything. We brought him in this afternoon and he confessed without hesitation. He's cooperating, so he probably won't face too much penalty."

"Little jerk," muttered McKenna. "I had the kid in a freshman class when I student taught there. I thought he would have dropped out before this."

"Anyhow," Rusty continued, "Gil paid another kid $200 to whack the cross-country coach over the head. The kid hid by the door until Marty came out. The punk saw his opportunity and clubbed Marty with a pipe. Marty's damn lucky his skull wasn't crushed. We picked up this kid, too. He had no compunction whatever about it when he clubbed the coach. He'd seen guys get clubbed on TV all his life. He thought the guy who gets hit wakes up a few minutes later, shaking his head. He had no idea that Marty Hague would almost die."

"Thank God Marty's going to be all right," nodded McKenna.

"What'll happen to the kid, Rusty?" asked Mickey.

Rusty shrugged. "The local cops have charged him on a juvenile warrant. He just turned sixteen a few months ago. Whatever happens won't stain his permanent record at all, I'm sure. The kid's been overwhelmed with guilt ever since it happened."

"Well, that's something, anyway," said McKenna.

"Then, Gil himself went out and backed off the lug nuts on the football coach's car. When Robbins got hurt, Gil figured the school administration would have no choice but to make him the head coach then."

"Right," said Mickey. "I remember you thought that's what they'd do."

Rusty nodded. "He got steamed when they appointed Pete Morley. Then he tried to undercut what Pete was trying to do with the team. Pete picked up on it early, before the first home game. Well, you know, he moved Gil over to coach the sophomores." Clint nodded. Rand took Mickey's hand. "Then Gil shot up Pete's house. He made the phone calls, sent the death threats, and so forth."

"Who killed Nancy Barnes and Jason Cohen?" asked McKenna. "I student taught in the Westwood Phys. Ed.

Department with them last year."

"The doctor we just arrested and some of the other cult creeps performed the operation that killed her," said Rusty. "You ought to prepare yourself, McKenna. Gil for sure got involved in that. I think he arranged the murders after they stole her liver for transplant."

Chapter Thirty

Malchus sat with Ruth in the conference room of the shelter in Aurora.

"You feel you have to leave?" asked Ruth.

"Yes, I do," said Malchus. "I have to disappear into another, more primitive country. I'm thinking Africa."

"The AIDS crisis?" Ruth asked. "And that's a continent, not a country."

Malchus chuckled at the correction. "Yes," he smiled. "I've been given a new life, almost two thousand years after I should have died, Ruth. Perhaps I should have left at once."

"Will I—we—hear from you?"

"If I can do it without endangering you and the kids, yes, I'll contact you. But I don't want other people showing up and taking you hostage again. If you can't tell them where I am, they can't hurt you."

"I could hurt them to a considerable extent before they hurt me," she said.

"You mean with the Cymreig. Yes, but Luke and Nicole have become vulnerable, as have Clint and McKenna although Clint could protect them well. The violent ones, however, don't know that."

"Because they don't know about the power of the Cymreig," nodded Ruth.

Malchus stood. "I am sorry," he said. "I haven't felt—well—like I feel about you, ever in my life. I didn't think I could fall in love. But. . ."

Ruth stood. She took his hands. "At some point, the faith of Abraham and Moses will have to reunite with those who follow Yeshua," she said.

"Yes, I know. I consider it inevitable. We worship the same God and shouldn't be separated."

"Er—" she said, looking at the ground.

"Yes," he said.

"I have a far better idea."

"What?" he asked, puzzled at this.

"Stay here with me and the kids," she said. "Share with me in the joy of them and their children."

He stood, looking at her in silence. "Do you mean that?"

"Yes, Malchus. I want you to stay here with me."

"I'm flattered. And touched to my soul." She glanced up at him with a smile. "Yes, I'm sure I have a soul again," he asserted.

"So. . ."

He hesitated, but then shook his head. "No, dear Ruth. No. You would be in danger the rest of our lives."

"I will be in danger without you here, also. I would be in danger if I came with you, also."

"I. . ." he tried to speak.

"Stay here," she said. "You've wandered long enough. You need to do a lot of writing. You need to rest, read, watch TV, eat good food, learn to play bridge and have fun with others."

She could see that she had tempted him. "I. . ." he began. Ruth released his hands. She put her arms around his neck and kissed him.

"Oh, my," he said later. "I don't know what to say."

"Say yes," she said.

Chapter Thirty-One

Nicole and Luke looked at one another. "Can we call it finished?" he said.

She stepped back and looked around. "Yes," she said with finality.

"My God, we've survived the first real test of our marriage," he said. "We actually painted a bathroom without killing one another."

"How many couples fall apart at this point?" she wondered.

"I don't know. But I think we'll look back on this as the real turning point in putting our lives together."

"You may be right," she said. She kissed him. "Now, we have to set up the nursery."

He sighed. "When does this ever end?" he asked.

"I don't know. Anna told me that she's never stopped worrying about McKenna, and she's what, twenty-three or twenty-four?"

"I meant with the house."

"Hey. We'll do it together, just like we did this room."

"Just think," he said. "We've painted and wallpapered an entire bathroom. And we can still consider intimacy."

She giggled at her husband. "Who's considering intimacy?"

"You must be kidding," he leered.

She sighed. "Just an idle question."

Chapter Thirty-Two

Clint and McKenna sat at the kitchen table in their tiny apartment, tired and worn out, an almost empty pizza box on the table before them.

"How many houses did we see today?" he asked, raising a weary glass of wine.

She laughed at his attitude. "Seven. Do you want that last piece?"

"No, I don't want it. Are you sure it wasn't twenty?"

"Yes, almost positive."

"Did you see anything you liked? Please say yes."

"You want to find the right place, don't you? The one I'll be happy in?" She continued grinning at him as she took a bite of the last piece of pizza.

"Yeah," he groaned. Then he shifted his tone. "That is, I mean, yeah! Oh, yeah, of course!"

"Very good answer," she said, and gave his head a condescending pat. He laughed.

"Thank you," he said. "I've been practicing."

"It shows," she affirmed.

He sipped at his wine and took her hand. "We're rich, aren't we," he said.

"Yeah, pretty much," she agreed. "The Government of the British Virgin Islands will take a big cut, but the gold and jewels in the chest will leave us pretty well set. Malchus and Luke and Nicole, also."

"Do you think I could start working on my doctorate?" he asked.

"Only if I can," she said.

"It's a deal."

The phone rang. Clint stood and walked to the phone. He said, "I'll get it. Though I don't know why. No one ever calls me." He cast his eyes skyward, the picture of martyrdom.

"Oh, brother," she said with a loud sigh, rolling her eyes. "Welcome to the church of St. Clint the Pathetic."

He snickered, and then tapped the on button. "Hello, this is Clint."

"Hello, Son," said his father. "Your mom's on the extension."

"Hello, Clint?" said his mother.

"Yes?" said Clint.

"We were wondering when you were coming to see us," said his mother.

"You were wondering what?" asked Clint, incredulous.

"Yes, we heard about the treasure," said his father. "We'd love to hear the story."

Now, Clint recovered enough to catch on to the scam. "You would, huh," he said.

"Oh, yes," they said.

"Uh, huh. Yes, I see. Please delete this number from your phoning list. We cannot pretend to be interested. Goodbye." He pressed the button to disconnect and turned back to the girl who had so brightened his life.

"Who was that?" asked his wife, taking a bite of pizza.

He took a deep breath and managed to calm down. "Nobody important," said Clint, and replaced the phone on the charging unit. He grinned and tapped his wine glass to the glass his wife held.

"Cheers," they said together.

* * * * *THE END* * * * *

Title: ACID

- Author: Jeff Lovell
- Publisher: TotalRecall Publications, Inc.
- HARD COVER ISBN: 978-1-59095-116-3
- PAPERBACK, ISBN: 978-1-59095-117-0
- EBOOK, Nook, Kindle, ISBN: 978-1-59095-118-7
- Number of pages: 352
- Publication Date: 2013

Rick Howell, living in the shadow of two women who have the power to change reality, must risk his life to stop the genocidal exploits of a desperate lunatic who wants to acquire their powers. The discovery of a mind controlling drug opens a pathway to frightening mental abilities for Rachel Farrell, who can move backward and forward in time at will, while Donna Riske, Rachel's best friend, can control the thoughts of others.

Title: The Coven of the Spring

- Author: Jeff Lovell
- Publisher: TotalRecall Publications, Inc.
- HARD COVER ISBN: 978-1-59095-113-2
- PAPERBACK, ISBN: 978-1-59095-114-9
- EBOOK, Nook, Kindle, ISBN: 978-1-59095-115-6
- Number of pages: 336
- Publication Date: 2013

An ancient secret, with frightening new powers, emerges to terrify and destroy.

Grace DeRosa, a gifted research chemist, lives with her husband Jim and their seventeen year old daughter Crissy. Grace finds a hidden spring in the woods near Salem, Massachusetts. She discovers that the consumed water imparts unique and fearful powers that lead to the ability to read minds, create terrifying mental pictures and force the user's will on others.

Title: Emerald

- Author: Jeff Lovell
- Publisher: TotalRecall Publications, Inc.
- HARD COVER ISBN: 9781590950807
- PAPERBACK, ISBN: 9781590950814
- EBOOK, ISBN: 9781590950821
- Number of pages: 348
- Publication Date: 2015

Emerald begins with a pirate assault on a merchant vessel. Blackbeard, or Edward Teach, terrorized the east coast of America from Nova Scotia down to the Virgin Islands. This book shows how people with a unique mental power called the Knack fight against the evil of pirates from 1715 to the present day, and even includes a long look at the court of King Arthur, and his chief advisor Myrthynne, who also had the most powerful manifestation of the Knack. This book, then, flows in several time periods and pulls together romance, villainy and a dramatic treasure, all of which frame a love story between a woman with the Knack and a man devoted to loving and protecting her.

Title: The Cape

- Author: Jeff Lovell
- Publisher: TotalRecall Publications, Inc.
- HARD COVER, ISBN: 9781590952078
- PAPERBACK, ISBN: 9781590952085
- EBOOK, ISBN: 9781590952092
- Number of pages: 228
- Publication Date: 2016

People say that *Der Fleigen Hollander—The Flying Dutchman*, as it is known in English—vanished with all hands in the sixteenth century off the Cape of Good Hope. Yet the ship has been by reliable, truthful people all over the world, suggesting that the ship is trapped in a time warp somewhere in the treacherous ocean south of the Cape. When her father is kidnapped by the ship, Therese goes to find him and rescue him from the self-imposed, Purgatorial imprisonment. In the search she is joined by her mother and a lifetime best friend, who seek to help Therese draw his soul back from the pit of Hell before he is lost for all eternity.

Title: The Ghost Of White Island

- Author: Jeff Lovell
- Publisher: TotalRecall Publications, Inc.
- HARD COVER ISBN: 9781590951194
- PAPERBACK, ISBN: 9781590952092
- EBOOK, Nook, Kindle, ISBN: 9781590952092
- Number of pages: 348
- Publication Date: 2015

In 1715, a ship's carpenter tried to rape the 14 year old daughter of the captain of a British warship and was flogged almost to death. He mutinied and captured the ship, killing the captain and forcing his daughter into marriage. After falling in with Blackbeard, he abandoned his young wife on a cold, bitter rock called White Island, off the coast of New Hampshire. When he was caught and hanged by the British Navy, his treasure vanished into history. Many people believe that Martha, his reluctant wife, hid the treasure in the Isle of Shoals chain. This is the story of a search for those gold and jewels and treasure, protected by the Ghost of White Island.

Title: Gina and Colby

- Author: Jeff & Jacqi Lovell
- Publisher: TotalRecall Publications, Inc.
- PAPERBACK, ISBN: 9781590953259
- EBOOK, ISBN: 9781590953266
- Number of pages: 136
- Publication Date: 2016

A Magic Amulet Allows Two Teen-Agers to Discover how to Make a Difference in the World of Animal Poaching

Two teen-agers, different in every way, form an unshakeable friendship as a result of the adventures they share after meeting in Disney Springs. Transported through a magic amulet to a totally different culture and continent, they are offered an opportunity to make a difference in the lives of endangered animals.

Dangers abound as they face poachers and pirates in their attempts to rescue these creatures, and they discover a courage within themselves that leads each one to a positive change in how they view themselves and others.

Title: Jazz and Ella

- Author: Jeff & Jacqi Lovell
- Publisher: TotalRecall Publications, Inc.
- PAPERBACK, ISBN: 9781590953006
- EBOOK, ISBN: 9781590953013
- Number of pages: 104
- Publication Date: 2015

Jazz and Ella tells the story of Jazz, a fourteen year old high school freshman, and his best friend, Ella, who meet on the way to Disney World. A supernatural being gives them each a magic amulet, which the children use to transport themselves to new and different worlds. They meet and deal many situations that cause them to face their fears and even terrors; that suggest ways that situations can be handled; and they see some of the choices that they will have to confront as they grow up.

Title: Marina and Dan

- Author: Jeff & JacqiLovell
- Publisher: TotalRecall Publications, Inc.
- PAPERBACK, ISBN: 9781590953228
- EBOOK, Nook, Kindle, ISBN: 9781590953242
- Number of pages: 128
- Publication Date: 2016

This ancient Egyptian Adventure, part of the Mousegate Series, traces the story of Marina and Dan, best friends since childhood, as they wrestle with the concept of heroism and how it applies to them. When offered a unique, but potentially dangerous opportunity by a spiritual being, they must make a decision that will stretch them in ways they never imagined. Able to experience first-hand the miraculous events that have been talked about for centuries, they witness the impossible become possible as they walk with Moses during the ancient biblical era where the crossing of the Red Sea took place. Both their friendship and their faith is strengthened through the adventures encountered together.